Dust
Short Stories

By Emma J Myatt

ISBN 9781793014634

For Hame, Sam and Isla

Contents

Author's Note

I hope you enjoy reading these stories. They are some of my favourites from the last few years of writing. Some have never been published before. Some have been published in magazines and in anthologies after winning prizes or been shortlisted/highly commended in various competitions (listed at the end). I know it's a pretty bonkers mix of styles, but I wanted that.

I am currently working on a collection of linked/themed short stories, a novella and several random short stories, as well as a collection of science fiction stories, when time allows.

Lots of people have encouraged me on the way and I'm grateful for every single line of constructive criticism and encouragement they've given me. All of my friends have been wonderful. I'm lucky in that there are lots – you know who you are and I love you all. *A friend is the masterpiece of nature* – Ralph Waldo Emerson, I think, and how true.

And thank you as well to my family – namely my mum, brother and grandfather, the latter an artist who encouraged me when I was a very small girl who knew she wanted to be a writer. Hamish, for his endless patience and help proof reading, Debz Hobbs-Wyatt for her wise words, Alistair Lawrie for his lovely warmth and encouragement over the last five years, everyone else from Mearns Writers, my English teacher Mrs Gray, who way back then saw a bit of potential in an otherwise bolshy and skiving teenager and most of all to my amazing children, who are my reason for everything.

Emma, June 2019
emmajmyatt.wordpress.com
@EmmaJMyatt

Sandlight

When I'm in bed reviewing the day on my phone and feeling happier, looking at it from a distance, I see the figure. I frown at the familiarity of her, then give myself a mental shake. It's just a shadow. Or a mark on the lens. But the more I look, the more it resembles my gran, standing on the beach, between Jake and me, hand on her chest.

On her right breast.

In exactly the same place I found the lump in *my* breast. She's not smiling; she's looking right at me with dark eyes, like shadows. If she didn't look exactly like my gran I'd be completely creeped out by this but I stare and stare at her, wishing it is real. Because it can't be. My grandmother died years ago.

In the morning, it still looks like her. I've woken up pragmatic, decided to go back to the place I took the picture and take it again because there could be a way the light shines in that particular place or there could have been a smudge on the camera, or there could have been a hair across the lens. The figure could be any of these things. I'm not gullible. I live in a world of the concrete, the seeable, the real.

After breakfast I tell Jake we're going back to the beach. He rushes upstairs to our room to get buckets and spades and comes flying down, leaving a trail of yesterday's sand down the steps. The grains glitter in the sunlight reflected through the skylight like fairy dust.

'Let's go,' I tell Jake, before I change my mind.

I don't tell him why, but lead him back to the exact place – as far as I can make out – that we were in yesterday. I tell him we're playing a game and that I need him to stand where he was yesterday, if he could help me remember?

He makes superhero poses and I take picture after picture, trying to remember where I was standing. We're there at the same time of day; the tide's further out, but the weather is roughly the same: a northern English version of late summer, bright, breezy and just on the right side of warm.

We're digging a moat for a fort and I'm trying to resist the urge to look at the photos when Jake yells.

'Mum! Look! Palaeontologists!'

I follow his energetic gestures and see a group of eager looking kids following a bounding man in khaki.

'Oh yeah – from that shop, maybe,' I say, as I watch. 'I wonder if we can join them?'

It's something I meant to do, book us on a tour, but when I rang from the train on the way to Yorkshire, they were all fully booked. 'We could wander on over and ask. Perhaps someone's dropped out?' Jake's away before I've finished my sentence. He runs straight up to the man and I see his uplifted face, smiling and talking. The man stops, seems to consider, then nods. He asks Jake something and Jake points over at me. I wave, get up and walk over to join them.

'Hi,' says the man in brown. If I could have drawn a palaeontologist, I'd have drawn him. Longish blond messed up hair, untidy beard and various light brown layers with pockets wrapping up a human package of enthusiasm. He's good looking in an unkempt way. 'Your son's welcome to join us, if you don't mind following on. You're supposed to have filled out a safety form but if you're here, it'll be okay. We had someone drop out this morning, you see.'

'Absolutely. He'd love that.' I ruffle Jake's hair and he joins the group as they go off, the man at the front, explaining why these cliffs are so full of fossils. I run back and get my bag, leaving our towels and spades in our half built fort.

Jake talks about fossils and dinosaurs all the time. I've been let off the hook for my parenting fail, for forgetting to book him on one of these tours. I watch him running off, chattering to a boy about the same age, charging towards another adventure. Something in my middle lurches.

He's only got me.

As we walk along, the itching starts up again. The itching that led me, when I was a little drunk, to lie down and examine myself properly. If I'd not read that post on Facebook, about signs of breast cancer, I'd not have found the damned lump, and I'd still be happy, instead of a walking bag of nerves.

There's this – my grandmother died of breast cancer.

And this – the lump doesn't move.

And this – there's an indent now, where there wasn't before, into the once-perfect arc of my breast.

Then there's this – I'm prone to cysts and most women who go to the doctor find out they have cysts. Why would I waste anyone's time over it?

And there's this – Jake's about to start high school. Once he's there, I'll have more time. I can get it checked later on.

I find I've cradled my right breast in my hand as I walk along and hurriedly move it down. I feel fine; I'm fit and healthy and have no tiredness or pain or anything. So I'm sure I'm all right. It's just a bit of a worry, but once the cyst shrinks, or whatever cysts do, the lump will be gone and I can stop worrying.

The group stops and the man shrugs off his pack. He hands out tools and laminates to the children and bends down over a rock. He motions the children around him and I hear tapping and then, quickly afterwards, yells of delight. He holds up something black. Jake beckons me over.

'Mum! It's an ammonite! He found it, just like that!'

'Now, all over this area, in the base of the cliffs, in the rocks, maybe even in the sand, are fossils. Go and search, but before you start digging at anything, call me over to see. Okay palaeontologists, off you go!'

With shouts of excitement, the children scatter.

'I've spare tools, if you'd like a go?' The man's right next to me. 'I'm Malcolm. It's my father's shop that organises these tours.'

'I'm Gemma. Thanks for letting my son join. It's got me off the hook for forgetting to book.'

'You're a poet,' he smiles. 'On holiday here?'

'Long weekend away. I used to live in Yorkshire. I used to come here with my grandparents all the time. It's not changed much. We're off home tomorrow, back to work on Wednesday…'

At that moment one of the children yells and Malcolm shrugs an apology before striding off to see what's been found. I wander over to join Jake, who's at the foot of the cliffs, digging furiously into the sand.

'I read about a man who found fossils like this. They fall off the cliffs as they erode away during hundreds of years and get buried by the tides.'

'Can I help?' I ask.

'Yeah! But if you find it I have to dig it out. Deal?'

'Deal,' I laugh. Jake's too young for high school, I think again. This enthusiasm for life and this freshness he has – I don't want life to bash it out of him. Remembering my own secondary school days, I know this is what might happen. Within months of going, I was hanging around with a 'bad crowd' – according to my mother – and experimenting with drugs and alcohol. At the age of thirteen. I feel horror at this happening to my beautiful, innocent Jake. Where we live, kids can stay kids for a lot longer. Once he goes off on that school bus, to the nearest town, I'll have lost him. And if he's not got me there to back him up…

'Mum? What's wrong?'

I realise I'm crying. Twice in the last twenty-four hours. Not good.

'Nothing, Fossil Finder. Come on, let's get digging.'

We scrape the sand from the base of the cliff, through seaweed, stones, odd pieces of plastic. We work in silence, each intent on our task; me, trying not to think. In the quiet spaces my thoughts come crowding in, unwanted. I dig, and dig, and enjoy the roughness of sand against my fingertips.

Jake gives a yell. 'I've found something!'

I move around to where he is and help him remove sand from what looks like a rock. I'm about to tell him not to be too disappointed when our fingers find ridges.

'I think it's a fossil!' Jake's excitement mirrors my own. We each take an edge and work downwards, scraping sand away so we've digging around it.

'Mum…' Jake's voice is all awe. 'It's an ammonite.'

We sit back a little and look at it, a perfect whorl of ridges and lines, a spiral repeated into itself. It's beautiful, I think. I have an urge to cover it up again, let it keep its secrets safe under the sand. But my son has other ideas.

'Malcolm!' he calls, right in my ear.

I sit back, out of the way. This moment belongs to him. Malcolm bounds over again, an excited puppy, kneels down and exclaims. 'Jake, this is a good one. Right, this is what we need to do…'

He explains to Jake how to remove enough sand and get it out intact. I watch their heads bent over together and wonder if Jake's father would have been like this. They've never met and not for the first time, a ripple of pain passes through me at what I've denied them both. But what choice did I have?

Malcolm calls me over, part way through their work. 'This is amazing,' he says. 'It's split in half almost completely, but is undamaged. It must have happened through continued pressure but look, the surface has been protected by the sand. It's almost in two perfect halves, separated but still joined by a tiny piece of rock. Almost a shame to move it, but we might be able to get it out without splitting it up completely. If we can. It's a pretty rare find. Nice one, Jake.'

Jake seems to glow, the smile on his face is so big. I take some photos of them working and video it as they slowly lift the fossil up towards the light. I try to think about the years it's been there but my mind can't cope with the time frame. As they bring it out, and Malcolm calls the rest of the group over to look, I look at the hole they've left; a hollow of nothingness that has cradled the ammonite for who knows how long. I think of it rising and rising, up towards the light it once knew when it was alive.

I can't stop looking at the space where it was. Whilst the others are busy looking at the fossil I place my hand inside the hole, to where the sand is cold and damp and dark. It makes me feel sick and gives me a twist in my abdomen. I withdraw my hands in a hurry and put them under my armpits to warm them again. I stand, and walk back into the sunshine, away from the shade of the cliff. I look out to the sea to steady myself, but the rising and falling of the waves reminds me of breathing and I feel dizzy and sink down onto the sand. My hands are still in my armpits and I let my fingers go back to the lump and push against it, feeling it hard against my softness. It's still there.

Later, we're in the hotel room, the day behind us, happiness and tiredness in equal measures on Jake's face. He's cradling the ammonite, looking amazed he was allowed to keep it. Malcolm managed to free it from the sand in one piece but as the group handled and looked at it, it came into two parts, each as perfect as the other. Matching parts of a whole, like Jake and me. There have only ever been two of us and this is right. Since watching him dig out the fossil, I've had to push thoughts of his father out of my mind, to where they keep returning. The ammonite is a sign, I tell myself. Two is fine. Two is us.

Jake falls asleep with the ammonite on his bedside table. I can see flecks of crystal inside it, shining at me, reflecting the glow of the fading light outside. It's late summer already, getting dark well before ten o'clock. Two minutes ago the days were still getting longer and five minutes ago it was Christmas, and all I had to worry about was how to get enough money together to buy Jake the Lego set he wanted. One minute ago I found the lump.

My phone sits on the windowsill. I can't put it off any longer so I pick it up and scroll backwards. Jake, smiling; kids, brown and pink faces grinning at the camera, at what turned out to be the find of the day in Jake's hands; photos of the group walking, Jake digging and Malcolm standing with a proud arm slung around my son's shoulders. I don't know how much more I can think about today. Removing things from where they're buried, fathers, growing up, school… It's all been there all day bashing into me. One of those days you know is a crossroads. I don't get the point of this one yet, but I can feel some understanding rushing towards me. I reach for my drink, a can of cheap gin and tonic from the shop two doors up from the hotel. If I drink, I can stop the thoughts because I don't want to cry again. It's not the lump I'm worried about, I'm sure of it, because it'll turn out to be nothing. And I don't want to find out; Jake and I are going along just fine.

The next photo is one of the ones I took today before we joined the dig, the one I reconstructed from the previous day. Here, curiosity overtakes me and I scan each photograph. There's nothing. I go back a little and stop on the one with the person-shaped smudge.

It still looks exactly like my gran. I touch the screen, wishing for a moment it is her, knowing it's just a trick of the light, of the dark, of the screen. Her hand is on her chest, her fingers towards her armpit, her eyes, looking at me. Except none of it is her. It's a smudge.

My tears come, then, and with it the fear slams into me, knocking me to the bed, where I sob into the pillow like I did when I lost my gran, let the waves of pain wash over and over me. I was fifteen the year she died, and I sobbed then as I'm crying now, like a small child. I know we're alone in the hotel tonight; the other two rooms are empty and thank God because I can't stop once I start. Jake won't wake up; he's a very heavy sleeper. He's is too young to face this. Too young to lose me.

In the end I can't move, so I pull the blankets over myself, wanting to cover my head that's pounding now and fall asleep. I lie there thinking that in the morning I'll phone my GP and make an appointment. I try to recall the number but I can't and my mind plays tricks with numbers, teasing me with all the wrong ones. I'll call, once I've looked it up but it's probably just a cyst. It'll be good to be sure, though, to know Jake's got me. To be able to enjoy life again, instead of standing and watching it rushing past me, faster and faster, like a train out of control, the only end for it smashing into the wall at the end of the line. I promise myself I'll check the number and phone.

The last thing I see before I close my eyes is the ammonite, glittering at me, picking up what little light there is and throwing it at me. It looks alive, millions of years after it died it's reborn. Here in this room, it's alive. Jake might be dreaming about it right now; dreaming about it as a living creature, moving through the water that used to cover all of this land, before change came in unstoppable measures and reshaped the world.

My thoughts roll over each other as I fall asleep, as if I am the beach and they are the waves. The last thing I remember – or am I already dreaming? – is seeing the phone number for my doctor's surgery on a pad of paper, written in my gran's handwriting. Underlined.

⏳

There is one element of my job I hate: telling people they have cancer. All the other parts of my job I love – even the awful bits when we can't save them, because we tried, and we gave them every chance we could. Being a nurse is the job I was born to do, but every time I have to tell somebody they have a potential death sentence is as hard as it was the very first time.

It's the look on their faces as I – specialist nurse, neutral faced – walk in with the consultant. They know, the moment they see you, before the doctor delivers the news, before their lives begin to change forever, before you've even sat down. They know. Often you see them notice you, change colour in front of you, swallow, fix their eyes on the doctor. Most of them cry. Most of them are with someone, who hugs them. A few come alone. Some bring their children, perhaps as a buffer against the future. If their children are with them perhaps they think they're protected. Some bring their parents, some a husband or boyfriend. Many bring friends and if it was me, this is what I'd do. A friend can be more support than anyone you are too close to, because as women, often the urge is to comfort the partner first, before looking to yourself.

Gemma Barclay is the first name on my list today. It's Friday and it's been a hell of a week. I've lost two women, both of whom I expected to make it. I'm struggling to get ready for the clinic today; I look terrible and I need to push it all to one side. I need to forget the two women for the afternoon, and concentrate on the living, those who still have a chance. Gemma Barclay is thirty-two, she's a single mother with a twelve-year-old son, according her notes. As well as her background notes I have the results of her mammogram, her needle aspiration and her ultrasound. It was the needle that found it, the needle that probed her most secret spaces and found evil there. And we need to dig it out. I've done this hundreds of times during the last fifteen years. I've seen consultants come and go, women survive and women die. More men are coming now and we're busier generally; there are a lot of awareness campaigns that we didn't have years ago.

The consultant arrives. It's Dr Taylor today, peering around my door. 'Ready?'

I nod. She looks exhausted; I know she was on call last weekend and has operated many times this week. But she never complains, never gives anything other than her all. She's my favourite so far.

I follow her into one of the rooms. Gemma Barclay is sitting upright on the bed, gown around her shoulders, tightly drawn up to her neck. For a second I think someone else is in there with her; but it's a shadow cast by the curtain around the bed against the wall, because it vanishes as I move. She's alone. I wish she wasn't. Gemma doesn't look up at us as we walk in, but she sees our feet. I see her nod to herself, before she looks up and meets firstly, my eyes, then the eyes of the doctor.

She knows. Any doubts she had, any hopes, have already gone and the doctor's not even spoken.

Dr Taylor shakes her hand. They will have met this morning, before Gemma underwent all the tests. The doctor will have felt the lump, examined her, drawn on her and now she has to tell her the news. I see Gemma Barclay lift her chin and fix her eyes on the doctor; I may as well not be in the room. I know she's concentrating entirely on her now.

'The mammogram and ultrasound were inconclusive,' the doctor begins. It sounds harsh, to dive straight in like this, but it's the best way. There is no softening small talk when cancer lives in the room. 'But unfortunately the needle test showed some abnormal cells.'

'I've got cancer?' Gemma asks, her mouth tight.

'You will need to undergo further tests, but yes, I'm afraid these cells look to be suspicious. It's most likely to be tubular and the size of your tumour means surgery is necessary, probably radiotherapy and possibly chemotherapy. I'm sorry, this must be a lot to take in,' she adds, softening her voice as she takes in the expression on Gemma's face. She's drawn into herself, pursing her lips and is chewing the inside of her cheeks. She's holding on tight. I long to reach out and take her hand but I can comfort her later, after the doctor's gone.

'Sally here is your breast care nurse. She'll be your go-to woman for everything and you can call her with questions and for information. Are you alone today, Gemma?'

Gemma nods. 'I have cancer?' she says again. I know she's not taken in anything the doctor's said. Part of my job now is to sit with her and make sure she understands what's happened today, and what will happen next. 'You said suspicious cells. You mean they might not be cancerous?'

Dr Taylor leans forwards. 'Gemma, we are sure it's cancer. But we won't be able to confirm what type until we do a biopsy. We say suspicious cells when we know they are abnormal, when they behave and look like cancer, but have not been confirmed as a particular type. But we can say at this stage it is likely to be tubular. I'm sorry, I know it's difficult to understand. If it helps you, I can say this, that every time we've seen cells like these they have turned out to be cancer. Did anyone bring you here today?'

'My mum lives miles away. Gran died of cancer. Breast. She would have been with me, otherwise. She brought me up. My son Jake's at school. I'm a single parent.' She rushes the words out, looking into the middle distance. I try, as I always do, to put myself in her place.

'Have you ever been referred to the Genetics clinic?' Dr Taylor asks.

Gemma shakes her head and the doctor makes a note. 'We can find out what kind of cancer your gran had and test you for a genetic link. Did anyone suggest it at the time? What about other women in your family?'

'Just… me.' And finally, she breaks down. Dr Taylor nods at me and I move closer to Gemma.

'I'll leave you with Sally just now,' says the doctor. 'We'll be in touch with a date for your biopsy.'

We've done this a hundred times. Dr Taylor will remove the tumour and direct the treatment; I'll be at ground level, helping Gemma in any way I can.

'Thank you,' says Gemma quietly, as the doctor leaves the room. She turns to me. 'I should have come in earlier. I found the lump months ago, perhaps over a year. But I kept thinking it was something else, or that it would go. I kept thinking about Jake and leaving him. I kept putting it off. Is it too late?' I can see the desperation she's feeling as she looks at me.

'Not at all. It's good you came in at all. Earlier is better, but mostly these things move slowly, not as fast as you imagine.'

Her words come quietly at first. 'There's just me, and Jake. His dad and I… It was a one night stand. I was ashamed at the time, but Jake came along and everything was suddenly all right. It's not easy, but it's worked out. I'm a learning support assistant at his old school. He's just gone up to high school. What if something happens to me? What if I die?'

'We'll do everything we can to make sure that doesn't happen,' I say. 'You're in good hands, here.'

'So I have cancer?'

'You have breast cancer. Is there anyone you can call, to get yourself home? Should you be driving?'

'I came on the bus,' she mumbles. 'You know, deep down I knew it was something bad. But I thought it might just go away.'

'With your family history it must've been very hard to accept,' I tell her. She's stopped crying now but has gone pale; she's a shadow of the woman who came in. I wish she wasn't alone but having talked to her I can see why: she's tough, or thinks she is, and has had to manage on her own. 'How old were you when you lost your gran?'

'Fifteen. I found out later that she'd known for ages but hadn't told anyone. I was a selfish little brat and only cared about me. I was horrible, during those months. I can't imagine what I put her through. I can't die, okay? So there is still a chance this isn't cancer?'

She's in shock. Women often ask me several times, maybe hoping the answer will change. I bring her a coffee and sit with her awhile, until I'm happy to let her go. I don't usually do this but I give her my private number and ask her to call me when she's home. It's not that I think she'd do anything stupid, more that she's not in full control of herself. I give her a small bag containing leaflets and some notes explaining what's happened today so she won't be wondering, later. I watch her walk down the corridor, head high, chin out and I think, she'll be all right. She's a fighter.

I begin to get the room ready for the next patient. I open the curtains around the bed, and pick up the gown Gemma was wearing. Something slips away from it with the tiniest of noises, a swish I can hardly hear. I feel a tickle against my legs and feet and grittiness in my hands. I bend down.

Sand. On the floor are grains of sand, sparkling against the plain lino floor. Sand? I remember Gemma telling me she's a learning support assistant so perhaps she gets sandy at school helping the smaller children. But she's not been at work today; she's been in clinic all morning. Maybe it was in her bag? But then I remember it sat by the desk the whole time. There'll be some explanation, I think, as I fetch a dustpan and sweep it up, marvelling at the light inside the grains. I rub some between my fingers and love the feeling of it on my skin, a touch that takes me back to my childhood and trips to the beach.

Even though it's been a bad week, even though I'm emotionally drained, I see the sea and the sand in my mind and it makes me smile. It'll be winter, soon. Maybe I'll try and find a cheap sun-filled holiday and go somewhere I can truly relax. Or I'll be no use to all the people who pass through here, on their journeys.

It's only as I leave the room I notice the sand is there as well, shimmering on the floor, a trail leading down the corridor, towards the exit, and the light.

⧗

I recognise Jake straight away. He's the boy who found a rare ammonite fossil last year. I don't forget things like that. There's even a photo of him here somewhere, showing a shorter version of him holding a fossil and grinning a massive grin. He's with a man, today. In the photo he's with his mum. I remember her; she was quiet, attractive, doted on her son. This must be her husband.

'Jake!' I shake his hand.

He grins at me. 'Hi, Malcolm. I'm here on holiday. Wondered if there was room on a tour? I'd like to take Andy.'

The man nods and holds out a hand too. He's got Jake's eyes and hair. Perhaps an uncle? Jake called him Andy.

'I don't know what it is with you Jake; I remember this happening last time. Didn't you join us on the beach after someone didn't turn up? Today we've just had two cancellations. That pretty much never happens. Maybe you're destined to make another big find today? Jake here,' I address the man, 'found one of the best fossils in the whole of last year! There's a photo over there.'

The man walks over and squints at the notice board. 'Great pic,' he says. 'Your mum looks well. You guys had a good holiday then? Hope this one lives up to expectations.' He walks back to join us. 'It's our first holiday together, eh, Jake?'

Jake reddens and nods. Neither of them enlightens me further. I get them to fill out forms, tell them to come back at twelve for low tide and watch them leave, wondering. I'm nosy.

They're back early, coming through the door as Jake's telling Andy about how he and his mum dug the fossil out. I tick off names on my list. Once everyone's here we set off for the beach. It's a mixed group today. I mostly get kids, but today there are two other men as well as Andy, and a couple of older ladies.

Andy and I end up walking next to each other.

'You're Jake's dad?' I can't help myself. 'He was here with his mum the last time.'

Andy doesn't reply for a second. He turns to see if Jake's out of earshot. Jake's chatting to one of the women. He's obviously a polite lad.

'I'm his dad, yes. But I'm just getting to know him now. I only met him for the first time three months ago. His mum's ill. She's been having chemo and it's affected her badly. She's in hospital right now, after a reaction to something they gave her. She got diagnosed with breast cancer late last year.'

'I'm sorry to hear that,' I say. Bloody cancer, again. It's been trying to get my dad. 'How is Jake taking it?'

'He's putting a brave face on it. His mum's fighting, hard, but it's been just the two of them. It's a long story.'

He looks like he could do with getting it off his chest. 'I'm a good listener,' I say.

But Andy shakes his head. 'Not now; this tour's about me and Jake. But if you fancy a pint later and he's happy foraging in the shops for a bit, I could probably do with it. I'm not much of a talker but something about being here... Makes me feel like opening up a bit. I'm going to catch up with Jake. See if I can find something with him.'

I watch him run after Jake and fall into step beside him. They've got the same loping gait as well as the same smile.

The dig's not as fruitful as they sometimes are. We find a couple of small fossils and some parts of a broken ammonite. Jake and his dad don't find anything but they look to be getting on well, which makes me smile. Doing tours like this gives you tiny insights into people's lives. I get elements of people's stories, little snippets like parts of a broken fossil, and often I want to know more, construct their lives in my head but they leave and usually I never see them again. Jake and Andy laugh often, chuck sand at each other, bump fists and look like a father and son who've grown up together.

Back at the shop, Andy tells me Jake wants to wander round the town for an hour or so and that if I can manage that pint he'd like it. There's stuff I should be doing, but I feel part of this story; I'm not sure why. And recently, with my dad fighting his own battle, talking to others has helped.

There's a pub at the end of the road. Jake thanks me for the tour and I feel he's thanking me for something else, as well, as he grins at his dad and me. If I'd been lucky enough to have children, I'd have liked one like him. I'm still young enough, I remind myself.

Andy orders the drinks and brings them out, where we sit in what during the day is the beer garden but turns at night into a smokers' den. For a few moments neither of us speaks.

Andy takes a large gulp of beer and turns to face me. He takes a breath.

'Three months ago, a woman called Gemma contacted me. She said we'd had a one night stand after a club night, fourteen years and five months ago. I wasn't sure at first how she could be so precise, but then she told me. Jake. She explained she felt awful for not trying to find me earlier, but had her reasons for doing so and wasn't sure what I'd think her motivation was…

'She said lots of things and I should have been angry, but then she told me about being diagnosed with cancer and that she wanted my help. I'm married, have been for four years to Carey, who's without doubt my soulmate. Luckily she's a very understanding soulmate and as soon as I told her the story she told me to ask them over for dinner. Looking at Jake was like looking at myself. Carey and I haven't had children, though we do want to, perhaps more so now. Jake's very protective of his mother. I'm ashamed to say I hardly remember Gemma, I think both of us had pretty hedonistic lifestyles and I'm sure the one night stand we had wasn't the first for either of us. But there was never any doubt in my mind that Jake's mine.' His speech is rushed, as if the story's been waiting there for a while.

'Blimey,' I say, which sounds lame.

'Yeah, blimey,' Andy smiles. 'Jake's an amazing kid and Gemma has brought him up well. He's kind and caring and not like I imagined a thirteen-year-old boy would be. He's taken all of this in his stride. This holiday was his idea. Originally Gemma was supposed to be coming too and the two of them would stay together and meet up with me during the day, but she's not well enough. I didn't think I was ready for fatherhood, but I'm enjoying every single minute. Gemma is strong as a horse, full of Northern grit, she tells me, and I'm sure she'll pull through. I was a little nervous about coming but Jake's made it easy. He remembers you very well, hasn't stopped talking about this tour once. We tried to call but the line was engaged and then I'm ashamed to say I forgot, with the last minute change of arrangements.'

'I'm glad we had spaces for you. Is Gemma most of the way though her treatment?'

'It's her second to last chemo treatment, but three days ago she was admitted with some kind of allergic reaction. She's so strong, so positive though. Jake knows all about it and she's never once complained or seemed to feel sorry for herself.'

'It's all about being positive, my dad tells me.'

'He has cancer?'

'Prostate. The doctors tell him it's such a slow burner he'll die of something else twenty years down the line, and the treatment's good, so I've no doubt he'll be okay. It's a difficult time though. Seems like it's everywhere, all over the media, taking out famous faces left right and centre. So when it strikes… But you know what? If, every day, they sent out statistics for people who'd just had their ten year all clear that day, there'd be heaps more of them. I'm sure.'

We finish our drinks and fall into easy conversation. Andy's a good bloke, I can tell straight away and I am glad because if anything does happen to Gemma, Jake's got somebody. I find myself wishing for her survival with a force that surprises me, nevertheless.

The next morning, the weather slips into proper summer with heat and sun. I work in the shop all morning and have a group in the afternoon. The beach is busy and difficult to negotiate with a group of twelve. I keep losing them and they're all kids today, so it's like herding cats. When I get to my favourite digging place, I see Andy and Jake kicking a football around on the sand. It's not so busy here; the crowds tend to stick near the ice cream shops. The sand seems to glow and sparkle today; magic sand that might yield some gifts. I get the kids going and take a breather, looking out to the sea that is shining with thousands of diamond glints. Jake and Andy are sitting now. Andy sees me and raises a hand in greeting. I wave back.

Suddenly Jake leaps up with a shout. He takes off at a run and I look ahead. Two figures are walking along the tide line, their feet in the small waves. One of the figures looks indistinct, and I squint, to look through the brightness of the sun. The two figures turn into one; it was an illusion, the brightness reflecting the sea or something. The figure walks slowly, stooping slightly. It's when I see her smooth head I realise at once who it is. Jake runs at her and throws himself at her. They turn into one, silhouetted against the sea, a solid unit. My vision blurs as I watch them part, and walk towards Andy, holding hands. I want to join them, be part of this incredible reunion but it's not my place, not my family. I watch as Andy kisses Gemma on the cheek and their exclamations reach me. I wonder how she did it, how she got herself out of hospital and came here. She *is* strong, I think, and I realise I want to know her better. I can go and say hello, later.

I drag my attention back to the group. One of the children has found something and all the others are standing around, looking for me. I wipe my eyes, and smile my way back to the group.

On the way back I see them still sitting there, higher up the beach now the tide's coming in. Jake and his mum sit close, with Andy on Jake's side. I can hear them laughing from here. I can't resist; I have to say hi.

They seem to share the same smile as they turn to me and greet me. Gemma is pale compared to the two sun-kissed faces next to her but she looks completely content.

'She broke herself out of hospital,' Andy says.

Gemma's looking at me, smiling. 'Malcolm. I remember you. Still doing the trips?'

'Just the same. You look…'

'Like crap?' she says, laughing. 'I don't feel too clever but I had to get away for a bit. I'll be in trouble but some Yorkshire sun will do me a lot more good that the cold air of the hospital.'

'No, I was going to say you look like you're fighting. And you look beautiful.' I want to clasp my hands over my mouth. Where did that come from? She'll either think I'm over-compensating or a total creep. Jake stifles some giggles and Andy raises an eyebrow. 'I mean it,' I say lamely, not knowing if this makes it better or worse.

Gemma laughs. 'You don't need to be polite. Anyway, I need to thank you. In some way, it was coming on your tour last year that made me seek medical advice. Something about the ammonite we dug out. Sounds bonkers, I know, but it was the night after we found it I made a promise to myself to contact the docs. I was almost too late.'

'I'm glad you did. You look like you'll beat it,' I say.

'Oh, I plan to. It's got no chance against me, eh, Jake?' she nudges him and he lays his head on her shoulder. 'I was just telling these two how much I miss Yorkshire. Being here makes me want to move back. What do you think, Jake?'

'*Yes*,' says Jake. 'I hate my new school.'

'The schools here are good, apparently. And you know what, I'm always looking for enthusiastic Saturday staff to work in the shop…' I feel my face reddening and close my mouth.

'Mum! Can we?'

Gemma pulls him close. 'Let me get myself right,' she says, 'and we'll take it from there. But right now, I can't see why not. All this has made me want a completely new start.'

'Well. You know where to find me. If that ever happens, I'd be happy to meet up and show you about.' I decide to stop talking before I make a complete idiot of myself. Something's happened. Something that hasn't happened for a long time. I can feel it, and I think Gemma can, too. She holds my eyes just a second too long as I say goodbye. It only takes a moment to fall, I remember my father saying. Just a moment.

I turn back to face the town and set off, wishing I could sit and stay with them a while longer, but it's their moment. This story doesn't include me. *Yet*, whispers my subconscious.

Only once I look back, across the sand and water, to where they sit together. Another figure stands just behind them. It raises a hand in my direction and I take my hand out of my pocket to wave, thinking it must be someone who knows me. I turn back and walk towards the slipway before realising that there's something amiss in what I've just seen. I look back and there are just the three of them once more. Time to get my eyes checked. And my pockets; my hands are covered with sand – there must be some fossil remnants lurking in the grotty depths.

I brush the sand from my hands and it trickles back to the beach as if through an hour glass, all those tiny particles that were once part of other things, creating this beach that I know so well, yet don't know at all.

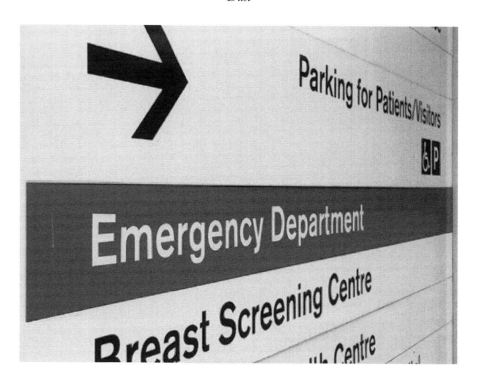

Your Lifejacket is Under Your Seat

She leans over and grabs the lifejacket, puts it over her head just as the cabin staff have demonstrated, and stands. She can see the exit, glowing in the gloom, beckoning, *this way, Charlene, this way;* an escape, unexpected but right there in front of her.

She treads on Deeg's feet on her way to the aisle. He can't speak; he's looking at her with a mixture of fear and admiration, eyes wider than they've ever been, seeing her for the first time. She waves a wiggly-fingered farewell and hoists herself into the aisle. The exit glows brighter and she runs to it, shoves against the hard metal and leaps, into blessed air – where her lifejacket turns into a parachute – into the unknown, into freedom.

'Did you pack my razor?' Deeg asks.

Charlene, who'd been gliding in clouds, shudders back to her seat, knowing she's wearing her rabbit in headlights look that he hates, backpedalling to remember what a razor is against the backdrop of the wide sky.

His sausage fingers are on her arm. *'Charlene?'*

She can ignore the promise of violence in his voice because they're in public. He'd not dare. His fingers dig harder.

'Wakey wakey,' he says.

'Yes. Your razor. It's in the case.'

His razor is an old fashioned, cut-throat one. He makes her give him a shave with it every day, a proper barber job shave that she had to go to barber school to learn. The other students were starting shops, or doing it as a way to make extra cash, toting their business on the internet. She's seen an advert: *Private, wet shave.* She's wondered if Deeg has ever had one of those; though he lacks the imagination to link sex with shaving. A small relief. His shaves are strictly morning rituals, designed to ease him into his day of bullying employees at the taxi rank.

They arrive at the hotel in Spain and Deeg's angry, having missed his shave due to the early morning start and the rush to the airport – her fault, for not waking him because she was too busy puking up last night's dinner in the toilet, too busy trying to retch quietly, consumed with trying not to cry and letting her fear show.

Deeg makes her shave him but she's got a plan. He doesn't see her slip on the latex gloves. She slips the razor to and fro across his wobbly cheeks and neck. Oops! In it goes, a little deep. His bulging eyes show it found its mark and she's away, ripping off the stupid apron he makes her wear, grabbing her bag and shoes stashed by the door, out into the corridor which leads to the outside world and into freedom.

'When we get to the hotel you'll give me a shave,' says Deeg, stealing some of her thoughts but, joy, not all of them.

She wonders how good the police are in Spain. She knows she's not in his will.

'I need the toilet,' says Charlene.

He raises his eyebrows at her.

'Please can I go to the toilet?' she asks, forcing herself to look at his red rimmed eyes. Forcing herself to keep her fingers by her side and not poke at those crimson squiggles in the corners, bursting veins that she hopes show some ill health. *Forgive me for my bad thoughts,* she thinks, again and again. *I'm not a good person.*

The plane is going to crash. As it's going down he'll either beg forgiveness or crush her hand in his fear.

She flexes her fingers and slides them under her thighs.

He's still considering. 'All right,' he says. 'But you'll have to climb over me.'

Charlene clenches her jaw and stands, hunching under the plastic underside of the overhead lockers. She slides a leg across and he grabs her crotch. He squeezes and pulls and grins at her with shiny lips. But Charlene feels safe enough to ignore him and she looks across the aisle, to a woman who's close enough to touch, a woman looking at her with perfect understanding. Charlene wants to cry, but Deeg hates her crying.

The toilet seems miles away.

'It's not *arranged* marriage, Clari,' her mother had told her in practised English. 'It's *convenience* for you. Save you from to look, now that no man take you. That boy. Took you from your life and then left you.' Charlene doesn't mention the real story; in their house it's a lie. It never happened. *That boy* wasn't warned off. She wasn't dragged to the chemist for a pill that would come too late. She wasn't pushed down the back steps by her brothers and she didn't have a miscarriage. Her life wasn't like a bad novel, so awful it could never happen, not in England. None of it was real.

'Deeg is from good family, Clari. He take care of you. Back in Bolivia, amongst our own people, he would be God. Look at him! The envy the village, you would be. We should have stayed but life, she goes on.'

'We should have stayed,' had once been the family *lament*: a word she'd learned on TV. Coming to England three years ago because of the earthquake, coming to stay with Geraldo, the cousin who'd renounced their freaktown religion – as Amy called it, and now she agreed – was the biggest mistake ever. No matter that the village was gone. No matter they were now one tenth of the population of Bemnites left in the world, because Deeg had offered a lifeline to the whole family and they'd start repopulating, right away. He never asked for her real age, choosing to believe the one on the emergency travel documents.

When Deeg found her birth control pills – given quietly to her at the hospital – he slammed her against a wall. She had time to think, *this'll show you, Mama,* before things went fuzzy. She woke up in hospital. Even Deeg got scared sometimes, she learned. He'd explained how she'd fallen down the stairs and hurt herself, silly girl. Charlene looked at his eyes and saw a promise and closed her mouth.

Deeg was such a God he went and became a Bemnite just to get her.

Her mother sighed, 'Such good man, this Diego. See what he will do for you, for us. He understands us.' Deeg was Argentinian so he understood the Bemnites' history and relationship with the better-known Mennonites, and, Charlene knew now, their naivety. 'Such small, brainless people, the Mennonites of Paraguay. And you're even worse,' he'd tell her, at night.

Charlene found out too late how many times Deeg had tried to get married; how many women had rejected him. Geraldo, with his empty bank account, introduced them, offering Charlene as a prize. She tried to tell her mother the truth but Deeg heard and after the night that followed, she'd never tell again. Never.

For a flash, Amy had been in her life. The curious next door neighbour, she'd questioned Charlene nonstop in the garden about their lives in Bolivia. 'Just like the Amish freaks,' Amy told her. After that Charlene wasn't allowed outside and Amy moved away. And then that boy, next door on the other side (whose name she still can't say), during her one and only rebellion, and then Deeg.

She runs to the pilot's door and bangs on it. He lets her in and he's a man like her father was, kind eyes, and yes of course he'll divert the plane and fly her to Turkey where she can disappear. Just say the word, Charlene. Not your real name? No problem. Here's a new passport with your proper name in it: Clarisa. Beautiful name. Right, here we are, Turkey. You run whilst we distract him. Run into freedom.

She opens the toilet door and closes it behind her. She dry heaves a couple of times into the sink, feeling her middle pull up sharp, too sharp. After the last time, any feeling there is frightening. How soon before she shows? She turns sideways and she can see, small but there, a tiny bump. The only mirrors at home are up high, so she can't see her tummy in them.

She has a bump.

He's too ignorant to think much about it, so at first he'll punish her for getting fat.

She pees, wipes, stands up again and winces as her wee is sucked out of the bowl with a roar. Could she fit down there? Sometimes she feels small enough. She could make herself tiny and push the scary flush and jump at the right moment and whoosh! Out into the air. Into freedom.

No matter how many times he tells he otherwise, she *knows* she is not stupid. She hangs onto this. She reads things; listens to the news; watches television when Deeg is at work; learns as much as she can. She can't leave the house but she can go anywhere through the screen and she travels the world and the space it spins in. Bemnites were real, but they lived in the past. Even her mother had changed now, accepted the new world, learned from Geraldo, apologised to her soft-eyed husband, *God rest him*, and got on with it. Deeg embraced electricity so it must be good; Deeg had a TV so her mother must get one too. Look at what he's done for us, Clari-*Charlene*. Her brothers even went to school.

She's clever, now; she knows about the world and how it works. Men who are not like her father were strange, at first, but they exist. She learned fast. If she runs and Deeg finds her, he will kill her. This is understood between them. She's *not* stupid, despite what he tells her every single day and so she knows that when she runs, she must never be found.

She goes to the front of the plane when it lands and makes everyone look at her. That man, she says, pointing, and she tells them everything. Hold him down, all of you, while I escape. And all the passengers become her heroes as they sit on his horrible body and she runs, into sweet freedom.

She goes back to her seat and waits for Deeg to let her in. He leers up at her and she lifts her leg up, squeezes over him, grimaces as he pinches at her, climbs back to her seat and his familiar, terrible smell. She gags, quietly, turning it into a cough. Deeg says, 'My turn, now,' and laughs at her. He grunts as he gets out of his seat.

He goes towards the toilet and some of the other passengers, who've been listening and worked out her whole life, run up behind him and shove him forwards. He lands against the main door and with his great weight it bursts open and he's born again into the sky, clouds welcoming him with cold arms. The plane goes down, everyone except Deeg is okay and she walks out of the hospital, after a few checks, into freedom.

'Spain! Clarisa!' If Mama uses her real name she's happy. 'Clarisa this is dream! See how far we have come. You bring back a proper baby!'

She didn't tell her mother that Deeg wanted to go to Spain to watch bull fighting and that he didn't trust her to stay at home alone. But she was happy; in Spain she would escape. She walked into all ten of their rooms in the big house that her mother said she was lucky to have. Each room held a memory of pain or fear. When Deeg wasn't looking, she scratched a tiny 'Adios,' into the wooden bedhead. Her will wavered when she saw her father's picture on the wall, and she wished she could take it, without making Deeg suspicious. Am I doing the right thing? she asked him. Then Deeg kicked her bottom, just for fun, as she was leaving the house and she knew exactly what her father's answer would have been.

When Deeg gets back from the toilet, sweat coagulating on his forehead, he kicks her again. She dodges but the woman in the seat next to her, the one in whose face she'd seen understanding, places her book with care on the seat next to her, stands in front of Deeg, and punches him solid on his nose. Blood spurts everywhere. Passengers laugh, as Deeg stumbles backwards and knocks himself out, and she's fallen into freedom.

Deeg doesn't kick her. He pinches her arm as he sits down, his cruel fingers making another *Deeg's property* mark on her skin. 'When we get to Spain, I will watch you every second of the day. Don't try nothing,' he says. And Charlene thinks, *When we get to Spain I will scratch your eyes out with my nails.*

The landing is bumpy and though she tries to imagine a bad ending for him, as the plane crashes, Charlene can't see one that doesn't have her in it. So she stops her silly fanciful thinking, as she's heard someone say on TV in a programme that reminds her of Benmites, with their old clothes and horses. If she's good, her baby will live.

Deeg is swept away from her as other passengers press from behind and she slips back towards the window. If she stays on, will the plane go somewhere else? He won't be allowed back on and she can fly away, into freedom. She sees him look behind, twisting his head with difficulty on his fat neck. The tide of people takes him, as if they've read her thoughts all the way to Spain. They flow down the aisle and she doesn't move. The cabin becomes hushed, like her house on a hot day when Deeg is asleep on the couch and she longs to be outside, but has to sit there, waiting for him to wake up.

She can see Deeg out of the window, trying to get back up the steps to get her but being spoken to by a flight attendant. She looks around. The woman from across the aisle is looking at her.

'Just you and me,' says the woman. 'But not for long. How old are you?' she says.

Charlene looks at her feet. 'Sixteen,' she says.

'Jesus. Get out now, while you still can. When you get home, call the 'Women First' helpline. Can you remember that? *Women First.* They will tell you how to get away. They will help you. Don't write anything down. Be strong.' And she's gone, hurrying away down the plane, shaking her head and rubbing her neck, as if erasing a memory

The words hang in the air. Charlene pulls them in and tucks them safe inside her, next to her baby.

She stands again. She wants to tell the woman that she can't wait another week. He'll find out about the baby and then he'll never, ever, let her out of his sight. How long before she vomits in front of him? She's been close, already.

Inside the airport the heat makes her vision shimmer. She looks at the departure boards as they wait for suitcases, forcing the words to stay still. One shines out – Los Angeles. The Angels, from where they flew to England. The Angels, whom, working backwards, will take her home.

Deeg pushes to the front of the throng of people and she watches as he falls onto the carousel and disappears through the flaps into who knows where. She runs, before anybody links her to him, and leaves the airport, into a waiting taxi and into freedom.

He turns to look at her and gives her a glance, eyes narrowed, which says, Stay there, girl.

She takes a tiny step backwards and more people slide in front of her, grabbing what space they can. She can't see Deeg's glistening hair any more. She takes another step backwards, and another. Now the door screaming EXIT is just behind her.

Deeg has her passport.

She shuffles forward again with heavy feet until she can see the lights gleaming from the bald patch he denies he has, that she once mentioned in an ill-planned moment.

He returns with the bags, his face frowning in a way she's learned to dread.

'I have to go to the toilet again. Now. Don't move.' He looks queasy instead of angry and her stomach unties itself.

And he's gone, and life has given her a gift. His stupid man bag is there on the basket at the front of the trolley. He must feel really ill because he's left it right there where she can grab her passport.

Perhaps there is a God after all because the Los Angeles flight is due to leave in half an hour. Perhaps the God that left her in Bolivia has come back to look after her because she finds the desk with ease. Someone, at least, is looking after her because there are some seats left and she pays with his credit card which isn't checked properly. She runs to security and there is no queue and she's safe in the lounge and he can't get to her and even if he could, she's got his passport and his money. The flight leaves on time and as she rises up to the sky, she cries, letting the tears steam up the window, hands on her belly, knowing she's flying into freedom.

'Just in case you get any ideas, girl,' says Deeg, appearing back by her side as she gazes at his ridiculous bag, worrying she's left the zip in the wrong position. He grabs it and heads back to the toilet, waddling in discomfort.

Clarisa, which means bright, shining and gentle, in her native language, waits until the toilet door closes behind him and then she steps away, light on her feet, her passport in her pocket, freedom ahead of her.

Wordsmith

In those last, miserable moments, before she finds *Wordsmith*, or, more correctly, before *Wordsmith* finds her, Cara is sitting at the table where it all began to end, the day he told her he had to escape.

Opposite her is an empty space but if she tries really hard she can conjure his image and place him there, smiling, taking her hand, touching her face or reading to her from a dog-eared book. They came here often, on dates agreed in a code only they knew. They took stolen illegal moments in a town where they both didn't belong, to drink coffee and eat surrounded by the stories of other people; millions of words spinning around them, enclosing them, as they wrote their own story. When they sat together in *Drink in the Stories,* it became their home.

Part of the painful beauty, perhaps, was in knowing it would have to end one day. He was here on borrowed time; all she could do was love him and the finite limit to their hours gave it an extra intensity. They'd slipped into magical weekends whenever they could, allowing themselves to disappear into each other in some hotel or other. It didn't matter where, just that they were both there.

She traces the grooves in the wood that she knows like the veins on her hand, the one she'd looked at when he told her he was leaving and he couldn't tell her when or how or where to. Even being there was a risk for him, she'd known that, and yet she'd not wanted him to leave. Everything had been a risk, any pattern was dangerous, yet this corner of *Drink in the Stories*, with its three walls of books and a narrow entryway, was theirs alone in a world that was full of everything and everyone else. So they kept coming back.

They'd met in the street, just outside. Life is chance, he'd told her over that first coffee. You being you and me being me and us bumping into each other. Just chance, and yet… And yet? she'd asked. It's like it was meant to be, he murmured, so there is magic too. She's not sure if that was the moment she got lost in him, or had it happened the moment their eyes met?

If he'd been a normal person and not on the run from jihadists intent on erasing him and all his words from the planet, would she have fallen so hard? If they'd had all the time in the world and all the freedom afforded to ordinary lovers and none of the risk attached that made every moment precious, would she have fallen so hard? Yes, she would, she knows, and without all the fear of losing it, every moment of every day, having to watch the news and try to understand things she's never wanted to. Like hate and faith and politics and why people find it so hard to feel empathy and why arguing about the name of God is so important.

Her thoughts tread a well-known path through the forests of her memories and she sips her coffee and looks at the stories around her. She'll not find his book in here; there are too many people trying to get rid of it and every bookshop has been scoured. The few copies that were bought before the fatwa was issued are well-guarded and kept out of sight. Nobody will own up to having one. She has fifteen that she's hidden for him, in a box, in a dark corner of her attic. It amazes her that nobody's discovered them, her or the books. Maybe it's because on the outside she's so ordinary as to be invisible to most people. The only person who knew her properly and made her soul stop feeling lonely has gone.

She can carry on, she knows this. Life before was all right, and life afterwards will be all right. Except that before she didn't have anything to miss, and now she does.

She tries not to wonder where he is but every moment, she does. She'll never be able to 'move on', even if there was anyone well-meaning around to tell her to. She has acquaintances; a family she's distanced from because they are Jehovah's Witnesses and she isn't and when she left, she was excommunicated, but nobody she could share any of this with. She's always been self-contained and complete, until now. And she knows this: love like that only comes once in a lifetime, so what would there be to 'move on' to? She also knows she'll keep coming to *Drink in the Stories* on the dates they agreed, just in case he can ever come back. He has to be able to find her. In this bookshop, something extraordinary – in the literal sense of the word – happened.

Prime numbered dates, that fell on a Thursday or a Monday. That was their code. Today is April 13th, and the next one happens to be Monday. Every seventh date, they skipped a meeting, just in case. Weekends had been spontaneous, and all the more wonderful for it.

She finishes her coffee and wanders over to the nearest bookshelf. They'd spent hours studying all the books in 'their' space and she knew when things had been changed around, new books added or other ones sold. She knows which ones they'd read together and which ones he'd touched, running a finger along a spine, choosing, reading her words he'd picked from thousands of others. Some of the books have hardly moved. She can almost hear them whisper – a timeless constant commentary all around her.

She sees a book that looks familiar. She's seen it somewhere; long ago, far away. She thinks, but the memory won't come. She frowns, and strokes the spine. It's a thick book, battered and faded, with an illegible title along the edge. She draws it out and weighs it in her hands; promising, she thinks, all those words. *Wordsmith* is the title, by Ellen Song-Smith. She's never heard of Ellen Song-Smith but knows she's going to buy the book the moment she picks it up. It says PROOF COPY in thick black letters, scrawled across the front. She can't stop the thought that comes: it's always belonged to her. She sits back down and opens the book at random.

He walked away from her, never once looking back, and they both knew that if he did, they'd run back together and they'd both be lost. She watched him until he was swallowed up by other people's rushing, drawn into the throng of life that was the city. And she turned, and walked away, her tears running fast and she not caring. She knew she'd never be happy again, for the cause of it was gone, all of her joy, was, in this moment, draining out of her, to die there on the pavement...

She stops reading and rubs her eyes. She opens the book again, somewhere else.

...and to know this is to be free. You cannot ever hold on to anything and life will never stop running, like a river it takes you whether you like it or not, but you choose to swim or to fight. After the war, I fought it for a long time whilst I tried to find my son. But he'd been taken; the currents had dragged him away from me.

She skips to another bit.

...I walk along the passageway through the knots in my mind as they tangle and trip me and cause me to fall and I get up, again and again, fighting, hard, because what else can you do and what else can you say? I'm getting back up, heading back in the same direction because however hard it is there is a way if you push hard enough... And there he is, walking towards me, and I welcome him in and say, this is my dream, and you can come in...

She closes the book and her hand hovers on the cover, stroking it. Short stories. What are the chances of random lines fitting her life like this? These words resonate with her, vibrate inside her, lift her. But there is so much going on, she reflects, that perhaps she could fit into anyone's story. This is an old story, after all. Losing love. The door to her soul left swinging open.

One last time, she reads. '*...if you stop looking, searching, trying to find him, you'll never forgive yourself and yours will be a lonely death,*' said the old woman to Charlotte. *Charlotte swallowed and thought, but he doesn't want to be found. The old woman smiled at her and seemed to read her mind. 'Precious child, he wants to be found so much he's wishing for you every moment of every day. Can't you hear him calling you?' Charlotte stood and...* She snaps the book closed, frowns at it.

She sits and finishes the cake she's not enjoying but has bought because it's his favourite, and checks email on her phone. Nothing. It's almost two months since he disappeared and she doesn't even know if he's alive. For her own safety she fears nothing; she's no dependents and perhaps it'd be a relief to not have to get up and face the hole that's been drilled into her life and is getting bigger every day.

She's made little attempt to understand why they want him dead. Crazy, all of them, she thinks, and wonders what made him take them on. What's wrong with a quiet life? They could have disappeared together and he could have renounced all that stuff he wrote that they want to kill him for. But she curses herself for her cowardice and for underestimating him. His integrity is one of the things she loves the most. His honesty and ability to focus intently on one thing at a time. When his focus was on her she burned with joy like pain under the intensity of it all.

She goes to pay. Nadia – known to her from a name badge and polite conversation over the till, despite Cara's intention to be invisible – nods as she pays. 'Not seen your friend for a while,' she says.

Cara shakes her head and does a sort of half smile that means, don't go there, we've split up. The sort of thing only a woman would understand. Also, how does she know 'Nadia' is Nadia? Her olive skin and dark watchful eyes and half-covered head could mean anything. This is what she hates, all this suspicion. She doesn't think she'll ever understand it.

'Looks like a good book,' says Nadia. Cara can now see she's trembling, as if she's sick. Her words are rushed. 'Only came in this morning. Someone left it, with a note asking me to put it in the small alcove, the one you always sit in. Said it was her favourite spot.'

'Oh,' says Cara, wondering if there is any significance here and deciding that no, chance sometimes is just chance. But she can tell Nadia is lying. Why would Nadia lie?

'Have a good day,' says Nadia as she hands over change, not quite meeting her eyes. Cara nods and leaves the shop, pulling her hat down low over her eyes.

On the way home she buys enough food to last her a couple of days. She's had holiday booked from work for weeks, and there didn't seem any point in cancelling it even though she wouldn't, as planned, be meeting him in Skye. She'd stay at home and read, and now she had the right book to get lost in. She'd wondered about moving, but her proofreading job here suited her; she could work from home whenever she wanted and the city was cheap to live in. She liked the wild unpredictable weather and the cold and the feeling of being at the edge of the world, even though it was really just the edge of a small island. And he's been here; that's the main reason, now. He knows where to find her.

It's the nights that are the worst, when she doesn't think she'll survive the desolation of being in the world without him. She's lost half of herself.

She settles under a blanket and begins with the first story.

I didn't see it coming. Before we met I thought I was complete; I lived my life, I took lovers, I laughed. But then I met him, and in an instant, it all changed. A layer was peeled away from the world and I saw in brighter colours. As a girl, I was sucked into the – forbidden, to me - Hollywood ideal of falling in love at first sight and feeling whole and living happily ever after. Of course the world got in the way and life's never like that. So when it happened I was lifted up high and all my cynicism was wiped away with these small, everyday words: 'I'm sorry! Wasn't looking where I was going!' as I stumbled into him, backwards, trying to stop my shopping bag from bursting. It was in his eyes, right there. Recognition.

Cara shudders. She pulls the blanket closer, and looks into the corners of the room. These are her words. That is, she could have written them. That was what she said.

She falls backwards into her life and is right back there, ten months ago, reddening as she straightened, gave up on the shopping and let it all fall to the ground.

Instant. Alchemy.

Life is a series of instances, of chances.

Charlie went red, too, though he wasn't usually given to blushes. She was flustered and naked-faced and looking wide-eyed at him, and he looked back at her and couldn't help it, a little of his real self pushed itself upwards and shone out of his face. He tried to cap it and shove it back down, but it was out; she'd seen it.

They scrabbled on the ground for tins and oranges and an onion, which tried to get away. In hindsight, he knows he should have followed the onion, picked it up and run away himself, because right then he felt the pull of feeling, a feeling he'd never known. She was familiar and new all at once, and as they stood and restacked her bag, something between them slotted back into place.

She regarded the onion. 'It must have heard me talking about a casserole,' she said, and he laughed.

'Speaking of which, it's lunchtime. Would you…?' He couldn't quite get the words out, but she nodded and in to *Drink in the Stories* they went, straight to the table that would become theirs. All the way he was torn, cursing himself for letting go, berating himself for the danger they would likely now both be in. Why had he not simply walked on? Because he knew her, didn't he? They sat for two and a half hours, and the only thing he didn't tell her was his real name. Oh, and the fact that some radical Muslims were trying to kill him because he'd written a book – his second novel – about a soldier in Syria who's a comedian and who makes fun of ISIS and gets them all to change their minds by making them laugh at their ridiculousness. Hard to believe he'd not meant it in a contentious way; he was just sick of all of it and thought a new slant might make people see it differently.

Things got serious very quickly and his agent advised him to disappear. Aberdeen was as far away from Cornwall as he could get without a passport, so here he was.

When they left the bookshop café, they each wore the same stunned look: a questioning of reality. He looked at her and saw it reflected right back at him. There was no awkwardness about their parting. He simply said, 'Same time tomorrow?' and she nodded and that was their beginning. He told her about the fatwa the following day, after they'd made love in the afternoon's shadows in her bed. He'd made sure they weren't followed but he knew he'd never be able to go there again. They needed rules and maths seemed like a good place to go.

'Prime numbers,' he told her. 'And a pay as you go phone.'

He sweated about it but he couldn't walk away any more than she could. They were two realists thrown together by a fairy tale idea that neither had believed in. The only thing he didn't tell her was his real name. With her, he was Richard. On the book he was AJ Rawson.

Eight months later, he had to disappear. They were onto him, his agent said. She didn't know how, but they'd tracked him to Aberdeen.

'Change your appearance, and go again,' she said, and this time she'd sorted him a passport. He became James Clarke, Human Resources Manager.

He took a bus to Manchester and got on a plane, all of it in a blur because all he could feel was the pull to go back. Could he have taken her? Maybe. But the risk to her was too great. The last time he saw Cara was on the street, in a crowd, after they left the bookshop.

He ran away, a coward again, and he found himself in South America, wandering from country to country, avoiding conversation, trying to forget her face. Failing.

Many times he tried to write but now he was someone else the words would not come, the sentences tied themselves in knots and punctuation stripped out the feeling so the words were wooden and dry. In the end he decided it was kinder to them both to stop, so he threw away his pens, zipped his laptop into the bag and wondered who he'd be if he'd not written that story.

He'd known it would annoy people but he'd never expected the violence of the response. His own feelings were strong – the whole thing, all of it, all of the madness and the misunderstanding and the murder needed addressing and laughter was his way. He'd once been Charlie the class clown. He found writing humour easy, and thought that perhaps if people could learn to laugh instead of hate, he could change things, for deep down he was a fighter. He believed in having morals and sticking to them. Cara he envied; she wasn't uncomplicated but she simply rose above anything she didn't understand or couldn't change and lived her life making the changes she could – proofreading charity newsletters for low fees, proofreading for nothing if they couldn't pay, charging those who could, such as Shell and BP. She made smaller changes. What had made him think he could change the world in one novel? The arrogance... Charlie sighed and stretched in his hammock and felt himself sink down, low off the ground, swinging from side to side, wishing for Cara, only Cara, a balm against all of the madness.

'Cerveza, por favor,' he said again, as a beach seller drifted past and he let the alcohol wash the feeling away.

The old couple sits at the tide line, backs to the dunes, watching the waves and sifting through the sea's gifts for stones and shapes. She makes mobiles from them which she hangs on the porch and he knocks in nails when they get blown down.

'A red rock,' she says. 'How?'

'Iron, maybe an old brick? Somebody's house.'

'Mmm. I wonder where the rest of it went. To the eleven corners of the earth,' she says.

'Why eleven?' he asks, taking her hand.

'I like prime numbers,' she says, and laughs a laugh that belies her age. It's the laugh of a girl from long ago, a girl who fell in love with a boy and lived happily ever after, eventually.

He takes her face in his hands and kisses her, like the boy he once was. That's who she sees, anyway, like the girl still in the mirror. Wrinkles are what other people put on you, they'd decided long ago.

Letting their guard down wasn't easy; he still looks over his shoulder once in a while and she hates a ringing phone or calling Screen. Mostly, the Screen is switched off, just in case someone from the past should contact them. The only time they leave it on is when they forget or on the agreed dates with Nadia. Nadia's aged well, her olive skin smoother than theirs and they can't blame the lack of worry; she's worried enough for both of them to carve gorges into her skin. It's her lightness that stops this. Her ability to shrug off the weight, feel it, let it go and move on. Right back at the beginning she used to try and get them to do it too, but the old woman acknowledges now that she never was a good student.

Hand in hand they walk along the shore to their house, a wooden structure that seems to hang together with luck and love and the plants that creep all around it. It's time for their rest; she insists on it, so that they can stay up longer in the hush of the night with the shush of the sea. Every afternoon they lie behind gently blowing curtains playing on the sea breeze, under a canopy of stars. The stars she put there to remind them – hand stitched every one onto the four-poster's ceiling sheet – to remind them that everything on earth isn't all that exists. That there is magic.

He takes her hand and she lays her head next to his shoulder and they lie, just touching, sometimes meeting in dreams and welcoming each other with a smile of recognition. It was like that right from the very first time it happened, as if they'd always known that one day they'd be able to stroll the corridors of each other's minds, step through the tangle of sleep and visit the purist parts of each other in their dreams. If she'd not experienced it, she'd not have believed it, like the time she met Nadia in a dream, months ago now, and they were in the bookshop and they communicated, somehow, without words. When she woke, it was with the idea for *Wordsmith*. She often dreams of *Drink in the Stories*, where it all began.

They make love and it doesn't always work and this is the one thing they acknowledge about age. But it never matters: it's the closeness that counts, the touching, the climbing back into one another's souls, making the connection stronger and stronger in case it is ever tested again.

Then one afternoon, there is a knock at the door, three quick knocks, to be exact, business-like and harsh. She doesn't know why, but fear paralyses her. She looks at him and sees, like that very first time, recognition.

It's not magic, as much as having an extra sense. An unreliable extra sense. Like love, like those times people say they fell in love at first sight. I didn't believe it until

I saw them together, like one person split into two. They were twins. They belonged. Love and this extra sense are connected. I first knew it when we still lived in Saudi. My grandmother had come to stay from Sudan; I was nine years old and when she left I knew I was never going to see her again. I don't know how, and nobody believed me, but it was a strong feeling in the shimmering air that made me rush to her and wrap myself around her legs and beg her not to go. I later found out she knew about the cancer already, she must have done, because she was so far gone with it when they tried to operate that they could do nothing except sew her up again and give her morphine. I discovered this much later and it made me think, did she have this extra sense, too? Or did she just feel ill?

After that it was sporadic: me knowing who was on the phone, dreams where I'd seen something that hadn't happened yet, small guesses that turned out to be correct, when I could never have known. Subtle stuff. Many Muslims don't like to hear things like this, especially the ones in my family, so I kept quiet. My mother would have said, 'Nadia, you dreamer. Get your feet back down on the earth and work.' I tried not to have the magic but it wouldn't leave me alone, and after we moved to Scotland it became more frequent, stronger. Scarier. The more I learned about life, the more I found I already knew, and I didn't know how I knew it.

When I hit puberty, late, it all got worse. I told my family, and Mother had Words. She and my sister sat me down and told me to stop this nonsense and what would Father have thought? And although I knew he would have agreed with me that there was a possibility of magic – after all, who is Allah if he's not magic? How can he hear us? – I had to obey them and stop talking my nonsense and accept it could never be true.

Until I saw them in the bookshop. I'd worked at *Drink in the Stories* for a year and knew every book and every corner and read as many as I could. I was alone in the city, Mum and Alina had left but I was, had always been, more willing to take on my new country as my own. I had a slight Scottish accent and although I wore a scarf, in deference and in respect for Mother, it was a wispy thing that didn't cover me. It was a token, a sign I'd not quite left their world.

I watched them come in and immediately got a *feeling* about him. She looked like she was in shock, joyful shock, and he looked terrified, but they both – strangely – looked happy.

They came in on odd days. I never managed to work it out as they didn't follow a pattern. I looked at them and wanted what they had. For all my knowledge of this extra –

mystical – layer in the world, I'd never discovered the magic of love, only the reality of disappointment. The Scottish men I'd met were solid, earthy beings, Muslim men confused me – either the drinking types or the devout types. There was nobody like me: a person of three worlds, or perhaps more. I lost count of all the identities I'd had. I tried to soak up their magic when they came in. They didn't talk to me except to order food and pay and buy books; they didn't seem aware of anyone around and yet they had an awareness of place that confused me. He kept an eye on the door and she kept an eye on him and I saw worry and fear pass over both of their features several times each visit.

Eavesdropping was easy; behind their alcove was a space where we stored cases of juice and flavoured water. I could slip behind there and hear what they had to say – and that's how I learned who he was. Like me, he was of several worlds. But unlike me, he'd trodden in one he didn't fully understand and left ugly footprints, stamped on our beliefs. The anger I felt was tempered when I actually read the book (I worked in a bookshop, it was easy to get hold of a copy though they claimed to have destroyed them all) and discovered what he was trying to do. He was trying to transcend everybody and everything and create understanding through something we all have in common: humour. I got it straight away but I also understood how he'd missed the point, got it slightly wrong, said too much, too soon, as if the world wasn't ready for him. I wanted to tell him but I knew if I told him I knew, he'd run. And for now, I needed them there.

Magic in action: their table was never occupied, even on busiest days, when they were there. Without fail, people would get up and leave minutes before they stepped through the door, never together, meeting in the alcove with clasping hands and desperate touches. I wanted some of their magic for myself, to mix in with my own.

One day, a flash. I was ill, feverish and shouldn't have been at work. I'd taken paracetamol and was carrying on, limping to the end of a shift that wasn't going to be covered by anyone as staff had been leaving in droves – the last oil push was on and many of them were tempted by the higher wages. Billy, the boss, told me on the phone from London to wait for a lull, stick a sign on the door and go home but I wanted to keep it open. What if they came, and it was closed?

And they did come. She was first, excitement and sadness in equal measures coming off her in waves of nervous energy. She couldn't decide what to order; she hovered, she dropped her change all over the counter when she was paying for a book. He often turned up after than her and she wanted to read, I supposed. I was about to tell her to pay at the end when the money fell everywhere and we both scrabbled to pick it up. Our hands brushed and the odd thing happened. Like Grandma, but worse.

I saw her old and alone and sad and tired. It was definitely her; eyes don't change. She was carrying the weight of sorrow and she was going to die alone. This, I knew. I swayed on my feet and held onto the counter for support and she didn't notice. That is how wrapped up in her love she was; she didn't notice me slip away like that. I put it down to my fever but it was later that I realised I was wrong. It was the same feeling, absent now for a long time, but come back when my guard was down.

I struggled to make sense of it and knew there was no sense to be made. Like that time in Saudi, and the tens of times since, I'd had a glimpse of something. I held onto the counter and waited until I felt solid, back in this world.

They came in three more times together and then she came in alone. I waited with her, although she didn't know it.

My first thought was that he was dead, but they'd have proclaimed it to the world, gleeful and dark, on video. Days passed and there was nothing and I thought, he's left her, but I knew that wasn't true either. And now came another one of those things I just knew and didn't know how: I had to get a message to that woman, that old woman. That old woman who may be in the future.

I'd never tried to harness the magic. Torn between myself and fear and my family who thought it was witchcraft and dreaminess, I'd just accepted I had odd *knowings* and I didn't mess about with it. I was fearful for my own soul, too. Religion may ask you to suspend all your disbelief and take on such faith that you accept whole invisible doctrines, but it doesn't allow for anything not in that doctrine. It's one of the biggest hypocrisies, but it still ruled me.

My mind, though, had other ideas. In my dreams I kept coming to the bookshop, long after I'd stopped working there, in a future where things looked much the same although the cakes were different. There I met the old woman I'd seen in the vision, that older version of the female half of the magic couple. She wandered amongst the shelves and in the dream I told her she had to keep searching and tell herself – the version of herself stuck in the present, with me – not to give up. Told her she had to send a sign, something she would follow. I could tell she'd been alone ever since and she was going to die alone and I woke up crying, every time I had the dream. She wasn't there to comfort me when I woke; nobody was. I had the dream time and time again, stronger when the woman had been in the bookshop that day.

On April 13ᵗʰ, which happens to be my birthday, I opened the shop at ten, switched on the machines, hummed Happy Birthday to myself and began mixing up the sandwich fillings. The air shimmered ; like it did that time in Saudi, and when I turned, there was a book, a battered, as if well-travelled, large book with PROOF COPY scrawled on the front.

I felt as if I was going to faint, my breath coming in gasps and a sprinkling starting around the edge of my vision, like visible static. I gripped the edge of the work surface behind me and shook my head. When I trusted myself to stay upright, I walked to the counter. *Wordsmith* by Ellen Song-Smith, I read. I knew exactly that to do with it. When the woman comes in, I said to myself, I'll give her a hint.

I walked back to the counter and began to make egg sandwiches. Began the long wait until she came in.

In the very last story, she reads her own recent history. And it isn't strange; by now she's understood that these stories are about her. It doesn't matter how; it doesn't matter that she doesn't know the name Ellen Song-Smith. It doesn't matter that none of this makes any sense. The message is: go and find him.

So she packs for a long journey, and two weeks later, she begins the search. The internet is helpful; there are trackers on various frightening sites which all want to kill him. His pen name nestles in lists, with other famous names well-known to the media. People who've written other books, drawn cartoons, sung songs. The good news is, they're all still alive. She feels he is too; the connection is still there, a light inside her.

She begins in Asia, travelling by feel, understanding the kind of places he'd want to go. She spends weeks getting lost amongst the drunken backpackers and the thinkers and the idealistic young students. She speaks to bar owners of all nationalities and she sits and she watches.

She can feel he's not here. But by now the hastily cobbled together money is running out so she takes a job teaching English. It's supposed to be a month but it turns into two and with every day she feels him slipping further away. What if he's gone back to Aberdeen? She left a cryptic message with Nadia at the bookshop with an e mail address that she can check from time to time, though she knows there are ways of tracing this. And what if 'Nadia' isn't Nadia? She's thought this before. Something about Nadia is a little off beat, wrongly put together, but she had nobody else to ask. She gets out her map and tries to remember every conversation they ever had, every ambition he ever told her, every dream he ever shared. He once talked of glaciers in South America, of wanting to see the way they'd carved the mountains, of wanting to stand next to one and see the ice shearing off into the sea, to feel that power and watch the shockwaves radiate out across the water. She gets on the internet and reads about Patagonia, and a glacier that is still growing, when all around it are shrinking. She circles a town and books a flight that will take her halfway around the entire globe.

Argentina is colour and edginess and music. She spends a few days acclimatising in Buenos Aires, catching up with herself, bits of whom are becoming scattered as she moves. When she's gathered as much as she can she heads south on a bus, watches the endless Patagonian landscape grow and shrink out of her window. Mountains fall and rise, plains stretch and villages appear as lives flash by the bus. She sees men on horseback, snow-capped peaks and feels harsh winds sculpting the land. Immediately she feels she's near him. This is a land to vanish in. This is a place so vast, so wild, anyone could appear and disappear at will. It's a land of magic and age and freedom. She carries the book by Ellen Song-Smith and reads from it from time to time. They are her words, some of them, but some of them are not. She looks in between them and can see him in there and thinks, what if he wrote some of this, too? But how can it be? And then her head twists into knots of unreason and she gives up and puts it away.

She checks the e mail address once a week. After a while, comes the line from ndeeeya85134@dits.com: 'He's not come back here. Thought you should know. Keep searching. I am a friend.' And she thinks she's being forced into trust and maybe this is a good thing. She doesn't write back, because of this lately developed paranoia that someone could track her down and get on his trail, which by now, she can feel she's on. But she imagines Nadia dashing off those lines and peering over her shoulder and she sends a hope to her to stay safe, because this world of madness isn't easy to follow and anything can happen to anyone; even though she thought she – and life – was ordinary, they're obviously not. She's not.

Recognition comes as a shock and a welcome home after weeks of moving. She sees the back of his head in front of her, staring at the ice wall in the distance but so very close, waiting for chunks of it to fall. For a moment she stands there and doesn't dare move, afraid he's an illusion. She edges closer, holding her breath, letting it in and out in tiny gasps until she's sure she's going to faint. When she's close, she sees him stiffen and put his head down. She can tell he's afraid to turn around, in case it's not her.

'I'm sorry,' she whispers when she's right behind him. 'But I *was* looking where I was going.'

It began as the odd email, a few lines across the distance. It became a conversation and as things relaxed and the world began to forget about AJ Rawson, I nursed the hope that they could live in peace and move on. After a few years, we were regular correspondents. She told me how they'd renamed each other – after all this time she still won't tell me his real name though she, at least, knows it now. She says she called herself Ellen Smith and he called himself James Song. He can carry it off, she says, because his grandmother was Chinese. I remember that book, and smile.

I got married, finally found love and the magic in me settled down, if it even *was* magic. I wasn't sure now if any of it had happened – anything can be rationalised, if you have enough imagination. None of it mattered; I had a family, Ellen and James had each other. I don't know where they lived; this was the only thing they wouldn't tell me. With Screens came a glimpse into their world: it was hot, they lived near the sea and with the coder, they could remain anonymous to any cyber spies. I don't know how all that worked; I was old fashioned and still loved books, even after everything went digital. I used the technology if I had to; I didn't try to make sense of it.

And then one night, years later, the dream. I was ill. I'd picked up a virus after travelling to my mother's funeral in Saudi. I was feverish, not quite in the world, and I saw them die.

I woke screaming, babbled to Roy, my husband, who was a practical Scot and who told me it was all a dream, but I knew it wasn't. I knew it. Just like the time in the shop, the world had shimmered. I'd been asleep but the feeling was still strong, recognisable after all this time. When Roy went to make me tea, I scribbled down what I could remember. Every detail had to be right. It wasn't a dream but the mind plays tricks; the more I told myself this, the more I believed it was a dream. I felt foolish, therefore, when I Screened them on one of our days, the following week. She was out; he was there reading, when I was beamed into their space.

I described every detail: the colour of their door, the clothes they were wearing, the guns. The killers remained faceless; in the dream I was behind them. They knocked at the door, a quick three raps, business-like. Even after all this time, they'd not forgotten or forgiven him.

'I'm afraid I've led them to you,' I said, and though it couldn't be true, any of it, I couldn't stop feeling this. I'd let them down. I'd caused them to die, sometime in the future. Just as I'd been able to contact her future self (Had I? Was that real? It was so long ago), I'd somehow contacted the killers, subconsciously. But something had happened to him, too. I wasn't the only one who'd become more rational. He assured me it was a dream, that he didn't feel afraid, that they would be fine. They'd Screen me next week and I'd see, they'd be fine.

'They've long ago given up on me, Nadia,' he said. 'We are living out our days in peace, both of us writing – we've even collaborated on a book of short stories. The proof copy arrived last week but the damn thing seems to be lost, I can't find it – can you believe it? The stories are partly about us, about how we met – her idea. We're happy; the world has forgotten my stupid idealism.' He grinned at me across the miles and I wished they were closer so I could protect them, and let some of their old magic brush off on me.

'Just promise me,' I told him, 'if someone knocks three times at your door, you'll run.'

I told him to give my love to Ellen and he waved at me and the Screen shimmered and I knew, all of a sudden and with a stab in my middle that I'd never see him again. I wanted to tell him to run, take Ellen and leave and not go back.

It was on the news two weeks later. I tried many times to Screen them, but the power has been playing up, as it does in these uncertain post-OilAge days and I never managed it.

The camera picked out a house on a distant shore, somewhere hot. I recognised something about it before I listened to the commentary. Roy watched me with concern as I scrambled across the floor to sit inches from the Screen, my hand fuzzing around the edges as I tried to reach out there.

I picked up on half the story: '...British couple. But the couple had obviously been warned, because the would-be murderers fired at what they thought were the sleeping bodies of James Song and Ellen Smith. They fired and ran, and then used flame throwers to set alight to the house. All we know is there were no human remains inside, only two mannequins in the bed – I think that's right – which were badly burned. These people seem to have had a warning. Rumours are circulating as to who they actually were. One rumour concerns a book supposedly written by Song under the pseudonym AJ Rawson, over forty years ago, but as yet this is unconfirmed. We understand the couple kept a boat nearby and it's thought they escaped on that.'

That night I held tight to Roy's hand. I thought of Ellen and James – for I will always think of them as that, climbing into a boat and drifting away from the shore, to start again, somewhere else. I wondered which names they'd choose this time. I knew now I'd been right; I'd never see them again.

During the following days, the news was full of AJ Rawson and Cara Wright. 'Mystery of boat escape couple leads to discovery of books' ran the headline across the bottom of the Screen. I watched as cameras showed a box of books being carried down from an attic in a house in Aberdeen.

There was a new print run and the old coffee and bookshop, *Drink in the Stories* – which still exists, somehow, as if it's been there forever – devoted a front window to the 'retelling of an old story'. I felt dread settle in – surely churning all this up again would threaten the fragile peace that existed across the world? It was only the die-hard militants who wanted to keep things going now, and everyone else wanted them to stop, even the worst leaders of the countries that had added fuel to the fire during the oil crisis years.

Copies of the book sold in thousands, even paper copies. The Screen showed people laughing together, Muslim and Christian, Jew and Hindu, Buddhist and Atheist, Muslim and everyone. Everyone and everyone. As multi-cultural and religiously-mixed as the world has become, we'd not quite yet managed to face that time when it was hell on Earth, when the fighting got really bad. I remember all the bombs, the endless Wars Against Terrorism, the never-ending promises by Western politicians, the threats, the bombs, the threats, the bombs… And finally, now they laughed at it. AJ Rawson was just a little ahead of his time.

Weren't we ridiculous? the laughter seemed to say. All that fighting, and for what? In the end it was stick together or die, so we stuck, and mostly the differences faded. We pray together now; we share the language of our beliefs, and although we still label ourselves, the lines are blurred. Humanity, finally and for most people, has come first.

I laughed then, and I kept laughing, and I hoped that somewhere, Ellen and James were laughing, too. And that maybe one day they'd find a way to laugh with me, face to face.

Inshallah. Amen. Shalom.

Not Employed Outside the Home

'**M**uuuuuuuum! I dunnnapooooo!' The yell comes from the downstairs loo into which my second smallest, Evie, disappeared a while ago. I'd forgotten she was there. I'm stirring porridge and trying to breast-feed my six month old, Oscar, who's strapped into a baby sling, at the same time. The twins are fighting over a toy car and Sara, my oldest girl, has the look of contempt she often wears on these crazy mornings; the look which says, 'Why did you keep having children, Mum?'

I shoot her an imploring glance and nod at the porridge but she rolls her eyes, shakes her head, and bends back down over her cereal. I can't blame her. Days like this I ask myself the same question: why did I? Then there are all the magic moments that make up for it, the happy family chaos that is the soundtrack to my days and nights.

Dean and I always wanted a big family - granted, that was before he got his latest job that involves much longer hours but we need the money and he needed the promotion so-

'Muuuuuuuuuummmmmm!'

'I'm coming,' I call back, turn, and promptly trip over the toy car which has now been thrown to the floor. I manage to save Oscar from being squashed and swear, softly, from where I've landed on my knees. Oscar, ripped from his breakfast, starts up an accusatory wail. I swear again, louder.

'I heard that,' Sara whispers.

'Sorry,' I mutter.

'MUUUUUUUMMM!'

'I'm coming,' I say through gritted teeth, hoisting myself and Oscar upright. He latches back on and is silent. The twins choose that moment to break into fist fighting and I grab Tom, the biggest and haul him out to the hall.

'Time out,' I say, placing him on the stairs.

'It wasn't me!' he says, indignant four-year-old voice full of fight.

'It doesn't matter. You two need separating.' I say, trying to be the firm but fair mum, when really I want to yell.

'But-'

'MMMUUUUUMMMMMMM!!!' Evie's voice has this incredible volume. It can make the hair on the back of your neck jump to attention. In supermarkets it's particularly effective at getting me to the front of queues.

'I'm here,' I say, managing the final two metres to the downstairs loo.

'My poo is huge!' she says, sitting sideways to show me and wiping poo onto the toilet seat. 'And I didded it in the toilet!'

'Evie-' I sigh, and bend over the loo. 'Well done.'

The clean-up job is made more awkward by Oscar's hungry guzzling, but I manage it.

'Porridge is burning,' Sara calls flatly from the kitchen.

'Could you stir it?' I yell back.

'No,' she says. 'I hate porridge.'

'Sara!'

'I told you, Mum, I didn't ask to be born into this madness.' She has the voice of a world leader at times. She stalks past me and up the stairs.

'I'll remember that when you ask me for a lift to the park later,' I mutter, just loud enough for her to hear. I can't blame her, though. For eight years it was just her, and now she has four siblings under four. One day she'll love it, I tell myself, over and over.

Tom has escaped from Time Out and the twins are rolling on the floor when I get back in and they scare the cat who runs under my feet at just the right angle for me to tread on her tail. She yowls, which makes Oscar cry. The porridge looks like a huge geyser, puffing itself about in the pan. The smell tells me it's beyond saving.

'Cereal!' I say to the room and grab all the boxes, several bowls and spoons and plonk them on the table. I take the burning pan outside and place it on the doormat where the chicken immediately appear, looking at me expectantly. 'Don't eat that yet, it's hot,' I tell them, laughing at myself for expecting them to understand, or indeed, listen, and lift it to the top of the log store. They'll get up there eventually but not until it's cool enough.

I turn to go back in and see two of the chickens behind me, running towards the cat's food bowl. One of them poops on the way.

'For goodness sake!' I say. Oscar has finished and is playing with my hair. I put him in his baby-bouncer and grab the kitchen roll, wiping up the chicken mess and chucking the kitchen roll in the bin in one smooth movement.

'Poo-pro,' I tell myself, and laugh. You've got to laugh. I tell Dean that often at weekends, when he has to face the chaos he's largely away from during the week.

The twins have got hold of the Frosties which means-

-Frosties all over the floor.

I open the back door again and in come the chickens, squabbling over the spilt food. I guess Frosties will be like speed to them but who cares. 'Express eggs,' I mutter, and laugh again.

'I'm glad you find this funny,' says Sara from the door. 'It's just... Why couldn't I have stayed an only child?' She steps over the chickens and crunches through the Frostie mess and puts on her shoes.

'Have a lovely day, sweetheart,' I say.

'I will, because I'll be away from this,' she says, voice so full of disdain it drips off her tongue.

'I love you, Sara,' I say, fighting the urge to snap at her. As my friend Faye, mother of two teens tells me, this stage will only last for another six years...

Sara sighs and gives me a rare smile. 'I love you too, Mum,' she says. 'Good luck.'

I'm still reeling in shock as she leaves for the school bus. She told me she loves me. A moment as rare as a hen's tooth, as Dean says. I smile. I'm doing something right, after all.

I step on light feet to the table to where Evie has poured milk everywhere except into her bowl, the twins are squabbling over the packet of cornflakes and Oscar has almost bounced himself off the edge of the table. I give myself a mental slap, lift him down and look for my coffee in the mess. I grab it and take two life-giving gulps. I glance at the clock.

7.45am.

Only 12 hours until the day ends...

After the twins have been dropped at Playgroup and Evie at Twos Time, I go home to deal with the chaos. Oscar falls asleep in the car so I park in the drive and leave the monitor on - safe in our small village - and go inside to sort out the house.

I make beds

wash dishes

hoover carpets

and make a coffee

all before Oscar wakes. I bring him inside to a slightly less crazy house and play with him for a bit. Then it's time to pick up the other three and make lunch for us all.

It's a nice day and a picnic is always less mess so I chase the chickens into the coop, pick the least chicken-poopy bit of grass and spread out a rug. I bring out various healthy snacks, giving the twins and Evie jobs to do, regretting it instantly as Evie drops the apple slices, the twins spill the plastic jugs of juice and Petey, the younger twin, sits in the spilt juice to make mud pies.

I decide singing is the way to sanity so begin a slightly manic rendition of the Wheels on the Bus, to which my rabble join in at the top of their lungs.

By some miracle, I get enough food in them all to keep them going for the afternoon. They're all looking sleepy by now so I strap Oscar into the sling, stick the other three in front of the TV (I was never going to be the kind of mother who stuck kids in front of the TV but sod that, the TV is my sanity.) Then I face the clear up. I tip the rug's crumby contents onto the grass and let the chickens out again. I throw all the plastic plates into the dishwasher and switch it on. I remember there are some e-mails I have to send so whilst everyone's asleep or TV-drugged I grab my tablet and settle on the battered sofa in the kitchen with Oscar snoozing against my chest.

Whilst I'm typing I'm beginning to feel sleepy and I think, a quick nap never hurt anyone. I feel myself slipping away into the most delicious doze when...

'Muuuuummmmm! I dunnnnaaapoooooooo!'

'Ohforfffffssake.'

I'm glad Oscar can't understand what I was about to say but I apologise to him anyway. He is woken by Evie's yells too, so I take him through to the lounge to place him on his rug where the sight I'm greeted with makes me want to swear Properly. Put it this way, the kids weren't sitting quietly watching TV.

The chocolate is everywhere. On mouths, hands, sofa, carpet.

Tom looks at me, brown smile gooey and happy. 'Yumyum,' he says.

'Where did you...?' And then I remember: last night Dean and I had left a family bar of dairy milk on the windowsill, after nibbling at it whilst watching a movie, during which we both fell asleep. I meant to put it away this morning but then there was porridge and Sara and poo and fighting...

'Muuuuuuuuummmmm!'

'I'm coming,' I yell.

I grab the remaining stump of sucked-on chocolate and give the twins a wet-wipe each. There are wipes placed all over my house, always within reach.

'Clean. It. Up,' I say in my scariest voice.

Gulping, the twins grab a wipe each and attempt to wipe their faces and hands. It helps, a little.

'MMMUUUUUUUUUMMMMM!' We're back up to supermarket level. I run to the loo.

'Look at this one and I didded it in the-'

'Oh that's lovely now don't- Okay. Never mind!' I wipe my daughter, the loo seat, her bum. I wash my hands and her hands. I look at myself in the mirror for the first time all day and see I've still got yesterday's mascara decorating the area under my eyes.

'Bloody hell,' I mutter. I've been out like this. I take off my specs -

which makes me realise how dirty they are - and wash my face.

'Muuuuuuummmmm! Tommy done sick everywhere!' yells his brother from the lounge.

Somehow, I survive the rest of the afternoon. At around three I remember I've not got tea on and in a fit of domestic goddessness I conjure up a beef casserole. We eat it, I clear up the aftermath. Then it's another hoover, clothes in the wash, milk for everyone, Oscar to bed, Evie to bed, the twins to bed, all at different times with different stories.

Sara gets home from Drama in the middle of this and takes one look at me and pours me a glass of wine. I don't know whether to hug her or worry about what my daughter thinks of me but I don't care because wine is exactly what I need. Oscar's fed; I can pump and dump. Not the best Earth mother behaviour but at least I'll feel sane. With the other four asleep I sit with Sara and look at her homework and talk about her day. With peace around her, Sara is lovely and chatty and my gorgeous loving daughter again. These are some of the best bits of my day. I'm doing okay, I remind myself. I can do this.

She goes up to have a shower and I fall into the battered kitchen sofa. The room is tidy; it smells like the house of a mother who cooks healthy food; everyone's still alive. I pour myself another glass and toast myself, put my feet up and lean back.

Dean arrives home in a flurry of cool air and practicality.

'Hello love,' I say.

He looks at me. 'Well, at least one of us has had an easy day,' he huffs. 'My day's been awful. I've never stopped. Wish I could just sit there with my feet up. You've no idea..

Legs

Legs and I are up in the clouds; she, glowing like some mountain goddess and me, a mere human. For me, this trip is about becoming braver. For Legs, it's an escape from her latest unsuitable relationship. She has this knack of falling for the bad boys, like so many beautiful women.

The air up here is clean and has a sweet biting tang, almost acidic, as I draw it in. There's a magical clarity around us as I look at the silver peaks reaching upwards; clear space in which anything could happen.

On her very first day at our school she was jeered at in the playground for her height. Her height that was all *legs*. She got her nickname on day one; I'd had to work hard at recognition for mine. When I went over to her afterwards, after she didn't take the bait, didn't crumble or cry, she grinned at me.

'It's better than at my last school,' she said. 'There they called me Antelope.' She stuck out a slender hand. 'I'm Antonia. 'Legs,' I guess now.'

'I'm Tim,' I said. 'They call me Tiny.'

Antonia – Legs – grinned down at me. 'Why's that, then?' she said, standing up to her full height.

'No idea.' I looked up at her and smiled back. And that was how we started.

'Ready?' Legs yells into air that twinkles with ice crystals. This morning, there'd been a grim recklessness, a danger in her eyes I'd not seen before.

'No,' I say, looking down the steepness of the slope.

'One, two-'

'Three!' I finish for her, momentarily brave, launching myself down the piste.

My stomach shifts as I plunge down, knowing I'll only get one chance at a head start and giving it everything.

'You-!' yells Legs behind me and I laugh at having surprised her.

I don't turn until I absolutely have to. It takes all of my guts at once but the alternative is gaining more speed and losing control sometime around the first bend.

I lean and shift my hips, and make a messy turn that nearly throws me, following with a better controlled one to the right. With a banshee screech Legs screams past – too fast! – I think, and doesn't turn until the last moment, flying around the corner, all long limbs and ski poles reeling. She's going to crash, I think, but being Legs, she makes it. I follow, onto the next straight, dodging other skiers, where I promise myself I'll catch her.

She always was ahead of me. First in height, then in maturity, alcohol, cigarettes and love and everything teenaged. From that first day in the playground, we stuck together, an unlikely friendship that somehow worked and protected us both from loneliness. For all of my missing inches, I was her safe place. Though she could have shielded me physically from anything life threw at us, I was the one who held the umbrella, firstly through the storm of her parents' break-up, the time she got suspended from school, and over Dave, her first proper boyfriend.

I had to find out from graffiti in the toilets at secondary school: **Dave n Legs**. When I asked her, trying to keep my voice steady, she nodded.

'Why didn't you tell me?' I said, wondering if she'd seen my inner thoughts, the ones I wrote on my sheets at night.

'Thought you'd be angry,' she said, shrugging. 'The fact that he's older, and been nicked, and all.'

'You can go out with who you want,' I said. 'We're mates, right?'

She nodded, eyes shining. 'I'm so relieved. Cos I want to tell you all about him!'

And she did. Every last detail.

When I'd caught her up in inches, I stood a little straighter.

'Now we're finally twins,' she giggled, putting her nose in front of mine, so close, and waving her hand across the tops of our heads. 'You're like my brother, now.'

'Yeah. Sis.' There wasn't much more I could say.

She's fallen. I change direction to end up by her side as I so often have, to help pick her up, but she is up and away again before I have chance, molecules of snow from her fall still floating down around the space where she's been. I ski right through it.

'Right,' I murmur, and bend myself forward to be more aerodynamic.

With every bit of courage I have, and going faster than I've ever done before, I catch her up. She turns to see me there and her whoop of joy is worth the terror I feel. She's always been braver. That was how she lived, by throwing herself at life and seeing what happened. Would she have still done that if I wasn't there to pick her up? It's something I asked myself often. She was there for me, of course, but in a different way. I was the safe place so I couldn't afford to fall very far. I didn't want her to see me that weak, telling myself it was for her, instead of to protect myself from meeting my own cowardice.

I catch her up again as the piste becomes a beautiful long straight. I ski around her, and wave, making a silly face as she skis back around me. This way we double helix our way down the mountain, our genetic ski code swirls mixing and crossing, writing our story on the snow.

I'd often wondered what our children would look like. I'm all torso and she's all legs. Would we have had a perfectly balanced mix? Someone with limbs that all matched? I take a quick glance back at our ski tracks. They are equal in all respects, perfect arcs that cross each other in regular swoops.

When I turn back, Legs is right in front of me. There's nothing I can do.

We go down in a tangle of limbs and yells and poles and white, our combined weight scoring the ground, scorching the snow, scraping the ice in painful places. Everything slows down and I have time to think, *this is going to hurt us both* but there's nothing I can do except slide, tangled with her, everything in the wrong place. There's snow down my back and front, up my sleeves. My right ski is off, knee bent in the wrong direction. I hear our skis crash into each other.

We stop at the edge of the piste. Her head is next to mine, but her eyes are closed.

'Legs?' I say, and in my tone I can hear things I want to stay hidden.

There's no response.

'*Legs!*' I yell.

By now a small crowd has gathered. I suppose it was quite dramatic, our fall.

'Ca va?' someone says. Hands start to touch us, to pull us apart, but as painful as it is, I want them to go away.

I can't remember how to say stop in French. Legs has rolled closer, so that our foreheads are touching. I try to take a breath. I move closer to her. Her cheek is touching mine. But when she opens her eyes, the first thing she does is look at me in horror.

Legs' latest relationship has been her longest, yet to me, most painful sounding. She always picks the guys she wants to fix, those who *life has dealt a rough hand*.

'He's lovely, underneath,' she'd say, after I hugged away the pain from her latest hurt.

This one is called Tony, and she sees this as a sign and wants to be called Antonia again. I refuse, in a small rebellion for the solidity of our friendship.

Tony is an idiot. He's older than her – they all are – and is divorced, has children with another woman, not his ex-wife. There's nothing bad in that except he doesn't look after the children. Legs says he's too ill to work, he's got health issues and just needs some love to make it all better. I cringe. She's going to sort him out, of course she is. I like Tony the least of all her loser boyfriends; Legs hasn't smiled properly since she met him. Tony doesn't like me either which gives me great satisfaction.

We came on this last minute holiday because Legs caught Tony flirting with his ex-wife by text, and she finally ran out of patience. We each booked a week off work as soon as we could and found a last minute skiing deal. Skiing was *our* thing from school. We'd been on two trips together and had developed a fiery rivalry on the slopes.

That first glance chills me, then she starts to cry. Legs doesn't cry very often.

'Are you all right?' I say. She looks at me though her tears. There's something different in her gaze.

She nods, then, 'My leg,' she says.

I look at the tangled mess that is us and our skis and see that her leg is pinned under mine. But my leg is pinned under my ski, which is the wrong way around. Helpful hands seek out what's happening and gently lift and turn my ski, putting me the right way around and freeing Legs.

Our faces are still close together. She's stopped crying. Is this it? Is this the moment I've been waiting for? Why have I never been braver? I think. I open my mouth to say something but she's in tears again.

'I'm pregnant,' she says, and it's so far away from what I was expecting that I can't take it in.

'What?'

I can only watch her as she puts her hands on her abdomen, and gently prods herself all over.

She looks at me. 'I'm sorry,' she says. I stare at her. I've wanted this moment for most of my life. But all I can see is her with a baby – that looks like Tony.

'I thought… you know,' she says, all her confidence gone.

'No, I don't know,' I say. A chill has crept into my voice. I look around and see people beginning to ski away, to leave us alone.

'It was a mistake,' she says. 'He doesn't want to know me.'

I don't know what to say.

'I found out the night before we flew. Or I wouldn't have come. And just now – I wanted to pretend it wasn't happening. I didn't think I'd fall. What if…?'

I get up. Brush the snow from me. Shake it out of my jacket.

'Tim?' It's the first time she's used my real name in years.

I step back into my skis. I take one last look at Legs. She's sitting in the snow. Every instinct wants me to go to her. But I look down the hill and my body follows my eyes and then I'm off, down towards the shadows of the trees.

When I look back to where she's still in a heap, unmoving, I see my solitary tracks. Uncertain swirls, half-formed DNA, as I ski away.

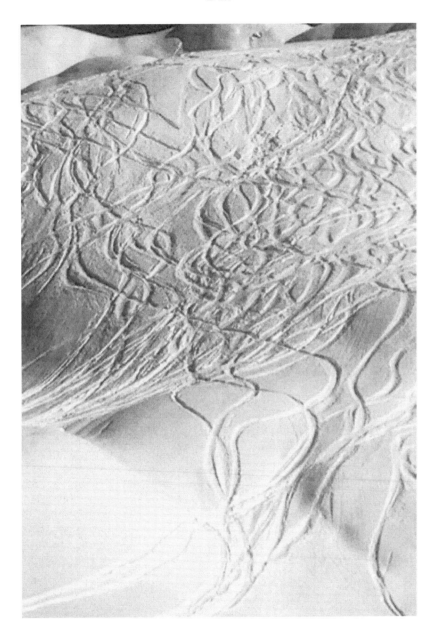

Gifts

The dew had turned the spider webs into Havisham Lace, gentrifying the rotten wood of the gate. Zoe didn't want to push the gate open and ruin the web but there was no other way in; creepers and bushes left a gap to walk through down the path but didn't offer a way around.

She could just turn around and leave, forget this ridiculous idea and leave the web intact. She stood still, feet refusing her brain's command to go. Just as her head was about to win the battle, the front door rattled and was tugged open and Mr Barr's head appeared.

'Come in, then,' he said, and Zoe's feet obeyed him and her hands pushed the gate open and the spider, she imagined, sighed.

'Hello,' she said. 'I'm not sure I can do this.'

'Come on in and let's talk,' Mr Barr said, wincing and with difficulty heaving the door open wider. It scraped heavily along the floor, catching letters and leaflets in its wake. 'Damn thing,' muttered Mr Barr.

He ushered her through a dusty, cramped hallway full of shoes, haphazard stacks of boxes, rickety towers of books and plastic bags, and into a room to the right.

Inside, time had stopped in various places during the twentieth century and left different eras competing for space in the room. Zoe was at once in the forties as she looked at the walls, the fifties as she looked at the sideboard, and a mixture of other decades in the bookshelves, the photographs on the piano and the carpet. She smelled her uncle in the cigar smoke that was captured, bitter, in the curtains and the musty male old aftershave smell reminded her of her father. There was nothing female in the room apart from a crocheted shawl thrown over an upright chair.

'My late wife's chair,' Mr Barr said, something in his voice telling Zoe she mustn't sit on it. He sat down on the piano stool and looked up at her. 'For singing, it's better to stand.'

Zoe nodded, her mouth clamped closed.

He played a few notes and hummed along to them. 'Forget talking, you're here to sing. Yes? If I play some scales,' he said, 'try to follow them and hum, like this.' He closed his eyes and swayed a little as he followed the notes, perfectly.

She nodded again, but when he stopped humming and played the notes alone and naked, her voice stayed silent.

'Try again,' he said, hitting the notes harder.

Zoe felt her eyes fill and eyed the door. The crochet-shawled chair was in the way, however, and Mr Barr was blocking the way she'd entered.

Mr Barr took his hands off the keys and looked at her.

'I'm sorry,' she said, controlling her voice with effort.

'Is there a song you like to sing?' His voice was gentle.

The only time Zoe sang was with her two small children. They were at playgroup just now, and she was wasting precious tidying-up time here. What was she doing?

'I don't really sing.' Except in my head, she wanted to add.

'What about when you were a child?'

'People used to laugh.'

'I see.' Mr Barr sat up straighter. 'You have children. All mothers sing to their children.'

Zoe only ever sang when her husband Tully was away, in her smallest voice, to Zak and Lucy as they were falling asleep. And she sang the song she'd loved at school, 'When a Knight Won his Spurs.' It reminded her of her own childhood and she knew that the secular village school wouldn't dare sing hymns, so she'd have to pass it on herself. She wasn't a Christian anymore but the song was about being strong and beating your demons and she'd certainly beaten a few of them lately. This is just another demon, she told herself.

'When a Knight Won his Spurs,' she said.

'Ah!' said Mr Barr and launched into a churchy rendition of the song on the piano, forgetting most of the words but making Zoe's eyes fill again. This time the tears overflowed down her cheeks.

'Oh for goodness sake,' she muttered, wanting to give herself a slap.

Mr Barr stopped playing again.

With an unexpected grandfatherly caress in his voice he said, 'There's only you and I here, Zoe. Nobody can hear you. Now try the first line. Just that. Say the words aloud, first, and then try to sing them. Nod when you're ready, and I'll play.'

When a knight won his spurs, when a knight won his spurs, she thought. That's all.

'When a knight won his spurs in the stories of old,' she said, then steeling herself, ignoring her fear, she nodded.

Mr Barr played a short introduction and she forced the words out, wavering and thin, reedy sounding to her ears, absolutely not in tune. He stopped playing and there was a silence in which she waited for the ridicule.

'Good,' he said. 'That'll do, for today. Now go home, and sing that line over and over, whenever you can.'

'That's it?' she said.

'That's it for today. Come back next week. You can start paying me then.'

The following week, she sang the line more loudly, and there were less tears. Mr Barr applauded.

'Now,' he said, 'sing it all.'

Zoe looked at him, swallowed, and nodded. And he played, and she sang.

When she was done, he applauded again, turned to the chair with the crocheted blanket and nodded. 'I agree,' he said.

There were rumours about Mr Barr's sanity – and sobriety – all over the village. Apparently he was too drunk to play the church organ one day so lost his job as Sunday organist which led to parents withdrawing their children from his music lessons. He didn't drive anymore after losing his license for drink-driving.

Zoe had heard he talked to himself and had once insisted that his wife had bequeathed him her ability to play the piano. There were people who did swear he'd become a better player since she died. Zoe hadn't believed any of it but she'd just seen him talk to his – dead – wife. Should she leave?

On the other hand he'd just become the second adult who'd ever heard her sing in all her adult life, so she had to stay and see this through. (The first had been Tully, when she'd not expected him home, and finished singing to the twins to find him standing in the doorway, listening. Don't give up the day job, he'd said, meaning it of course as a joke, not knowing her relationship with her voice.)

She smiled.

'Let's do it again,' he said, 'and this time I want you to *feel* the notes coming from the back of your head, through you, not just in your throat. He played, and she sang. And this time, she sang louder.

'Very good,' Mr Barr said when she'd finished. 'Now, let's practise individual notes. Let's get you tuned up.'

At the end of her hour, Zoe left and jogged home, elation picking up her feet and spurring her on. That night she raised her voice with the children, letting the words flow from her out into the room, where they danced up to the ceiling and fell down to the children's sleeping faces, kissing them her courage. Whilst making dinner she hummed along to the radio, making Tully smile.

'I'm having singing lessons,' she told him. 'On Tuesdays, when the kids are at playgroup.'

'Why?' he asked.

So she told him about the ridicule when she was at school. About how she'd been asked to get up on stage and audition for the school play and how this had involved singing a few lines of a song. How everybody had laughed, even the teacher. How she'd been laughed at for many other things anyway, and how this had been the last straw. Although buried deep inside her, it felt easy letting the story out, after all this time and years of marriage.

And then she told him about how since she'd been diagnosed with cancer and it hadn't been the scary thing she expected, she now wanted to take on every single fear she had, and beat them all. She'd beaten cancer. Everything else should be a breeze, right?

Tully took her in his arms and kissed away the tears.

'I'm proud of you, my fighter,' he said. 'It never had a chance against you, so you damn well go and beat the rest of what's holding you back.'

She stepped back and looked at him.

'You think I don't know?' he said. 'You have so much in you, waiting to get out.'

'You never stop surprising me, Andrew MacTully,' she said.

During the third lesson, Zoe realised she could tell when she was out of tune. Mr Barr taught her to listen to herself as she was moving through the scales. He tuned her in, as he called it, tweaking her voice here and there, getting her to sing a perfect scale. Halfway through the lesson, he stopped playing and looked at her.

'You had cancer?' he asked.

'Yes. Breast. Caught it early, kicked it into touch.' She wasn't surprised he knew; although quite new to the village she'd worked out how the grapevines worked. It was useful, had meant she didn't have to explain it all, again and again.

He opened his mouth to speak and suddenly she knew exactly what he was going to say. She listened whilst he said, I ignored the symptoms and Prostate and Late stage care, and she wanted to cry but knew she mustn't.

'But it's all right,' he said, looking over at the crocheted shawl on the chair.

Since the children had been born, Zoe had found it hard to grab hold of life and make it slow down. It went too fast, it flew away from her and suddenly her children were growing and she felt like she'd missed a year or two and the cancer months had stolen more time and she was running to keep up. There was so much she wanted to do with her life. Singing was just the start, and she knew it would get easier.

During the next four lessons Zoe's voice grew in strength and her confidence in it grew alongside. Soon she was belting out numbers from musicals – not her choice – as Mr Barr smiled and hammered the keys with a gusto she hadn't seen in him before.

She turned up for her ninth lesson to find the house dark and cold.

This time the village grapevine had failed her. She strapped the children into the car and drove to the hospital, an hour away. He was lying propped up in bed, attached to tubes and wires.

'The piano's yours, if you want it,' he said. 'Teach your bairns to play. Keep you singing.'

'Oh, I won't stop singing, not now,' she said. She took his hand. 'I've not thanked you properly.'

He waved her words away. 'When you first approached me for lessons,' he said, 'I'd not taught for years. Not since I lost my job. They wouldn't ever believe it was a one-off. Maud was gone and I only drank in the evenings. That one day, I forgot myself. Teaching you reminded me what I could do best – play. If this hadn't got me,' – he indicated his abdomen – 'I'd have gone back part time. So I've you to thank for that. You have a lovely voice emerging there. Don't keep it from the world any longer. Go out and sing. In fact that's your next lesson. Go and find a remote outdoor place and sing your heart out, loud as you can. Then come and tell me how it went.'

'Deal,' smiled Zoe, and they shook hands. She rounded up the children who were in the waiting room, being watched over by a nurse at a desk, and they made their way to the exit.

Running feet caused her to look behind. A nurse caught her just by the lift.

'Are you Mr Barr's family?' he said.

'Just a friend. I don't know his family.'

'Right… It's just that you're his first visitor, and he's been in two days. There are things I need to discuss.'

'I don't know; perhaps they live far away? I can make enquiries in the village? I'm new there but it's not big so somebody will know.'

'Yes, if you could that would be good. I would say time isn't on our side, here,' he said.

'You mean…?'

'As you're not a blood relative I can't give away much, but Mr Barr isn't a well man.'

'Oh. Well, I'll do what I can. And I'll come back very soon.'

That evening both children spiked a fever and Zoe was on her own. She rang Tully who was away with work and asked him to take on the task of asking about Mr Barr's relatives. For the next few days she ran about looking after the children, clearing up sick, feeding them hot lemonade, keeping them on Calpol, worrying endlessly about their temperatures.

Tully came back and asked questions about relatives. There were some guarded comments about family rifts but someone said they'd tell someone else to find Alan's son. Zoe had never heard him called Alan. It wasn't until the following week when the children were better, that she remembered her next lesson. She dropped the children at playgroup and drove herself up Cairn O'Mount, parked in the hilltop car park and walked as far away from the car park as she could. As far as she could see there was heather and rocks and the huge sky above her.

She opened her mouth, and began to sing. She started with When a Knight, moved on through some of the songs in *My Fair Lady*, and as she sang, she felt her voice get louder and stronger. She wished Mr Barr – Alan – were there so she could show him.

The last song he'd taught her had been Memory, from *Cats*. It was a difficult song but one she liked, having seen the show when she was a child. She faltered through the first lines, feeling stiff and out of tune, but something changed inside her when she got to the second verse.

From somewhere – inside her? the sky? – she felt this burst of pure sound fill her. At once, all she had to do was open her mouth and let the music out. It drenched her, the music, and she felt herself transported out of her body as the notes filled her and filled her again. She'd never experienced anything like it. The music was coming through her, but she could grasp it, take control of it, bend the notes whichever way she pleased.

This is being a singer, she thought, this is it. This is what people feel up on stage, when they know the notes will come out right, when they know they command the tune… Zoe sang and she sang. She went back and sang all the songs she'd practised with Alan and this time they were even better.

When she stopped, her heart was racing, her breathing ragged and inside her was a fizzing, an emotion, a bursting of energy. She stared at the sky and laughed out loud. Where had that come from?

She looked at her watch and swore.

In the car the radio was loud but her voice was louder. She sang along to every song she knew that came on. It was easy. She didn't have to think about it. She felt as if she'd suddenly learned all the lessons Alan had been trying to teach her, at once. She was a Singer.

She picked up the children, grabbed them a snack from the shop and drove straight to the hospital. She'd be early for visiting hours, but never mind.

When they got to the ward, there was nobody on the desk. 'We'll go and surprise Mr Barr,' she said, and shushing the children, they walked to the ward at the end, where Alan had been in the sunshine the first time she'd visited.

The bed was empty.

'They must have moved him,' she said to the twins. She found a nurse, who tutted that they were early.

'We're looking for Mr Alan Barr,' Zoe said, and saw the news on the nurse's face immediately, stark and sure.

'… just two hours ago,' the nurse was saying, but all Zoe could feel was the music inside her, soaring.

Leucothea
I

The sea is biting cold. I am cumbersome with all the equipment; using a dry suit requires more of everything, especially strength. I'm thigh deep in the sea, tiny tears in the neoprene allowing arctic water to creep into my bubble. I shiver, wishing I'd checked the suit more carefully before remembering that it doesn't matter.

I wade out in my fins until I'm waist deep. My mask is still around my neck and I fit it over my eyes and nose. I put the regulator in my mouth and breathe the cool air, feeling my lungs fill in a way they don't on land. I wade deeper, the rocks becoming slippery with seaweed. As the water is about to close over my head, I notice a boat on the horizon. People out fishing? Have they seen me? Nobody is supposed to dive alone. I have a very good reason for doing it but I'm not about to explain it to anyone.

I duck quickly and the cold closing over my head makes me gasp for breath. My chest tightens and I can't breathe properly. I begin a count in my head to slow things down, until I've got myself under control. I let some air out of my jacket and feel myself sink more heavily onto the seabed with each step.

I check my air and depth gauges: everything's in order. I've enough air for about forty-five minutes, which is plenty. I let myself fall forwards, clear my ears and swim horizontally. I imagine myself Leucothea, feeling my body moving the way a sea spirit would. I clear my ears again and tune into the underwater clicks and whooshes, disconnecting myself from the world above.

This is my element. Always has been.

I'm gliding above the rocks, letting the current carry me along. Seaweed sways below me. I hear myself singing my diving tune; a song I always find in my mind when underwater. I am suddenly so grateful for this last experience of life that my eyes sting and fill. I blink rapidly to push the tears back because I can't lose it now. I concentrate instead on keeping the pressure in my ears equalised.

At twenty metres the water is clearer and a deep solid blue. A final checklist runs through my head: notes, all addressed and ready; car, left open with notes inside; house, everything in order; will, written. The relief I feel, combined with the weightlessness ignites a happiness within me and I stretch out my arms and soar, turn on my back and see the sun shimmering on the surface of the water way above. A few sunbeams break through and flicker towards me until they dissipate to nothing. The boat is long gone and I'm all alone again.

I turn back to face the seabed once more and begin searching for the wreck. Once past that, I know there's a deep trench. I check my depth and air and see that I'm close to the halfway mark, the point at which I could still turn back, have time for a decompression stop and surface with air still in my tank, as all good divers do. I let go of the gauge and promise myself it's the last time I shall look at it, until the deep blue of the trench is all around me and above me and I am safe.

The wreck looms before me like a live thing, seeming to drift closer as if it is *me* that's still. My breath catches. I swim close to it and lay a gloved hand on the rotting hull, seeing how it is becoming part of the sea. Eventually it'll relax down to nothing, sigh itself into the seabed. I pull myself up to the deck, lop-sided and broken. Fish glimmer everywhere, bringing the dead boat to life. I see an eel peer out at me from a rusty hole in the deck.

Something catches my eye in the old wheelhouse. I look up but whatever caught my eye has gone, all I see is the flick of a large greenish tail, disappearing behind the boat. A seal? Porpoise? Usually they're more curious than afraid.

I swim on, kicking and pushing myself over the wreck and down the other side, towards the trench. I see it immediately, a jagged hole in the rocks, which widens and stretches until it looks as if the seabed is trying to tear itself in half. I kick harder and let myself glide over it until the edges are too far apart for me to see, all is blue and dark. That beautiful depth. My ears hurt and I have to kick upwards slightly to clear them, before going down once more.

I stretch out my arms and legs again and allow myself to float down, taking nothing but the desire to be free. I can feel the heaviness inside me lifting. The guilt is ebbing away after months. I'm paying back what it was I took. I give in to the feeling of freedom, dimly aware that my air is getting harder to suck. My ears are sore again, but it doesn't matter. I have a go at clearing them and they pop a little.

I am letting go.

Something darts across my field of vision. A large animal – dolphin? The seal again? It briefly rouses me from the warm contentment which is spreading as I descend.

'Go back,' sings a voice. Is it in my head? It's in my head. It's my life force (never my soul) urging me one last time not to give up. I expected this, I expected a bit of fight from something deep down within me. 'You don't belong here, Laura, go *back.*' The voice is insistent, no longer singing. And it knows my name.

And suddenly there is a face in front of me. Part of me knows I must be looking at a seal; they are curious and she'll be wondering what I'm doing in her world, but it's such a human face that for a second I am angry. I wanted to be alone. I reach out and push it away and I see sorrow cross the curiosity in the eyes. Then the face is gone with a silky flick of movement.

My air is nearly gone. I can still manage little sips, but soon there will be none. Then suddenly, it's gone. I let the regulator fall from my lips and close my eyes, seeing red against blue, a flower of death bursting out into the water. I open my mouth and in rushes the cold heavy water. I feel it going down my throat. I welcome it.

And then there is a mouth on mine. A soft, cool mouth. I open my eyes and see green irises before me, hair flowing around us. And I feel myself being pulled and pushed upwards.'

I finish reading. I can never tell the man in front of me how I long to be back there. 'You were very lucky that those fishermen found you. *Incredibly* lucky there was a decompression chamber close by,' Dr Collins says.

'Yes,' I say, still unable to forget the green eyes.

'You wrote this in the present tense,' the doctor says, indicating my statement. He calls it a Cleansing Piece, all the suicidal ones had to write them about how we didn't die. And we have to keep reading them aloud. It doesn't help, but he thinks it does. I suppose he wants to see my reaction to it one last time before he decides my fate.

I'm not sure how to respond to this so I say nothing. But I think, it's because I've never surfaced.

'Laura? You understand why I'm asking?' He's said all of this before.

'Yes, I did. It felt very real. But I know it wasn't. It was just hallucinations brought on by the narcs. I mean nitrogen narcosis.'

'How do you feel about it now?'

'It wasn't real, and I'm aware of that now. I no longer feel suicidal and I look forwards very much to going home and starting again. I can't believe how stupid I was. Guilt makes you do funny things.' He has to believe me; I can't stay within these pale yellow walls another day.

'So you don't feel guilty now?'

'Yes, I do, but I will make amends in other ways. I no longer feel I have to pay the world back with my own life.'

'Strictly speaking Laura, it *wasn't* your fault, as we've discussed many times. You are in the clear.' Dr Collins leans back in his chair.

In the clear. Strange words. Of course, the man in front of me can't see the mess of bodies in the shallows; the crimson blood as it blooms out into the clear blue; he can't hear the screaming; see the shocked faces; the broken deck chairs, the speedboat forced way out of its element onto the sand. He didn't find himself waking up in the cockpit to all that, the creeping horror of realising it was All. My. Fault. I see it all, every day. I know how it ends, every time.

'And I'm feeling good about that. Like I said, I look forward to starting again,' I say, looking at him, unblinking.

There's a silence which stretches and I'm worried, before he leans forward and tells me I'll be under observation and that there are conditions but all I really listen to is 'leaving us' so inside I'm rejoicing.

There are awkward goodbyes then I exit the building and walk to the bus stop. I've made sure nobody is there to meet me. They kept telling me it wasn't my fault but I saw the way nobody could look me in the eye afterwards; felt the way I could silence a room just by entering it. My job was the only blessing, sitting alone in my office, writing reports about the state of the sea, diving whenever I could, before I realised I didn't deserve a place in the world any more.

I scan the bus timetable. There's only one place I can go and I notice with satisfaction that the right bus will be here in just a few minutes. What I'm doing is right, then. It's a sign. I let my bag fall to the pavement next to me and turn so my face is in the sun. I close my eyes.

Which is a mistake because immediately I see red against blue, life bleeding out into the water. Horror-stricken faces, a twisted deckchair flung up the beach.

I open my eyes again. It'll never go away. And if it ever does, then I have no right to be alive. I should not even have been *in* the boat that day due to my back injury but I hadn't wanted to miss the beach party, our end of project celebration.

The bus arrives and I get on, pay the driver some money, feel my breath hitch in my throat as he looks at me and smiles, in case he can see my thoughts. He lets me on. There are only a few people on the bus and I'm sure nobody has noticed me. Life outside glides past, wobbling slightly through the dirty glass as if we are all underwater.

I think about the green eyes staring into mine. The eyes that knew everything but were still wrong. That was exactly where I belonged. I wish that *thing* had let me stay. What awaits me now is a dead life, if that is possible. A life of deadness. Deathlife. A living death? I've never agreed with myself how to describe what it's going to be.

Cranmore House, the place they've told me I'll stay for a while 'until I get back on my feet' will by now have been informed I'm coming and if I'm late they'll come out looking for me. I will the lumbering bus to go faster.

I watch other people's lives drift past: dog-walkers shoppers street cleaners toddlers toddling cats jumping garden walls containing flowers women chatting drunk men staggering from the pub smoking pushchairs casually held in one hand, rolling people eating man running a policeman talking to an old woman girl cycling. All of it, all going on all of the time. The minutiae of life. A million tiny events every second. In any moment, all of it could be taken away. The bus driver could have a heart attack and crash through those school gates; that red car could have a blowout and pin the cyclist against the wall; the mother who's chatting on her mobile could let go of her child's hand for an instant and the child could run in front of the bus.

I suddenly feel sick. When my thoughts start spinning like this I find it hard to hold on to what's real. As if any of it is!

I will the bus to move faster and miraculously it does, everything speeds up and it's my stop and I get off leaving my bag exactly where it is and bolt for the doors and ignore the shout behind me and make for the right street and run up the hill and see the sign saying 'Fosse Cliff' and feel the pull of the sea tugging me ever forwards, drawing me in until I can hear the gulls and see the massive blue stretching out before me and I'm at the top and I don't know exactly how I got here but here I am and here is the only place I was ever really headed.

I breathe. I stretch out my arms and just like I do when I'm underwater, I gently let myself fall forwards.

II

Ray gets a couple of extra minutes this morning before it hits him with a nauseating flip in his abdomen, the little reminder that it isn't all a dream. Usually it gets him right away, but this morning he lies half-asleep listening to Win humming in the shower, thinks about her soft warm body and rolls onto her side of the bed, to lie on her pillow and smell her night cream. As he does every day, he thanks whatever it was that brought her to him and filled up his aloneness and made him laugh. Then he remembers It, all over again, and it's all spoiled.

He checks his left leg; it's the same as it has been all week since it got a little worse – perhaps slightly stiffer. It's hard to tell. He makes a fist with his right and smiles slightly; it feels a bit better. Maybe. He does struggle to decide sometimes – if he's feeling rough in his head his whole body feels wrong. If he feels good, if he's having one of those random days full of joy like he did yesterday, he feels better all over and can kid himself he's going to beat It.

Win's still humming and splashing so he opens his bedside drawer, reaches right to the back, to the old cigar box he's had since he was a child, pulls it out and lifts the lid. There they are, next to the leaflets full of support group numbers and information about It, the little pills that the doctor says will help, will delay the onset of symptoms. He pushes two out and dry-swallows them. The shower stops so he shuts the box and shoves it back in, closing the drawer. He tries to remember when his next appointment is. It's perhaps sometime this week. He'll have to phone and check, which he always has to do seeing as he can't write it down on the calendar. Win would keep him right, of course, which is probably a good reason to tell her, just as good as the reason that if he doesn't, she'll probably leave him. I'll never lie to you, he'd said, when she'd told him about John, her ex. She'd fixed him with her deep blue eyes and said, No, Ray, I don't believe you would. It took him less than two years to begin hiding stuff from her and he knows, just as he knows that you don't get a gift in life without getting an equal amount of good stuff taken away, that she will not forgive him when she finds out. If she finds out.

'Morning Raymond,' says Win as she emerges from the bathroom in a cloud of steam.

'Morning Winifred,' he replies, winking and placing onto his face a bright smile. 'Sleep well?'

'Til you snored. And you must've been dreaming because you kept twitching. Your left leg kept kicking me. Were you dreaming about footie?'

Ray looks at her and frowns, feeling a cold ball settle into his stomach. 'No, no I wasn't. I'll get up,' he says.

But Win's already bustling out of the room, still in her towel, calling over her shoulder, 'Stay and relax, you're not working til eleven today. I'll get you the paper and a coffee.'

'Win,' he starts, but she's gone. He stares at the space where she just was. 'I don't deserve you,' he whispers. He lifts back the covers and looks at his leg. Twitching isn't good. Twitching at night, when he doesn't even know – that's worse than not good. He feels sick. He holds out both his hands. Are they shaking? His right hand looks like it is. He makes two fists and slams them down on the bed, either side of him. If the shakes start, it's bye bye bus, bye bye life and probably, bye bye Win. And losing Win would be the end. If they'd not been married when he got diagnosed, he'd have told her. The fact that it came a month after his wedding – one month! – had just thrown him. He shakes his head and is still shaking it when Win walks in, his coffee in one hand and the other holding the paper close up to her face. She's saying something about it being a terrible shame.

'What's that, love?' he asks, mostly to divert his thoughts. He doesn't really want to know at all – no more bad news – but she's reading it.

'I've not got my specs on but looks like someone's thrown themselves off the cliffs. A girl.'

'I don't…'

'Oh my God, says here she got off the Number 43 bus – isn't that yours? – and they're looking for people who might've seen her before… Wait til I get my specs.'

Ray grabs the paper and stares at the photograph on the front page. He recognises her straight away. She looks younger in the photograph, wild black curly hair down to her shoulders, a big open smile on her face and her eyes, wide and full of life, smiling as much as her mouth. Ray remembers faces. Yesterday she hadn't looked like that. He'd noticed her because she hadn't looked right and he remembers thinking, man trouble? She hadn't looked directly at him but he'd seen her eyes – they were dull and the whites were red. And the way she'd got off-

'Ray?'

'Oh, God,' he says. The way she got off, she'd left her bags and run and with a thud in his middle he remembers the stop they were at when she ran. He puts his hand to his forehead. 'She got off by Fosse Road, the nearest place to Fosse Cliff. Jesus. She got off, running, left her bags and ignored me when I shouted after her and ran in front of the bus and across the road. I was angry. I looked round and saw her stuff there and thought about how she'd ignored me and I felt angry. I let her go. I closed the doors because I was late and I drove off. And I didn't think about her much, even when I had to take her bags in at the end of the route and get them booked. Shit. Shit, shit *shit*.' He puts his hand over his mouth.

The bed creaks as Win sits next to him and looks over his shoulder. They both read:

CLIFF DEATH

Dust

By Tamsin Brown

Yesterday morning a young woman – who has been named locally as Laura Jones – fell to her death from the top of Fosse Cliff. Miss Jones, 31, had been under observation at Hallmead Hospital after a suicide attempt last year. She left the hospital yesterday morning on the (Number 43) bus after being discharged to travel to a nearby supported living environment. It is understood that on the way there Miss Jones walked to the top of Fosse Cliff where she then fell to her death. There are not believed to be any suspicious circumstances. The police have asked anyone – especially those on the same bus – who may have seen Laura Jones yesterday to contact them as soon as possible on 0865 5500 500. Miss Jones' family have been informed. More on page 4.

Ray doesn't speak but finds the right page.

Continued from front page

Last year the Echo reported that Laura Jones had been involved in an accident which claimed the lives of four people, including one child. Miss Jones was taking strong painkillers for back pain and was driving a speedboat just off Fosse Sands when she fell asleep and the boat collided with two families on the beach. Miss Jones reportedly had not been informed she should not operate any machinery while taking the medication and she did not know what the side-effects could be.

According to one of her friends whom the Echo interviewed at the time, Miss Jones tried to end her life because she could not live with the sense of guilt she felt. According to one source the doctor who prescribed the medication has been under investigation about the incident.

'I'll have to call them,' Ray says.

Win takes his hand. 'If it was suicide, she probably made her mind up a long time before.' Her voice is gentle, careful.

Ray says nothing. He is remembering a time when he sat in his car, at the top of a hill on the way to Portsmouth and wondered how much hosepipe he'd need. He'd just left the doctor's where he'd gone for a follow up appointment after being told the stiffness was probably repetitive strain injury after driving for so many years, but they'd give him these tests *just in case* so in he walked expecting to be told he'd need a bit of time off work, perhaps some physio and then *wham*, in a few seconds everything was different. He'd sat in his car for six hours, thought about ways it could be done, wondered if he had the guts and decided he had, if not for Win. They still had leftover wedding cake at home. Hadn't even got all the honeymoon pictures printed. So he drove to the pub, ditched the car and got drunk and when he got home, Win was angry for a while but he hadn't had to tell her and after that first day it got easier not to.

He looks at her now. 'I'm going to get a shower then I'll call them. I don't think I'll go to work today. I'll call Mike and get cover. I don't think I'd be safe.' He looks at the time. 'Don't be late for work, I know you've got that day trip today.'

'It's okay, I can stay a bit longer. The oldies can wait a little while.'

'Honest, Win, I'm fine. You go. They've probably been looking forward to it all week.' He manages a smile.

'If you're sure you're all right…'

'I'm all right. It's a shock, to be sure. I should have… I wish… Oh hell, I don't know. Maybe she didn't kill herself.' But he remembers the sadness he'd thought was man trouble in her and thought, she did mean to. I just didn't realise it. He'd been happy yesterday, he remembers that. All around were folk getting on with their lives as he drove; he'd felt as if he was driving through a beautiful picture, with tiny important details of life being played out all around him and he was in the middle of it with all these people's lives literally in his hands and he'd felt strong and safe and *happy*. It had been a gift day, a truly happy day when he usually had It hanging over him too much to do anything except pretend.

He'd had all those people's lives in his hands including Laura Jones'. He shrugs off this thought so Win doesn't see it and kisses her. 'Go, I'll see you tonight. Fancy an Indian?'

He holds it together until he hears the front door close and then he holds his face in his hands and sobs.

After his shower Ray feels able to call work and the police, with whom he arranges an interview in the afternoon.

He thinks of Win, pushing wheelchairs around the garden centre, holding papery hands and helping old ladies choose plants. He tries to imagine her pushing him around in a chair, or walking next to him as he rides a mobility scooter. Shame makes him close his eyes. It could be years before you lose your mobility, could be years before it gets really bad, the doctors had said. But he knows different. Those little pills that hide under the leaflets are not helping. The symptoms are only getting worse and this is not a good sign, he knows it. He tries to push away the truth because if he thinks about it too much, and stops telling the doctor, No, no worse at all! then he might as well have bought the hosepipe after all because it's all going to end really soon anyway. Those pills are his religion. If he stops believing in them, he has nothing.

He opens the bedside drawer again and takes out the cigar box. He opens it and pulls out the leaflets that have been folded up in there for the last fourteen months. The first one he opens is numbers for support groups. Apparently there are lots, all, if he believes the pictures, attended by happy hand-holding couples smiling into the camera as if to say, Yeah, I've got Parkinson's but it's great! Look at us! Look how happy we are!

He knows what Win would have done by now, called every single one and taken him there and met people and got him involved and he would have gone, to please her, because he'd do anything to please her. All he wants is to make her happy and all she says she wants is to be with him. But now? As if she is right there in the room, he hears her voice in his head. Raymond Baillie, do you honestly think that would make any difference to me? Don't you remember our wedding vows? I love you, and I'm here for you whatever happens. Do you really think I'd leave you? Be ashamed of you? Think you less of a man?

And suddenly something in him shifts. He feels on the brink of an understanding. He breathes, and lets it come. First comes the knowledge that he has to tell her because she deserves to know and she is the best friend he's been waiting for his whole life, all fifty-two years of it. When he's not with her it's like half of him is missing. How has he thought it was all right *not* to tell her? How has he even considered it was okay to try and cope with this on his own?

'What have I been *doing*?' he says. He looks again at the picture of the girl from the bus, and then he knows all of a sudden he knows what he has to do. He thinks about her eyes and imagines what she was holding inside her – the lives of four other people.

He imagines himself driving his bus, pushing the truth deep down inside him until even *he* doubts it's there, hiding it and hiding it until one day his body literally stops working and he suddenly cannot steer and there is a car coming the other way around a corner, a car full of a family and the bus goes straight into them.

'There but for the grace of God go I,' he whispers, and he picks up the phone.

III

Ray? It's me.

I'm going to be late home.

No, go ahead and eat, I can warm mine.

I can't explain now, but I need to be here.

Sorry?

About what? Can it wait until later?

All right. Yes, I love you too. See you later tonight.

This isn't heaven. I know that voice, it's Winnie, one of the volunteers. She's standing by the edge of my bed. This is not my bed! This is the bloody hospital. They've brought me back, again! It's in my notes, DO NOT RESUSCITATE, clear as day. Why won't they just let me go? I'm ready – more than ready. I've had my life and it's been good and now I'm just taking up space. Let me go and see Maud.

'Why won't they just let me go?' My voice doesn't sound right.

'Frank? Welcome back.'

Winnie's bending over me, smiling. 'I said, why-'

'Don't try to speak, let me get a nurse.' And she's gone.

I look around me. My head's awful stiff and it feels like it's stuffed with sawdust. I know what's happened though, I remember it all. No memory loss, like last time when I woke up and had no idea of anything. We was at the garden centre. Winnie was helping me choose something for David for his birthday and then I felt it coming on me and Winnie helped me sit down and I thought, this is it, Franky-boy, this is where you leave the world. And I smiled at Winnie, I remember that, and then here I am. So I guess it's me heart again, and they've zapped me back to life with those paddle things and I'm back. Again.

Winnie reappears with the nurse.

'Yes, just after you left, I heard him saying something.'

'Mr Willis? Can you hear me?' The nurse is loud.

'I'm not bloody deaf,' I tell her and see Winnie smothering a smile behind her hand. I give her a wink. She's all right, is Winnie.

'You're in A and E. You collapsed at the garden centre. Do you remember?' Winnie speaks around the nurse, who looks a little annoyed.

'Yep. Me heart, I'm guessing?'

'Actually, they don't think so. Not this time. You collapsed and we called an ambulance, but you were all right – I mean your heart was working fine, you were breathing, just unconscious. They said your blood pressure is really low and-'

'Thank you, would you mind waiting outside for a moment? I just need to check a few things with Mr Willis.' And before Winnie can object, the nurse is shutting the curtains around me right in front of Winnie so she has to step back.

'Oh,' she says. 'I'll be just outside, Frank.'

The nurse speaks to me as if I'm seven, prods and pokes and shines stuff in my eyes all efficient like but then gives me a kindly smile. Maybe she's okay. 'A doctor will be along to see you soon. You're probably going to have to spend the night here,' she says.

'Thanks,' I say. I'm not feeling all that thankful though to tell the truth. Body hurts, I'm so old people most don't see me anymore, my family don't visit. It's time for me to go, like I said. The nurse squeaks off across the shiny floor and a few moments later Winnie reappears. Winnie's one of the folk who still sees me. She often tells me I'm her favourite at the Inverluthe Daycare. *Daycare.* Makes us sound like children.

'You don't need to stay,' I tell Winnie.

'I'll stay til you get a proper bed, or they chuck me out. It's fine. I've rung Ray and he's fine. We didn't really have plans tonight and even if we did, I'm not passing up an opportunity to spend an evening with my favourite man.'

'If I knew you wasn't joking I'd tell that man of yours,' I say.

'Oh he's fine. He doesn't mind sharing me,' she says and winks. 'Now. If you're here for the night I can ring one of the others at the centre and get them to pop home for you? Doesn't your neighbour have a key?'

'Mrs Sharman. Yes, she does.'

'How do you feel?' Winnie takes my hand in hers.

I consider for a moment. 'I'm tired, my body's worn out, I think my time should be up. Let someone else have a go. I don't think the end's too far away.'

Winnie looks upset again. 'But you're still young, mentally, and compared to some at Inverluthe, you're a spring chicken!'

'*Sprung* chicken, maybe. What's that saying – had a hard paper round?'

Winnie laughs. 'Yeah, that's the saying. You were a fisherman weren't you?'

'Yes. Just up the coast. Used to fish these waters too, sometimes. Loads more fish back in the day. All gone now and all these bloody quotas – so much gets wasted! It's a crime. We knew, us folk back then knew how to keep the oceans happy. We cared for them. We threw back tiddlers, we didn't use those dragging nets they use now… It was a different world.'

'You're not wrong there,' says Winnie.

I've got a story inside me I've never told anyone. And if I'd died today, it would've die too. I think it should be told. Winnie's a good listener. But would she believe me?

'While we're on the subject… Would you mind if I told you a story?'

Winnie looks around the bits of the ward we can see. It's busy. 'Don't think anyone's going to come anytime soon,' she says. 'I'd love to hear a story.'

'It's a true story,' I say. I wonder where to start. I've never told a soul. Don't know why. Just never found the right time. And, just like I had that thought a second ago, another thought pops into my head like someone else has put it there: I *have* to tell her, right now.

'Would you pass me my jacket?' I say.

Winnie turns to the pile of folded clothes with my jacket placed neatly on top. She puts it in front of me. I reach to the inside pocket and take out a small drawstring bag, made of green velvet. I hold it in my right hand and close my fist over it. Although I've held it every day for the last fifty years, it always gives me a slight sort of jolt. Like it's alive a little bit. This is probably why I've never told anyone the story.

'Maybe I shouldn't, after all,' I say and Winnie nods.

'Okay. Whatever you want. But some things just have to be told. I need to tell my Ray that, he's holding back a story from me, I know it. He'll tell me when he's ready, I know that as well. Telling things makes them real.'

It's this that decides me. She's right, nothing is real if it's stored in your head. Telling it gives it life I suppose.

'Right,' I begin. 'This story is fifty years old and I never even told Maud. I wish I had. Still hope to be able to if we end up in the same place. You religious, Winnie?'

She shrugs. 'Some days I am. Others not. I think if there was a God he'd not let half the stuff that happens, happen. But there's too much *stuff* out there for there not to be *something*. So, not sure. What about you?'

'I think there's a God. But not like any God we talk about. This God's a dangerous, dark bloke who is as much about war as he is about peace. See, you can't have one without the other, can you? But I believe in heaven, and hell. Hope I go wherever Maud's gone.' I pause. Been thinking about her an awful lot, lately. She's been gone nearly seven years. I'm fed up of being alone.

'I was a fisherman up the coast. Like I told you. Fished for whatever we could get and sold it at the market. Maud was a teacher at the local school and we did well. She used to come out and help me during the holidays. Sometimes I'd take other blokes out to help, sometimes it was just me. There's a small island off the coast about five miles north of Fosse Bay near where we used to drop our lobster and crab pots. If I had time I'd pull the boat onto the beach and walk a little. The island's still there but it's got buildings on it now, they've made a bird watching research thing out there. Back then though, it was deserted. Got real peace out there. I loved the family but with four young kids it was pretty noisy. Fishermen get used to solitude, you know? So sometimes I'd stay a bit longer than I should and just sit, and watch the waves.' Those were fine days. I felt glad to be alive, glad to be a fisherman. Glad of God, whatever he was, for making all of it. I smile at the memory of myself, young and strong, resting on that beach.

I reach for a sip of water but Winnie's there already, passing me the glass. I see my hand shaking a bit as I tip it towards me. Winnie's kind hand closes over my own and helps guide it to my lips. I have a long drink and lay back for a moment.

'You're a good un,' I tell her. 'Ray's lucky.'

'So I keep telling him. Only if he behaves, though! Fancy, all this love at our age.'

'Shush woman. You've got thirty years on me. Plenty life left.'

'I hope so. Me and Ray have a lot of plans.'

'It goes quick, but you can fill it up and make it slow down,' I say.

'So, you're on the island…?' Winnie prompts me.

'I'm on the island. That island. Was my own bit of paradise. Never took anyone there and only a few folk used it for fishing so usually just me alone there. So, this day I'm lying on the beach watching the shags and the terns and the gulls. Thinking about jobs I needed to do to the boat, and the fact that Maud wanted me to take a holiday but it was the best season for fishing. I remember. I was looking at the rocks and suddenly it seemed like one moved. Rocks always look different – the light, the tides, the waves – you think you recognise them but they seem to change every day. I could've seen this one before. Wasn't sure. But it moved. I swear it. I watched harder. Nothing happened and I decided it was a trick of the light. But just as I moved my head, I saw it move again. This time I wasn't wrong, I was sure of it. So I gets up, and goes to have a look.' I can't help but chuckle, remembering.

'What?' asks Winnie.

'Telling this, it's strange. It's never been told but it's like the story wants to come out. You're going to think I'm nuts, though. Send me off up to Hallmead.'

'Frank, not much surprises me. Trust me, you're sane. That's not going to change.'

'Well, we'll see,' I say, flexing my hand around the green velvet bag. 'I walked over to the rock. It was like a normal rock every time I looked at it and I knew the beach pretty well and was sure it was a rock I'd seen before. Maybe. But every time I looked somewhere else, it kind've flickered. Shimmered. And then I looked back and it was just a rock. Thought I was seeing things.'

I could still stop, save Winnie's view of me as a nice sane old man. But she's listening so hard and anyway this story wants to be told. I can feel it. In my hand, the green velvet bag is warm.

'I walked right up to it and bent down. And I saw a face. Honest to God, I jumped back about five feet. I think I shouted something. From where I was, it was just a rock again but then I went closer and looked and looked and there it was again, a face. And it was in pain. How can I describe it? It looked a bit like a seal, and that's what I thought it was, a hurt seal stranded. But it had green eyes, bright green eyes and long hair which could be seaweed at first glance but I could now see was hair. And it was all curled up so the face was sort of tucked down below this, this *tail,* a shimmery, silvery-green dolphin tail. But not a dolphin tail, cause I've seen plenty of them. Well, I just stood there and stared. And these green eyes stared back. I dunno what possessed me then but I reached out and touched it. And this mouth appeared from nowhere and hissed at me! Like an angry snake. No words, just a hiss. And something snapped at me and I turned and ran.'

Winnie's looking at me like she's really interested.

'What happened next?' she's whispering.

'Well, I thought I was ill, seeing things, like. I turned towards my boat and started running. But then, I heard this call. This singing lonely call. It sounded like it was in pain. Sort of like a cat and a dog and a seal. Peculiar. I stopped dead and looked back at the rock thing, certain it'd come from there. There were no words but it was calling me back. Like I imagined a siren to sound. Singing to my soul.' I can't help it, the memory makes me shiver.

'So I went back. I was scared. Really scared. And aware I was all alone out there. But when I got back the thing had gone less rock-like. It was now a soft wet shiny *thing* like a seal, like a fish, like a –mermaid. No other word for it. But not a pretty mermaid like you see in kids' books. No, this was a frightening creature. It had green eyes and skin of all shades of blue, green and red. It seemed to change colour. It held my gaze with terrifying eyes then looked down at its tail and then I noticed the nets; had missed them before. It was all tangled up with nets and wire. It was stuck.'

We stare at each other for a moment. Winnie looks like a wide-eyed child. She believes me, I see that right away and I'm relieved. We both turn at the squeaky sound of someone walking up the ward. A tall young man in greens is looking at me, the nurse by his side.

'We've found you a bed, Mr Willis,' the nurse says to me. 'Doctor Baldwin here just wants to do some tests before you leave this ward. Thanks for staying, but you can go home now,' she says to Winnie.

Winnie looks at me, and I say to the nurse, 'Please, could I have five more minutes?

I'm giving Winnie here some directions to my house so she can bring me clothes.'

Winnie smiles brightly. The doctor is frowning. 'We'll be really quick,' says Winnie.

'All right. I have another patient to see here, which I can do first. But when I come back I really will have to ask you to-'

'It's okay, I'll be gone,' Winnie says. They both nod and walk away.

'What happened next?' Winnie leans forwards. 'Are you all right to continue?'

'I'm nearly at the end,' I say, and know it's true. 'Well. I squatted down – a bit nervous cause I'd seen this *thing* hiss and knew it had teeth but it needed help. And there was intelligence in the eyes. Like human intelligence but cold, so so cold. I reached out my hands toward the net and nothing happened, no hissing. So I reached out both hands and tugged at the net a little. The creature gave a growl of pain and I knew this was going to be difficult. The net was all twisted around and cutting into its skin. To make it short, in case that doctor comes back, I got out my knife and cut away all the net and stuff. The tide was coming in so I got wet but I didn't care. The creature didn't make a sound except these odd hisses when I hurt it accidentally. Eventually, I got all the net off. By this time I was kneeling in the water up to my neck. It tried to move its tail and although it must've hurt, it could move okay. It swam right up to me and put its face very close to mine, then it put a hand – I didn't even see its hands before – behind my neck and pulled me forwards, right under the water. Well, I thought I was a goner. I tried to push myself up but this thing was *strong*, much stronger than me. I could do nothing but be pulled forwards. We ended up in the water and I thought I was going to drown. But it put its face right up to mine again and I heard words in my head, *Thank you,* and something was pressed into my hand and I felt a slither next to me and then I was alone, face down in cold water, wondering what the hell had just happened.'

The telling of this has worn me out. I open my hand and hold out the green velvet bag to Winnie, who takes it. I see she's got tears in her eyes. I see she believes me. I smile. 'That's it.'

'Is this what it gave you?'

'That's what it gave me. Look inside.'

Winnie opens the bag and slides the stone into her palm. 'It's beautiful!'

'Isn't it,' I say. It's the colour of the creature's tail – all colours, flowing in and out of each other. It shimmers and shines and seems to glow, somehow. Winnie gazes at it.

'Take it,' I tell her.

'I can't, it's-'

'Soon after this happened, we had a tough time in the family. That's probably why I didn't tell Maud about what happened on the island. Long story, I'll not go there now. But this stone – this stone seemed to help me. It's got this kind of energy. Hold it. You'll see what I mean. It helped me. I don't need it anymore. It's right I should pass it on, and as nobody else knows the story, I feel you should have it. In case you ever need some help with anything. I used to sit and hold this and sort of feel recharged.'

She's trying to protest when the doctor comes back. I hand her the bag and she slips the stone in. 'I'll come and see you tomorrow,' she says. 'We can talk about it then.'

'Thank you,' I tell her. 'For listening to a mad old man.'

She leans over me and whispers in my ear, 'You're not mad. Thank you for the story,' and she gives me a soft kiss on my cheek. She turns, and she's gone. And so's the stone. I feel light. Like the water vapour that rises from the waves.

John Smith

Fire; incinerating last year's disappointments. Anna stands apart from her husband; she can't see his face in the dark even with the glow of the flames. But she can see John in every scene the fire makes; she watches him as if she's a seer and the fire's the crystal ball. There he is with his own family, his children. They have his raven hair and they're laughing, running around their own end-of-year burning. He smiles, but she sees him glancing back through the flames, back down the years to her as if the fire's a two-way mirror.

She remembers him as she does a hundred, a thousand? times each day. She thinks of the fires they shared on beaches and in jungle-heat. She'll give up trying to find him. It's a resolution she tries every year.

She remembers so clearly drawing the playful heart next to his name and details in the Filofax that made her feel organised, so organised she said she'd keep the future safe for them both after he showed her his scrappy notebook with its loose leaves. He went into *People met whilst Travelling,* on his own page.

How many times had she meant to copy the address, write his mother's number – 'she'll always know where I am' – in a second place? And the Filofax stolen just days after they parted, with a promise: *When I'm settled…*

The first firework jerks her back from that time, thirty years ago. It lights the sky pink.

A new year. A kiss from her husband.

Low Tide

Maggie doesn't need to spray the blue shirt with water; her tears slide down her face and nose; landing as little seas of sorrow. She hisses them away with a press of the iron and they leave tiny tide marks against the blue.

Pull yourself together, she tells herself. And she does, as she always does, sniffing away the feeling, as waves clear a beach. She finishes the shirts and hangs the blue one – his favourite – at the front.

An hour later she finds herself standing in the kitchen before a pile of breakfast dishes, staring at the wall, no idea of how she got there.

Then for a moment, it's all clear. Her life, their life, the future, the past. The never-ending cooking, hoovering, dusting, ironing. The fact she's unemployable, because she's been unemployed for too long. What a joke, she thinks, looking at the pristine house.

When Andrew comes home she listens for his keys clattering into the wooden bowl on the hall table; the shake of fabric as he takes off his coat; the silence as he doesn't call out Hello! the way he did, once. He goes straight to his study. She hears the door close.

As usual she takes him a tray of dinner. Neither of them knows it, but this is a test. With his silence, he fails, and something shifts in Maggie's soul.

In the morning, after a breakfast of minimal conversation. Andrew goes to work. Maggie wonders how he'll cope. He can't cook. She does the bills.

In his meeting, Andrew is uncomfortable. The blue shirt feels too small, it clings and constricts. Whilst important things are discussed he loosens his collar, sweats. It crosses his mind he could be having a heart attack.

There's a mark on the sleeve. A small white ring, irregular. Toothpaste? He rubs at it. For some reason, he thinks of the dog he had as a child, and how he sobbed when it died.

Someone asks him a question and his mouth goes dry.

Someone else asks him if he's okay and he mumbles something about needing a glass of water. He stumbles from the room, eyes burning with what he thinks is shame until he sees himself in the gents' mirror. He's crying? He stares at his reflection, which wobbles back at him. He sees, in the mirror, more of the marks; small white clouds against the blue. He rubs at another, and the same sad feeling stabs at him. He pulls at the shirt.

Something's wrong, he thinks. He needs to go home. Maggie might be there – though he realises he's no idea what she does with her days. He needs to change that, he decides. They need to reconnect.

On the way home is a flower stall and he buys roses. As he holds them against himself they drip water onto his front, blending in with the unknown white marks.

Maggie will know how to get rid of them, he thinks.

Howja Know?

'They're coming back for me,' Wee Stevie says. He's shoving down his sandwich and biscuits as if he's not eaten all day, which he probably hasn't. I don't think he's been to school either as there's no sign of a fight on him.

I keep my face composed and ask, 'Who's that then, Stevie?'

'The blue people.'

I'm not sure what to say; I'd thought I'd heard the end of this story. It's not unusual for a child in difficult circumstances to invent a fantasy, but Stevie's twelve – in my eyes too old for that sort of escapism. Plus, he's under no illusions about the state of his life; he knows what alcoholism is and understands the social care system; he can describe any drug to me and I saw him carrying a knife, once. I took it from him and he gave it to me, shrugging. His dad appears every few months, makes his mother screech and throw things and then disappears again. Stevie told me he once asked his dad if he could go with him and his dad answered by laughing, and shoving him back to his beaten-up front door.

But Stevie doesn't complain. He wakes up each morning, and he survives. And I watch over him.

We met in the newsagent's downstairs. In a block of flats where net curtains are one way mirrors, I knew all about him. I knew social services were involved, occasionally the police; I knew Wee Stevie had been fostered a few times, always coming home to the care of his skinny, sallow-faced mum and his older brother, who pretended to look after him. I watched him for weeks after I first moved in, before deciding that even if it got me into trouble, I had to help the child. I'd seen the way 'neighbours' ran past Stevie's door. I didn't want to be accused of meddling or anything worse, so I planned the whole thing as I'd once planned lessons, from having full cupboards of kid friendly junk food, to meeting Stevie downstairs and asking him to help me with my shopping.

His nickname's apt; he's small-boned and scrawny, with a cheeky grin and what my mother would have called a 'streak of the devil' in him. I know from overheard conversations he's been caught shoplifting, stealing from other flats, fighting, smoking, hanging out with groups of older kids who drink and take pills. But there's something about him. Feral as he is, he shines with an intelligence that comes across as belligerence, glows with promise that he could do a lot better if he were given the right circumstances.

Or perhaps I just missed children. His mum didn't care and my son was lost to me – it felt like fate.

The first time he came to my flat he grabbed all the food on offer and ran, to sit and shovel down food with grubby fingers in the stairwell opening near his house. I watched him, smiling, through my curtains. The second time he ate a couple of sandwiches before taking the rest and walking out; the third time he stayed until the plate was empty.

He called me Mrs Theal, even though I'd told him my full name, and I wondered where he'd got the manners. I didn't change it; it gave us a distance. He knew I was a retired teacher and he'd looked at the younger me with a young man and a boy and a baby, peering out of ageing photo frames. He never asked, but I told him anyway.

'My son,' I said. 'That's Derek. He and I fell out a long time ago.'

'Why don't you make it up with him?'

'Because I don't think he'll talk to me. I once said some very hurtful things to him.'

'Howja know, if you don't try, Mrs Theal?' he grinned in a way that showed me his promise, all over again. He reminded me of other rough diamonds I'd tried to shine during my career.

He mentioned the blue people on about his eighth visit. 'They come for me in blue shining spaceships with lights in the night,' he'd said. 'They're nice. But they always bring me back.' It seemed like the description a much younger child would've given. Stevie usually spoke with gangland swagger behind his words. When I tried to ask him what the blue people were like he said they wanted to be a secret. I told him that not all secrets were good and asked him if they made him uncomfortable. He grinned at me. 'Told ya, they're nice,' he said.

I kept a closer eye on him from then on, and I noticed that next time he was removed from his home, he mentioned the blue people again, after he'd been brought back. Ah, I though, of course. It's the police, the blue shining lights are emergency lights on the car; the nice treatment he'd spoken of is him being properly looked after. And whilst I harboured a jealousy that I was unable to do this for him, I was thankful there was someone looking out for Wee Stevie. Things went quiet across the way, across the gap of space that separated our corridors, and I thought, maybe things are improving.

So when he tells me they're coming back for him, I pay attention.

'I thought things were getting better,' I say.

'Oh, come on, Mrs Theal. You know me mum's not going to get better. And Rob's leaving. He's away down to England to work in a club. Next time they come, I don't think I'll be coming back. They're kind and they have this really sick stuff – stuff like you'd never believe. Their spaceship's massive, there is food and things like tablets you can play on and they make you well if you're ill. And you never know til you try, do you?' He fixes me with his grin.

'So when are they coming?' I ask as casually as I can.

'Tomorrow,' he says. 'It's still up to me but if I want to go, I can.'

The following day I watch like a hawk. I eat and drink by the window, looking at the whitened world through the netting. He doesn't emerge until the afternoon, when he's shoved out of the door by his mother. I feel myself grow rigid and hot as I watch her, swaying, swearing at her son, slapping the door as she screams, 'Get out!' He runs to the stairwell and vanishes, a quicksilver blur of boyhood, disappearing.

I grab my shoes but I'm not as fast as I think and by the time I make it down the stairs it's too late; he's vanished. I ask around a little but half the people I speak to don't bother to answer. I wish some blue people would come for me, too. This is not where I want to live.

I buy all the things Stevie likes and lug them up the stairs. I wait all day, but he misses his sandwiches and biscuits and doesn't come home.

Still, I watch.

I wake up, stiff, with a sore neck where my head's been flopped to one side during the evening. I'd dragged my armchair over to the window to be more comfortable whilst I waited for him but all I've done is given myself a place to nod off. I check the time: half-past nine.

'Damn,' I mutter. I go to the loo and make a coffee; hobbling back with still-sleeping legs while the kettle boils.

I watch and I wait. Wee Stevie doesn't return and I begin to think this is a good thing, a positive sign, because it means he's been picked up by the police and will now be awaiting placement with a foster family, maybe the same ones who've had him before; the ones who return him fatter and cleaner.

My eyes start to play tricks on me and I see kids everywhere, but they turn into stray dogs; teenagers kissing in the shadows or cats, hunting. I'm starting to think I should just go to bed when I see him in a flash of movement, a skinny lad being chased by bigger lads and flashes of steel. I want to call to him but he'd never hear me. Suddenly I see blue lights reflected in the windows opposite, flashing and shining to the right, and Stevie swerves and runs towards them, hands outstretched. There's a flash and a whoosh like tyres stopping on gravel and the blue lights reverse and disappear. My eyes are playing tricks again because it looks like they're going upwards but of course they can't be.

The bigger boys disperse, yelling at each other. I breathe out.

Minutes later, the police come screaming back, haloes of blue hanging above them. By the time I get down the stairs and onto the grass there are six officers and three cars and a jumpy audience, watching from a distance.

'We had reports of fighting. Someone called and said there were knives. You see anything?' a policewoman calls to the onlookers.

I walk over and quietly tell her about Stevie and the bigger boys and the police coming.

The woman nods. 'Steven Parker. Makes sense – always in trouble, that one. But we're first on the scene so it can't have been a police car he went in. Are you sure?' She looks at me and I shrug.

Of course I'm sure, I think later, as I sit with a sherry by the window. Of course

I'm sure. Just as I'm sure that if I call him, Derek will still refuse to talk to me.

I hear Wee Stevie's voice in my head: *Howja know, if you don't try, Mrs Theal?*

So the next morning, whilst the TV's showing pictures of the flats with a photo of **Missing Boy, Steven Parker**, overlaid, I pick up the phone and key in the last number I had for Derek.

I don't need to look it up.

Colour Therapy

Gill's ancient Casio beeped *social worker o'clock!* Seconds later, there was a knock at the door; Marie's smart rat-a-tat which vibrated through the flat. Gill jumped off the sofa and put a hand to her chest before standing up and walking to the door.

In the hallway was Marie, with two very large holdalls. Gill raised her eyebrows and Marie waved the unspoken question away.

'Later. Some gifts. How are you?' Marie went to embrace her and Gill stiffened, before remembering that it was okay, that she'd asked Marie to do this, to practise being normal again. Being open again. Being the self she knew was still in there somewhere.

Gill opened herself to a brief hug and found her smile. 'I'm okay,' she said, 'it was a shock, obviously, but I'm all right. I'm fine. I'm safe, right? And he's, ah,' She couldn't say 'going to die' in case she somehow got the blame for killing him. She didn't tell Marie about the sleepless nights, the fears, the regression to the person she'd been a year ago.

'I'm so sorry – it must have brought up – all kinds of things.'

Gill nodded, but stopped herself from speaking. Marie was now a friend as well as her social worker, although Gill didn't know if she could trust her with everything. Once a social, always a social, her mother used to say.

Gill put the kettle on whilst Marie walked through to the lounge. Gill braced herself, and didn't have to wait long.

'Oh my God, Gill!' Marie's voice was too loud. Gill flinched.

'This is incredible! This place really feels like yours, now. Your home. How did you do so much?'

Gill, hiding in the steam of the kettle, imagined it though Marie's eyes. Every wall was a different colour now – several shades of a different colour – and the patterns were even more intricate than before

They crept around the windows, up and down the door frames, in depths and shapes which pulled the viewer in. Gill smiled, as she made the tea.

Carrying it through to the living room she felt again the shiver of excitement that walking around her flat gave her.

'You like it?' she smiled at Marie, an open, smile which shaped her face into a heart.

'I love it,' the social worker replied. 'It's amazing... it's...' and she brushed a tear from her eye. 'I'm so happy for you.'

Gill didn't trust herself to speak – again, the trust issue. If she told nobody, she'd be safe.

'Can I see what's in the bags now?' she asked, thinking how like a child she sounded.

'Not yet. After I've gone, is probably best,' said Marie, not meeting Gill's eyes.

ONE YEAR EARLIER

Marie entered the flat first. Gill was stooped, head low, breathing harsh and Marie wanted to go in and turn on the lights so her new charge wouldn't trip and fall the very first time she walked into the flat.

The lights were too bright and Marie cursed herself for not checking it out first. The hospital was bright; she'd wanted Gill's first entry into her new home to be as far removed from hospital triggers as possible.

Gill followed her in and leaned against the hallway wall.

'That's the lounge, ahead; the kitchen is to the left here and there are two bedrooms off to the right. The bathroom's next to the kitchen,' Marie said.

Gill nodded but didn't move.

'Come on through. Let me show you the kitchen; I put some food in for you.'

Gill followed her through to the small clean room. Marie had put flowers in a vase but all Gill could see was white and an off white/magnolia colour. She shuddered.

'Do you want me to stay a bit?' the social worker asked.

Gill shook her head. 'Thank you,' she muttered.

'I'll be by in the morning. Go and explore. This is yours, now, Gill. Nobody else is here. I know this is what you want but if you find it overwhelming in any way, call me, okay?'

Gill nodded again.

After Marie had gone Gill walked from room to room, running her fingers along the back of the sofa, turning on the tap in the bathroom, on and off, on and off, just to see the water run. She nodded at herself in the mirror, and then switched off the lights.

The next time Marie came she brought art pads, paint and brushes. Gill glanced at them and didn't touch them for over a week, thinking, how dare she? But they called to her, those colours, and demanded that she open them and let them live. The first time she sat down she painted until all the paper was used up. That night she dreamt about her ex-husband, and the way he used to jeer at her paintings and how he – drunk – burned them all one night, because she burned his dinner. In the dream he was fiercer, darker than in real life. In the morning she hid the paintings and it was weeks before she let Marie see them.

The next time Marie came, she brought three times as much paper.

The weeks went by and Gill felt life returning. Life in the hospital had been empty but safe. Life in her new flat was every day a challenge – far from safe but interesting, an adventure, days full of firsts and one day she caught herself passing in a mirror and saw that she was smiling.

She'd painted over fifty pictures, over fifty unique, slightly surreal, colour-filled dream scenes of fabulous creatures and things she was at night and people she'd seen at the hospital and Marie's eyes, eyes that she was beginning to trust, before she first signed her name. It was tiny, printed in the bottom right hand corner of the paper, *By Gill*, so tiny it was hardly there.

'But it is there,' said Marie, squeezing her shoulder. 'You didn't let him beat you. You still exist. He, on the other hand, is locked up, stripped of his name. You have your life back.'

Gill shivered and Marie, realising she'd broached it all too early, was angry with herself all the way home. She'd wanted to be Gill's social worker since she first heard the story, so similar to her own. The next time she went, however, Gill showed her a painting of a grey cell, surrounded by the outside world like a flowergardenjungle, all around the outside. Inside was a very small man.

Gill's name at the bottom of her paintings grew larger and her paintings grew bolder, filled with new colours, shades she imagined she'd invented herself. One day she woke up and realised the flat was far, far too plain.

Marie laughed when she walked in. 'Oh,' she said, 'this is YOU. Now I can see you.' And Gill laughed back, her face feeling doughy and all out of practice at laughter.

Colours and patterns grew in layer after layer, getting ever more intricate. Gill began to love the flat; it was no longer a way station on her way back to normal life – now it was her home. Colour was her home. She existed in shades of green, yellow, red, blue. She found herself in deep purples and rose pinks. She saw her moods in the blues of the sky and the craziness of a rainbow. She found herself in the swirling patterns that covered her kitchen cupboards.

And then one day, eleven months after she'd moved in, she'd noticed, as if for the first time, how grey the village was. Her flat was an oasis of colour amidst a desert of grey. One morning, she knew exactly what to do about it.

It was Marie who brought the first newspaper cutting round.

'Mystery Painter Baffles Villagers' one head line read. In another a plea – 'Police Want to Talk to Mystery Artist' and in the last one Marie gave her was something that made Gill shiver deliciously inside. 'The Colours Make Us Happy, say Residents'.

'Don't suppose you know anything about this?' Marie said, eyebrows raised. Gill looked at the cuttings again, glad of the red in the cupboards which might hide her blush in their glow.

'No,' she said, shaking her head. 'Not at all. Nothing.'

'Because,' Marie continued, 'I'd hate whoever is doing this to get into trouble.'

'Hmm,' said Gill.

'If somebody found out who it was and that person had a bit of a background that people might misunderstand – well, it might not go too well.

'Hmm-mmm,' said Gill.

'However, people do seem to be enjoying it. And you, Gill Anderson, look positively radiant.'

Gill tried to stop. But the greyness was everywhere she looked. She forced herself to travel farther afield to get art supplies in case anyone saw her and worked it out.

One day, a year after she moved in, saw a headline herself:

'Monster Husband to be Released on Compassionate Grounds'. Before the shaking took her over completely she scanned the story.

...Paul Anderson – terminal cancer – early release – wife so traumatised after years of abuse that she was hospitalised for five months – will be guarded at private hospital...

That night she painted nightmares all night, thinking that if she let them out, they wouldn't get to her first. All the next day her pictures were dark. But the day after that, she went out and did some decorating. The old phone box now had a facelift.

Her overriding concern, to her surprise, was her lack of art supplies. She'd run out of DIY shops where she'd not be recognised and she still wasn't able to travel too far. The paint she had left was dwindling.

/

'Can I see what's in the bags now?' Gill asked, thinking how like a child she sounded.

'Not yet. After I've gone, is probably best,' said Marie, not meeting Gill's eyes.

Gill waited until Marie's car was off away down the road before she unzipped one of the bags.

Inside she saw trust and true friendship, spelled out in tin after tin of outdoor paint; brushes in all shapes and sizes; thinner; brush cleaner; and yet more paint.

Tears fell onto the colour charts as she opened the second bag and saw more and more tins; every shade glowing at her, the promise of healing in every shade.

She looked outside at the fading light and the grey lampposts, and wondered how she'd get to the top, as she decorated them, every single one, so they could stand there as individuals, instead of uniform posts, as they sent light out to the world.

The Clearing

'I don't want to do it,' Charlotte said.

'You drew the short straw. Random chance. You have to,' said Hannah, exotic and new, self-proclaimed leader of the group, girl who most girls wanted to be, including Charlotte.

Charlotte looked at Hannah's brown eyes, fixed on her. Something unnamed moved inside her. 'Okay,' she said. 'I'll do it. When?'

'Tonight. They always walk down the lane at half-past six. Take your phone and snap them,' Hannah giggled, 'doing whatever they do. Then we can threaten to show Joe's bitchy wife the pics and *persuade* him to let us back into the Den. It's genius.'

Charlotte nodded and the rest of the girls in the group giggled, before linking arms and marching off, leaving Charlotte staring after them, wondering how this new girl had so easily taken over and wishing she had the thing that Hannah had. Whatever it was.

Two hours later Charlotte was hiding in a hedge at the end of the lane, waiting for Joe and Ben to go past with Ben's ancient dog. Perhaps tonight they wouldn't go. Maybe the dog would hear her, and she'd be busted. She shifted on her haunches to get more comfy. She'd give them five more minutes and then go home, Hannah or no Hannah. Her mum thought she was at Hannah's, doing her homework – as if that would ever happen. And as if her mum cared – she was too busy writing letters to her solicitor. Charlotte wished herself back in time to Before, pre-separation and pre-Hannah. Instead of sitting in a hedge she'd be sitting doing her homework at the kitchen table, whilst her mum cooked and her dad whistled his way in from work and they chatted and asked each other questions and laughed about times before she even existed. Tears blurred the greeny inside of the hedge but she daren't wipe them away because here were footsteps and low voices. Damn.

Joe and Ben passed within feet of her. The dog strained towards her, sniffing, but then caught another scent and pulled Ben onwards.

She could just not go. She could say she missed them, say her mum had called her home. But she was a crap liar and this, if she could do it, would make Hannah notice her more.

The men's voices faded and Charlotte crawled out of the hedge. She could see them going around the first corner, towards the wood. As soon as they were out of sight she crawled out of the bush, brushed herself down and jogged to the corner, peering around it. There they were, about to enter the wood. Once inside, she could hide behind trees and follow them.

She waited until they went beyond the curtain of green and ran again, hiding behind the first tree. Here, she stopped and glanced around, self-conscious and embarrassed, aware she looked as if she were playing some hide and seek kids' game.

She was alone.

She slipped into the wood.

It was a different world. She hardly ever came here anymore; once, she and her family had walked here every weekend. Her parents had told her it was where they used to go walking to escape their friends, back when they first met at sixth-form college. They told her it used to be known as Lovers' Clearing. Charlotte knew it by a different name, now, one that made her go red.

Voices ahead told her the men had taken the right hand path, the one that led to the clearing and the pond. Her heart thudded. Suddenly she didn't want to see what – if anything – they were doing, Den or no Den. It wasn't exactly that great, the Den, anyway, surely they could find some other place to hang out? She began to back away but then Hannah's face, grinning at her for agreeing to do this, swam before her and she sighed and followed, down the right hand path.

Dodging behind trees she kept the men in sight as they walked into the clearing. So far nothing had happened; they were just two friends, out for a stroll.

She crept to the edge of the clearing.

Joe and Ben were sitting on a fallen log tucked into the screen of trees at the far side. They were laughing about something. The dog was still on the lead, Charlotte noticed with relief. If they let the dog off the lead the dog would find her and that would be that. What would she say to explain?

She crouched behind a tree, and got out her phone. She raised it and slid her fingers apart until the men filled the screen. For several minutes, they chatted and then they fell silent. Slowly, Joe's fingers reached over to envelop Ben's and they both looked down at their hands, as if in surprise.

Click, went Charlotte's camera. *Click, click.*

They raised their heads and the woods seemed to fall silent around them. Her heart thudded louder and something liquefied in her middle. She wished, suddenly, she were anywhere but here.

Joe reached around with his other hand and touched Ben's face. It was the tenderest touch she'd ever seen. It made tears blur her vision again. *That,* she thought. *That's it. That's what's missing.* But she didn't understand her own thoughts and instead focussed on getting the job done. *Click, click.*

She expected them to kiss and she wasn't sure she'd be able to watch it but instead they drew close and held each other, becoming a single unit, like a statue, with the dog at their feet. She took some more photos and watched. Joe's wife, she thought. The rumours, she thought. And she heard her dad's choked-up voice during that terrible time last Christmas: no smoke without fire, Charlie, as he explained what was going on between him and her mum.

The men broke apart and stood, holding hands once more. They murmured to each other and laughed and the look on their faces made her catch her breath. She'd never seen gruff Joe smile before, not like that. They turned and walked away, out of the clearing, holding hands until they reached the edge and then dropping them and moving further apart, as if preparing to enter the real world again.

Charlotte bent her head and sobbed as emotion, unfiltered, unnameable, crashed through her.

She grabbed herself from the inside and stood up, unsteady at first as the blood drained from her head too quickly. She shoved her phone in her pocket, walked over to the log and sat down, looking around her. The tree to her left was carved with letters. Poor tree, she thought, standing up to stroke its ruined bark. She traced her hands over the letters wondering at all the stories the tree had heard.

E ♥ T

H XX B

T n K.

Her fingers found D + L. 'Danny and Lorraine,' she whispered. The letters were distorted and swollen, but they were still there. She traced them with her fingers. She thought for a moment about running home, grabbing a parent by each arm and forcing them to look, to see that once they'd been here, just like Joe and Ben, and all the other people who'd lived and loved in this small clearing.

There were fresh initials, closer to the ground. She bent down to look. J and B, they said, in a carefully carved, tiny script.

Charlotte sat down again. She reached around and took out her phone, scrolling to the camera icon. One by one she deleted the photos. She scrolled to her albums folder and erased them from the recently deleted file, so they definitely didn't exist. She stood up, feeling lighter inside.

She was first to arrive at the park. When they came, a laughing mass with Hannah at the centre of their world, Charlotte's stomach flipped. She tried to tell herself she wasn't a crap liar but it sounded unconvincing.

'Well?' demanded Hannah, grabbing her hand. 'What did they do? What did you see?'

Charlotte drank in Hannah's tiny, temporary need for her as the girl's brown eyes drew her in and made her forget for a second what she was going to say. She held out her phone.

'Nothing,' she said. 'They went for a walk, I followed them, they went home.'

'Mannnnnn... I thought the rumours were true. Wouldn't bloody blame him either. His wife's a cow. Oh well. It was a good plan. I guess. Nice work, anyway,' Hannah said, giving Charlotte's hand a squeeze. 'I've got some vodka. Let's go and sit on the swings with it.'

'I'm off home,' Charlotte said. 'Mum'll be worried.' Her hand felt warmer. Tonight, she knew, she'd shower with it sticking out of the curtain to keep it dry.

'Suit yourself. Oooh look, here come the boys…'

Charlotte watched them forget her as a gang of testosterone burled into the park ahead of them. She watched Hannah's eyes glitter with plans and ideas and need.

She turned and walked back the way she'd come, blocking out the yells of the boys and the giggles of the girls and concentrating instead on herself. Inside she felt all wrong. It was like excitement: that feeling before stepping onto a roller coaster. She rubbed her stomach and the feeling intensified, like nausea. She was about to walk off a cliff. Something had changed within her; shifted like sand does in deserts. She'd been caught in a sandstorm. She was lost and she wanted Hannah to explain it all and lead her to the right place. But Hannah was gone.

She wanted to be at home. She wanted to talk to her mum. She wanted to tell her about the initials and about what she'd seen and the small awakening that she couldn't quite put into words inside herself. She wanted a hug from her dad. She wanted the evenings back, the ones where she did her homework at the kitchen table and her parents would laugh together and the radio played and they'd say to each other, Do you remember…? Do you? And they'd say, I do. I do remember.

Playing the Field

I was out with Danny, my guitar playing fair-haired boy I'd met in the pub, when I saw Mark, and suddenly Danny wasn't quite so attractive and his guitar playing went a little off-key so after a few days of quiet withdrawal and long sighs and the eventual 'I'm sorry, it's not you it's me...' I went after Mark and of course I got him, because if there's one thing I'm good at it's getting men to notice me. Mark couldn't play the guitar but he could play me and I fell smack into him for four whole weeks, properly in love, hearts and flowers, all that stuff. Then one day we were out walking in the park and at the end of a lead with a puppy attached I saw

Devon and he gave me that subtle look, even though I was with Mark, that subtle look that said, I would, would you? And I thought yes, I would, and suddenly Mark's helpful hands weren't quite so magic and I did the sighing and told him it wasn't him, it was me, and he left, almost in tears I think, and I went straight to the park. Devon and I walked the puppy round and round for hours whilst we talked until the puppy was exhausted and we sat and kissed in the shade of a sycamore tree and I thought mmm-mmm. And I fell in love, differently, all over again. The puppy grew and Devon and I travelled all over, exploring woods and streams and beaches and each other. One day though, when the puppy was now a large dog, Devon said the same thing once too often and I realised he wasn't as pretty as I'd first thought and around the same time I saw

Caroline in a café and Caroline smiled and the smile said, let's have a go, so we did. When I told Devon he was confused and his ego had been bruised so badly I doubted he'd be walking with any more women for a while but hey, he'd get over it. Meanwhile Caroline and I had some exploring to do and we discovered that we had a lot in common, more than we'd ever thought. Firsts; it was all about firsts, for both of us. I loved Caroline in the way you only love your first until I got tired of being the same end of a magnet and looked for my opposite once again and there, in the cinema, under a mop of hair was

Paul, who turned and saw us, saw me and smiled and Caroline saw and she knew the moment I did. I said I was sorry and told her that of course it wasn't her, it was me and I chatted to Paul the very next day when he rang me on the number I'd scribbled onto a piece of paper and slipped into his hand. Paul was a bit dangerous and a bit edgy and he lifted me right out of my comfort zone and he would have done except I discovered he liked white lines and the white lines made him at first very loving and then the next day, when he was coming down, downright nasty. One black eye was all it took and at the police station I saw

Jez, in for shop lifting, in for a caution, younger than me and cocky and cute. I gave him a lift home and then bought him a drink and he kissed the black eye and asked for Paul's surname. Turned out he knew of a friend of his who went and warned him, something, anyway, because Paul was on crutches the next time I saw him and Jez became my hero, just for a few days until I recovered enough to know I didn't need saving and I walked away, into the arms of a silver fox called

Mal who was older and reminded me of the dad I'd only met once, the one an old boyfriend always said I was trying to find, by going through men like a steamroller. His words. Mal was married, which I only found out after his wife banged on my door when I was banging her husband upstairs so he got the boot and I was alone for a whole week until the new guy in the warehouse at work suddenly introduced himself as

Andy and said I was beautiful and would I? Of course I would; I wasn't sleeping as there were no arms around me and I craved the warmth in the middle of the cold black night and the company in those small hours, lying awake. Andy treated me like a queen and bought me things and whispered in my ear at all the right times. I decided I loved him and I gave him myself in all kinds of energetic ways that he demanded and I learnt a lot about football and music and curry. For three whole months I cheered and clapped and ate mango chutney in a variety of places until one of the waiters gave me a wink with his deep brown eyes and I went back there the following night and discovered what the rooms above the restaurant were like. Enclosed in those brown arms he whispered that his name was

Ali and he was new to the UK and would I show him around? Of course I would, I said and I told Andy I was sorry and that it wasn't him, it was me, amongst deep sighs and a pushed out tear to make him feel better. I got Ali's name wrong, just once, and he couldn't forgive me, he said, and I would have to leave, after only three weeks and I was alone again, not sleeping and scared of the night until I met

Tim in the pub and he wasn't nice but dim, he was solid and real and he fell for me right away he said, but he knew I needed help.

What? I asked him.

He repeated, you need help. And he asked me some questions and listened, and by the end of our conversation I thought, maybe he's right.

He held me during the long night and I cried and I felt the precipice coming closer. Tim held me every night and said he loved me and that he wanted to help me.

Help me? I asked. And I began to be suspicious and the precipice fell away as I drew back until I was safely in the green green field away from the edge and I left Tim's one night and went to a club and met

Jamal who was sweet and sexy and a perfect balm for all that seriousness. Of course I didn't need bloody help. I was fine, all I was doing was playing the field and having fun. Jamal and I started to work our way through the Karma Sutra and we got to about page 96 before I knew what was coming every time and noticed a guy in the supermarket called

'Ben, here to help' and he grinned and touched my hand accidentally whilst packing my shopping. I wrote Jamal a letter, feeling that I really didn't want to have to explain, all over again. It wasn't him, it was me, I wrote. Ben and I went camping a lot and made love under the stars and it was all going well until I missed my period and I told Ben and he ran a mile, literally, ran a mile.

And my body began to change.

Soon I was two people. In the night, I could hold this new version of me, place my hands over its growing, kicking form and I wouldn't feel afraid. The kicks grew stronger and I withdrew into a world of baby equipment and focus and I grew huge, expanded with a whole new personality. When the pains began I called myself an ambulance because I was alone at home and it came and took me to a safe white world where I welcomed into being a tiny warm bundle who I named

Jack.

And it turned out I didn't need help, after all, I just needed to stop running for a while. I held Jack and stayed still and all the rushing thoughts I had calmed down as he fed and my world shrank and I was glad of it. My body grew soft and I felt ugly, but I felt Amazonian at the same time, a strong beauty was inside me and I simply didn't care about the surface stuff. Jack grew and I bloomed as a mother, into a flower I'd never imagined before. Jack and I existed in a perfect little world, in my council flat, happy, content, sleeping well. He lay tucked in beside me every night; my dreams were all about him and all the adventures we'd have as he grew.

One day there was a

knock knock

at my door and I opened it and there stood

Ben, terror in his eyes, a bunch of flowers and a wooden truck in his hands. Jack crawled out from the living room, into the hall and Ben's face softened and he bent down and held out his hands. And Jack, who wasn't great at going to people, stretched up to be picked up. They had the same eyes. Ben's filled with tears as he turned to me and said, I'm sorry - it wasn't you, it was me. Can we go out for a walk?

I thought for a while and said that yes, we could. And Ben held the door for me and helped Jack with his coat and off we went, down to the playing fields, where I took a deep breath and started explaining about how I'd played the field myself, for all these years. And Ben listened and explained that he was really quite similar and that perhaps, two people who were similar might understand each other quite well?

I looked around the park, saw a cute bloke jog past who gave me an appraising look that said, mmm-mmm, how about it? And whilst a part of me leapt to answer, oh, yes please, a greater part of me turned away, turned back to my son and his father and said yes. Yes, you're probably right.

I think I'd quite like to be understood.

The Perfect Stroke

She begins with a length underwater. Down here everything makes sense and she remembers being here before. She can hear her heart and feel every muscle in her body. She's free. She comes to the surface at the deep end, takes a breath, executes a supple turn and starts her swim.

Pull, kick, glide... Eleven strokes to a length, a longer glide to the wall and a silky flick to turn. Every now and then she throws in a few freestyle lengths to give her neck a rest. The blue swimsuit is an extra layer of skin, bending and flexing with her body. At the *pull* she reaches ever further, with the *kick* she propels herself forwards as hard as she can and at the *glide* she must be like an arrow, perfectly straight, tips of toes to tips of fingers. *Pull kick glide* goes her body over and over again in search of the perfect stroke.

There's always something wrong. One finger will be slightly in front of the other. One toe lags below. Her stomach is more clenched on one side. It's hard work. Her breathing, too, must be perfect; start the exhale just as her arms are reaching forwards for the glide. The exhale must finish just as her head is reaching its highest point. She wishes she could control which way the bubbles flow but they're haphazard, running up her face and past her ears.

Pull, kick, glide and she's pretty sure she's approaching length number 50, so she makes the length only take seven strokes, gliding spearlike, further with each stroke.

Someone's getting into her lane.

She swims right down the middle of the lane, fast, but the person comes in anyway. It spoils everything and wrecks her count but she's no choice except to finish the swim. She can't change lanes partway through. The person is a man – even worse – and he's wearing blue trunks. Her colour. She turns without giving him any attention at all and pushes off the wall, furiously reaching into the first stroke.

All the way up the pool she can feel him behind her like a shark and her breathing has to change to drive her faster. He must not overtake, that would just ruin everything. At the turn she sees him a quarter of a length behind and is relieved; they're a similar speed.

She swims on but it's all ruined. She wants to sink, simply let go and sit on the bottom and breathe there; be unseen until the pool is closed and she can continue on her own, alone. She's no choice but to leave the pool now.

At the shallow end she touches the wall and bounces up high from the bottom. She rises up out of the water and onto the side.

'Sarah!' she hears, from behind.

Head down, she makes for the changing rooms.

He's there, waiting, by the door. She stops. There's nowhere to go, only the fire exit and that would make everyone notice.

'Hey, Sarah.' His voice is gentle.

'What do you want?' she says.

'To talk,' he says.

She holds both hands out in front of her. 'No,' she says.

'Please, Sarah.'

But she squares her shoulders against him and slips past and leaves the building. A bus is there waiting.

The following day she's cautious. She thinks she remembers a man in her lane. It could have been yesterday so she should be careful.

She changes into the swimsuit she bought at the pool shop, a red one. She doesn't know if red will be all right, but it'll disguise her a bit. It makes her feel strange, wearing red. She's got a new hat, too, white with blue stripes. She can't afford goggles too but she wears a different pair from yesterday, an old pair she found in a drawer.

There's an empty lane which she takes as a good omen. She slips into the water. After a few deep breaths she sits down, curls herself over and kicks off, along the bottom. She covers the 25 metres with ease, flying along the bottom of the pool, touching the end, feeling as if she could swim forever.

She's on length 87 when her goggles start to leak. This is a huge problem because if she stops, she'll have to swim extra, to balance it out. She tries to carry on but her eyes sting and she can't endure it. She stops in the deep end and adjusts her goggles. She's just about to push away again when she hears two of the lifeguards talking in low voices.

'You'd never guess, would you? She's here every day. Can hardly see the scars. The attack-'

'Shhhhh, she's-'

Sarah shakes her head and swims off. None of her business. She hates it when people talk about other people. It's happened to her sometime, though she can't remember when.

She's on 89, trying to work out how many extra she'll have to do when it all goes wrong and a man gets into her lane. She shakes her head underwater. Was it yesterday there was a man? If she gets out he might follow her but if she carries on swimming he won't be able to talk to her.

Pull, kick, glide she swims and the rhythm calms her. The man sets off before her, just as she's about to reach the wall. She sinks down and breathes out a tower of bubbles in the water, watches them go to the surface and sees the man's feet disappearing. Ahead of her is all right; if he's ahead she can keep an eye on him.

At 99 she turns and swims back to the shallow end underwater. It hurts. Just halfway down the pool her lungs want to burst, but she pushes on. Spots dance in front of her eyes and a passing thought, *just breathe it in,* flits across her mind. She makes it to the end; she doesn't know how but she does. The air is clean and warm and she gulps it down.

'That was pretty good,' says a voice. 'Especially at the end of your swim.'

It's a man and he looks familiar but Sarah cannot place him. She's not got enough air to speak yet but she nods. She reaches up and pulls off her swimming hat, and notices it's not her blue one. *Strange,* she thinks, and then she looks down and sees a red swimsuit. She frowns.

'You have a lot of swimsuits,' says the man.

Sarah stares at him.

'I was here yesterday. And the day before.'

'Did we... Did we speak?' she manages.

The man smiles at her, and nods. 'We spoke. We speak often. I know a little about you.'

'I need to go,' she says in a hurry. Something is wrong with his words. Sarah pushes herself up out of the pool.

Outside he's there, waiting. He smiles a cautious, gentle smile. 'I'm sorry, Sarah,' he says. 'I thought, I thought you might have...' he sighs. 'It doesn't matter. Can I see you to the bus?'

She doesn't say yes but he walks next to her anyway. A bus is there waiting for her. A woman – again, familiar – is standing next to the big door.

'Hi Sarah,' she says. 'Good swim? Hiya, Duncan.'

Sarah's mouth opens as she turns to look at the man. He's smiling at the woman. Sarah wants to get back into the pool, where things make sense.

'See you tomorrow?' he says, as he turns away.

Sarah stares. And shrugs. The woman helps her onto the bus.

'He likes you. And he's okay. You can trust him; I've known him for years,' she says to Sarah. 'He's been made redundant. You should be kind to him.'

'What's your name again?' Sarah asks the woman.

'Moira, love. I'm Moira. Not having a great day today, are we? One of your bad ones?'

Sarah shakes her head. Tears prick her eyes and make the world go blurry. She watches the fuzzy cars and people and houses slide past. The woman, Moira, is talking in a whispery voice behind her. Sarah can hear what she's saying and it's about her and it's about that man, and she doesn't want to hear so she starts humming a tune she knows but can't remember the name of.

Pull, kick, glide goes her body, up and down and up and down and she's building a pyramid of strokes; she's been close to the perfect stroke a few times. It's a good day. She's seen Dr Memory, as Moira calls him, and he said she was making progress. Whatever that means. She can remember yesterday, and something last week.

When Duncan slips into her lane she smiles at him and says, 'Hi, Duncan.' The reward is a smile so bright it makes her insides go fluttery.

They swim together, side by side, and she likes the way his strokes match hers. He even shares her underwater world for a little while, before he runs out of air and bursts up to the surface. At the edge of the pool he laughs and calls her a mermaid, which she likes.

As they get out he says, 'Would you like a coffee?'

She discovers he's divorced and he's lost his job, which should make him feel sad, but he likes coming swimming and taking the dog for a walk and he doesn't mind, not really. 'Another job will come along', he tells her.

'How long have we known each other?' she says.

'About two months,' he says, studying her face.

She feels her heart lurch. She wants to run. He covers her hand with his own.

'It's all right, Sarah. I'm your friend. I just want to be your friend. Today seems like a pretty good day. Do you remember us talking yesterday? Moira said if you tried to talk about days before, it would help.'

Sarah looks and him and knows he is kind. He has a kind face. But she doesn't want to talk to him about yesterday, or *any* yesterdays. There is something, some clue lurking there on the edge of her mind. She knows if she goes digging for it, she could dislodge it. But she shakes her head.

'There's nothing. I better go. Moira said there would be a bus for me.'

'I'll come with you. You look bonny today, Sarah,' he says in his soft voice and Sarah feels a strange flutter deep inside her. 'I'd like to help you get better. Moira said any new friendships are good.'

'I'll maybe see you tomorrow then,' Sarah says.

Pull, kick, glide goes her body, over and over, making its own shapes in the water. Her green swimsuit makes her feel like a mermaid. *I'm in love with the water,* she thinks to herself. And every stroke feels close to perfect. Toes almost together, bubbles in a stream either side of her head, fingertips touching. Nothing else matters but this. Why can't she live in the water? Then life would be all right. All the odd stuff that happens when she gets out, the lines that blur at the edges; all of this is gone in the water. In the water she knows who she is. She's a swimmer, and she can count. She rolls over in the water like a seal, twice, at lengths 49 and 51 and the second time she feels the water caress every inch of her, feels some loose hair escaped from her hat, feels the wonderful weight of water on her back. It is beauty itself. She'll swim further today. It might make the counting hard, but she's sure she can manage it. It's the only thing that doesn't feel confusing.

But then it's all ruined. Just as she turns at the deep end, she sees someone getting into her lane.

It's a man. And for some reason, he's waving at her.

Chestnuts

Timber

I can't do this.

    I can't sleep.

    I can't be a mother. *This* isn't how it was meant to be. This isn't how *I* was meant to be.

I want it to stop.

It's unrelenting – a long bridge of work and work and work between each side of the broken night. All day long I long for bedtime and I count the hours. Then when I'm asleep I get little tiny blocks of it and I wake up to screaming and I think, I can't do this, and I feed and I go back to sleep and it happens again and again and again. I am angry with myself because this is what I wanted, all along. This is what I dreamed of, worked for and tried so hard for and now it's here all I can think of is a good long sleep and a lie in and a good movie and no soreness anywhere and no tiny being needing me every second of the day and a moment to myself. This is how fast my thoughts go.

I have a smile plastered to my face. Everyone says I'm a natural. The 'you're doing so wells' and the 'like a duck to waters' that I hear from vague acquaintances when I venture out don't help; they make me feel I must play along. The health visitor gets me to do this questionnaire to see if I'm depressed. I look at her and know I have to lie because she'll take the baby away if she knows what's really going on in my head, what dark thoughts are coming, uninvited…

Each day is a blur of trying not to scream and putting on a face and going out into the world. I strap the baby into the pram and parade around the shops, smiling at the cooing and the smiles. Returning them, giving them back because I don't want them. If you knew what I was thinking inside you wouldn't be smiling at me. If you knew what I thought last night, when I was woken for the fifth time in five hours and my nipples bled and I didn't know if that was okay, to feed with bleeding nipples, and there was nobody to call. Well. There are people to call but if I call and tell them how difficult it is they'll say I'm not a fit mother and they'll take the baby away.

The worst times are when Jacob is home. I've tried to make the house nice. I really have tried, but it's a mess, everywhere. There're piles of papers everywhere.

All of our post seems to be lost because I've tried changing addresses and it's just not happening. I've had phone calls from the new owners of our old flat saying that letters are still arriving and please could I arrange the redirection. Nicely. Everyone's nice when I'd prefer it if they were all horrible and spoke to me the way I want to speak back to them.

I wish I had the kind of mother I could call on for help, but Suze (she's never let me call her "Mum") is away on a yoga retreat in India. Or Sri Lanka. Or the moon. And remembering how she was with me, as a too-young mother, instils in me some protectiveness towards the baby. So perhaps she does have a role as Grandmother. GrandSuzer.

And my body.

It's not mine anymore. It only exists to feed the baby. It provides milk. It's a soft, lumpy mass. My curves are blobs. My tummy is a big soft thing that doesn't look like mine. When I lie down it flops to the side. If I tell anyone they'll just say it's because I ate too much when I was pregnant. I got too fat and this is what you get. I keep eating. I have to eat to make milk. I try the healthy things but I crave chocolate and chips and biscuits. I can see Jacob's eyes watching me warily, in case I get so big I fill the new house. I can't undress in front of him anymore. And sex? He tried once, and I wanted to kill him.

He's been away a lot. His new job, coming at just the wrong moment, means he's away from me for long periods of time. He's travelling all over the place, getting planes and hiring cars and decorating the world with his footsteps which are still so damn light. Not like mine as I pludge around the house, from room to room, looking at the piles of organising to be done and fading from myself in the light coming through the curtains.

I avoid mirrors. My eyes are grey and slide down my face and my skin is awful and if I put make up on I look like a clown.

During Jacob's last visit – for that's what they feel like – he softly asks me when I think I'll have finished the unpacking and I look from him to the baby to the piles of shit – and smell the smell of *real* shit from all the nappies in the bin and I want to weep. I want to punch him in the face. Why can't you do it? I want to ask, but it would just show him what a crap, inept excuse for a person I am.

The first three months pass like this, with me crying in private and entertaining thoughts of how it could change for me. The baby might not wake up one morning and I can sleep. This thought catches me unawares and shocks me to the core and makes me wonder for the first time – if I am not right. Because the thought of a long sleep beats the thought of losing the baby.

I am a terrible person.

I think that if Jacob dies people will come and take care of me and I'll have an excuse for crying every day and people will feel sorry for me and take the baby away for a bit, when he'll be safe and cared for. People can bring me food and stroke my head and tell me it'll all be ok and aren't I brave, bearing this so well? When inside all I'll feel is relief.

I am a terrible person.

One night, after Jacob's latest visit, in between trips – during which he was knackered and wanted feeding and looking after just like his son – something breaks.

The baby won't stop crying. I have tried everything. My breasts are sucked dry – he's bled me dry – and I'm so tired I sway on my feet. He's cried so much that I shake him.

Just a tiny bit.

And then I'm so consumed by guilt and the knowledge that I am a terrible mother that I put him down and run from the room and sit with my back to the cupboards under the sink and cry, and cry myself, wanting to cry so loudly that I drown out his crying.

There's a knock at the door.

And I'm relieved. Somebody knows what I just did and they've come to take him off me and I'll give him up and tell them thank you, because they can take care of him. I can't.

I run to the door and fling it open, ready for uniforms.

It's a small, oldish lady.

She's so small she has to look slightly upwards to meet my eyes.

What can she do?

What she does is this:

Gently pushes me aside, walks through to where the baby is screaming on his back in the lounge somewhere – I can't even remember where I put him down – and picks him up. I follow her, stunned into silence.

She holds him close like a real mother and coos and murmurs and rubs his back and within seconds – seconds! – he has stopped crying.

That confirms what a shit mother I am. This total stranger can calm my baby and I'm a broken, crap wreck who can't take care of him.

I cry even harder and stumble my way through to the kitchen. I go back to the floor, where my bum's left a dent from all the hours of sitting, below window level, so nobody can see that I'm not taking care of him/unpacking/feeding myself to make milk. I decided a few days ago that eating wasn't helping. That I'd feel better if I was thin again.

The silence is blessed. It's like a gift.

The small woman comes in, empty handed and I have to stamp down on the thought that she's taken him away and I'm glad.

'He's asleep in his cot,' she says. She fills the kettle and switches it on. She works her way through cupboards until she finds what she needs and she makes two cups of tea. There's no milk so she leaves me for a moment and comes back with a whole pint.

She pulls out a chair and pats it. Dumbly, I stand up, shuffle across the floor and sit on it. She hands me a cup, takes her own and sits next to me. From somewhere in her thick cardigan she produces a packet of biscuits and hands me one. Doesn't offer, just hands me one.

I eat it. I drink the tea. I listen to the silence.

'I'll tell you a story,' she says. 'I come from a long line of women who help. We always end up near people who need help.'

'I don't–' I begin.

'You do, and it's all right,' she says, patting my hand. 'It runs in my family. A usefulness. My mother moved in to help a woman when she had just had twins. The woman grew up right here, when it used to be a big old house that looked after orphans. The woman's husband had just left her and she had newborn twins and she only had one arm.'

I listen to this, feeling myself shrink. I have two arms and just one baby. Who am I not to be able to cope? I feel worse. I want the woman to leave. I'm about to get a lecture on lifting my chin and getting on with it.

'My mother saved all three of them. The woman was drenched in grief, sore, exhausted. The babies were tiny, needed feeding every half hour for days and days. She organised a wet nurse and cooked and cleaned and took care of the woman til she could do it herself. She was the first woman she helped. After that she did it over and over, and when I was fifteen, I started, too.

'One thing I've learned is that it doesn't matter who you are or what your circumstances are: if you need help, you need help. There's never any judgement, I just get on with it. I moved next door a week ago and I've seen that you need help and I'm here to offer. Been a while since I did it.'

I look at her, waiting for the punchline. Waiting for her to tell me what a terrible job I'm doing.

'Here's what's going to happen,' says the woman. 'I'm going to go home, and cook tea. You're going to have a shower, whilst your son is sleeping. I'll come back with food. You will eat and then feed your baby. I'll stay the night and help you, so you sleep. Tomorrow I'm going to take you to the doctor.'

This is it, then. They'll find out and I'll have him taken off me.

'The doctor will maybe give you some pills that will help. I will be here, helping. And one day, you'll wake up and know you can do it yourself. And at that point, I'll go. People get put together for a reason,' she says. 'I knew there was a reason I chose the flat next door.'

She pats my hand. 'Go and have your shower,' she says. 'I'll be back as soon as I can.'

When she comes back I'm on the sofa: clean, quiet, confused. It was so easy to do as I was told. She hands me a plate of lasagne which hardly touches the sides, as my brother used to say. She takes it through to the kitchen and refills it and I eat that, too.

The baby is still asleep, which is some kind of miracle. The woman disappears and brings him back.

'You *woke* him?' I say, feeling horror and anger in equal measures.

'He needs feeding before he goes to bed. Babies need routine,' she says.

She hands him to me and I feel a flood of pain and sensation in my breasts. Milk appears from nowhere, more milk than I've had. It wets my shirt and the woman smiles in approval.

'Good,' she says. 'Now feed your son.'

I pull up my pyjama top and he latches on, guzzling loudly. I look at the woman.

'What's your name?' I say to her. 'I'm Lynn.'

'My name's Janey,' says the woman. 'I was named after the woman my mother looked after. She said she had more strength in that one arm than a room of able-bodied people had in all their arms put together.'

'But she needed help,' I say, confused.

'We all need help. The strength is admitting it. Now, look down at your baby.'

I usually watched the TV when I was feeding. It took so long sometimes and I'd get fed up. I look down at the baby.

I get a different feeling. A round feeling.

'That's better,' Janey says. 'When you feed him, watch him. Be there with him. What's his name?' she says.

I almost say, the baby.

I look down at his face and for the first time, see Jacob's nose. The round feeling gets bigger.

'Harry,' I say. 'We named him Harry.'

Tree

My grandfather had scars on his hands. When I was little I used to run my fingers over the lumps and bumps, tracing them and asking him about them. He was a butcher, once. That accounted for one of the longer scars. After that he'd been a volunteer fireman and that was the burn on the back of his left hand. He had various nicks and dents from gardening, helping break up a dog-fight, (I was shouting so loudly at them, he told me, that they both ran off into the woods. And never came out. Trouble was, one belonged to my boss,) cutting himself whilst fixing the roof, and one faint, round one on the side of his thumb, like a tiny umbilical scar, that he said he'd no idea how he got.

'When I was a lad, it was there. I asked my mum once and she went all strange, so I shut up. My father left us when I was young so that was no help. It hurts, sometimes. I get this pain and throbbing, but there's nothing there. Used to bother me, but it's normal, now.' I forget where we were when we had this conversation but I remember how he held his thumb in his other hand, seemingly unaware of it. As a kid I had all kinds of theories about why his thumb had a scar. He'd been bitten by a dog. An elf had chopped a bit off him. It was spider bite, gone nasty, like Luke's at school. It was a witch's mark and one day she'd be coming back to get him. Neither Grandad or I ever found out the truth. His twin sister, Edie, is still living on, years after he left us, but she doesn't know either. The secret got buried with him. Before him.

Because of my grandfather's scars, I've always been careful with my hands. I've got dreams of becoming a surgeon although I'd have to get to university and will I get good enough grades? I don't know. It's one of my dreams. I'd also like to play guitar professionally, but I'm not in a band and I never play on front of anyone. I'd like to be a writer, but the ideas never leave my head for the paper. They are just dreams, but the one for Medicine is the biggest.

Whilst I'm waiting for A-level results I'm working as a labourer on an enormous building site. It's where everyone is working this summer, everyone. There are brickies, tea makers, sparkies' helpers, apprentice joiners, every job you can think of. Because of this new development a whole generation of us townies are going to have a trade we'd never have had otherwise.

I got the job after a woman came round school asking if we had any plans for the summer. Anyone who was interested had to go into this empty classroom and fill in a questionnaire. I thought I'd get picked for something in an office, but I got given a job as a labourer. It's my size. I'm stocky, but not as strong as I look. I tried telling her that but she said I'd do fine. When they told us what they were going to pay we all said yes, regardless of the job.

I buy working gloves to protect my hands. I don't care if I'm laughed at. Surgeons need good hands.

On the first day I return exhausted. I've hardly noticed anything during the day. I'd been planning to write a journal about the summer of working, as an introduction to the rest of my life, a memoir about being a doctor, but on day one I can hardly remember anything except endless carrying jobs, endless pain in my back and jeering from the real builders when I drop stuff.

I sleep as soon as I get to bed and wake up almost ready to quit, I'm so sore. Mum persuades me to give it another day. This time I try to notice more.

The first things I see are the huge old pillars. I hope they're going to leave them; they look ancient. The drive has been roughly cleared, bushes stripped back and already I don't recognise it.

We've always called this the Den, and it's where that we've been coming for years to play, get lost, kiss in. We used to build shacks, play hide and seek and scare each other witless playing Blair Witch. Some of the few good memories I have of Dad are from here, too. He used to bring us here to listen to the birds, and once he told us he used to hide from the bullies at school here. He clammed up after that.

'Scott?' Someone's yelling at me so I move away from the pillars and go and sign myself in. For safety reasons we have to sign in and be attached to someone all day because the site is so big. It's in case we get lost/skive off/fall into a huge hole. Apparently there are some cellars somewhere.

I go and present myself for work, and look around me. I'm determined to notice more today. The site is slowly being cleared. There are instructions to move only the trees that block the walls they're going to build. Most of the trees will stay, hence the name Chestnut Apartments. The trees will be incorporated into the design of the build – I've read the pamphlets. I'm glad because this place all cleared would look wrong.

Mum told me it's been years getting this off the ground and that I should feel proud to be working on it, but all I can see is a summer of pain and worry about my results. I need AAB, though it there is a bad year of grades they will drop one or more of them, and I'm predicted CCD. There are always resits. Fleetside prides itself on a 99% A-level pass rate, even if it's second time around. Not like the comp, which has the smallest sixth form in the world – about eight children.

I'm told to go and start hauling bricks from what looks like an old outhouse. It's a huge mess of rubble and plant life and rubbish. I pull on my gloves, sigh, think of the money and get on with it.

After ten minutes, I scream. I've found a skull and some bones, lying by the trunk of a tree, almost part of the tree itself. People come running from all directions thinking I'm hurt, and they laugh when they see what I'm pointing at.

'Dead animal, that's all,' says the guy I'm working under. 'Stick it in with the rest of the shit, in the skip.'

Carefully I pick up the skull. It's large and I wonder, dog? fox? If it was a dog, whose dog was it? Did someone grieve for it, when it never came home? Next to the dog are some smaller bones – perhaps something the dog caught. I imagine it stuck out here, slowly dying until one day it just doesn't wake up... I shake myself and chuck the skull into the skip with everything else. Its spirit has already gone, I tell myself.

By lunchtime I've cleared half of the pile. I collapse, exhausted, into a heap by the last remaining wall. It's blackened. We all know the story of this place: it was an orphanage that burnt down. There are various versions of it. The one I like best involves robbers and kids standing up to them and not letting them in, and the robbers torching the place as revenge. All the kids escaped except two apparently.

The day drags and drags as I haul rubble to the skip. As the day rolls to an end my arms feel twice the length and all I can think about is a meal and a hot bath. Mum, however, has other ideas.

'It's Aunt Edie's birthday. We're going to go and have tea with her,' she says, completely out of the blue.

'Mum. I'm knackered. Please tell me I don't have to come?'

Mum gives me her stern look and I shut up immediately. 'You Aunt Edie has done a lot for you. Don't ever forget that. She's promised me she'll help with your tuition fees – if you get in.' She storms from the room and I gather she's had a bad day. I make a coffee and wake myself up.

Half an hour later Mum yells at me from the front door, 'Hurry up, Ben.'

In the car she says, 'I'm sorry. I'm grumpy today. Had a message from your sister saying she's not coming on holiday with us. It's upset me, that's all.'

'How come?'

Mum looks at me and raises her eyebrows.

'Oh,' I say. 'Rupe.'

Rupe is her boyfriend, pierced and antagonistic, has a theory on everything.

'She says she wants to spend the summer with him.'

'God,' I say. 'Why? Her ears will be bleeding by the time summer ends… So is she staying with him in York?'

Mum nods. 'Says she's too old for a family holiday. I said, "fine." But this is the last one we'll be paying for. I don't mean that. We can always go away together. I don't want that ever to stop. But…' her voice hitches and I put a hand on her arm. Since Suze went away she's become weird, unrecognisable as our daughter and sister. She's bolshy and cross about everything, changing more each time she comes home.

'It's just a phase,' I tell Mum. 'Like the punky one.'

'Mmmm,' says Mum. 'I don't know. Worst case scenario is Rupe gets her pregnant and we're stuck with him in our family for ever.'

'She's not daft, Mum,' I say. But I think, she is, really. I know Suze better than anyone and I know her crazy, devil-may-care side. I miss it.

'Everyone's daft when they think they're in love,' Mum says. 'Like I was.'

I've not seen my dad since I was a kid, so I can't comment. I've never seen him as an adult. He was always a distant bloke who appeared from time to time and took us somewhere fun, bringing us back late, dirty and skint. Whatever Mum gave us to spend was gone. So she stopped giving us spending money and he stopped coming. I don't need to know what he's like. We're fine, the three of us. Well, two of us, since Suze has defected to the camp of Rupe. I laugh a little and Mum looks at me.

'What's so funny?'

''I dunno. Just thinking of Rupe being some kind of weird cult leader, brainwashing women and girls. I could picture him dressing weirdly, having odd rituals.'

'Strange sense of humour you have,' Mum says. 'Here we are.'

She pulls in to Greenacres and parks the car near the entrance. We walk through the door and sign ourselves in.

Sandy, the owner, comes out to greet us. 'She's not too well,' Sandy says. 'Says she's tired and doesn't want to eat.'

'I'll talk to her,' says Mum.

We walk along the cabbagey corridors and find Edie lying on her bed in her room. She's watching a game show, mouthing the answers before the contestants do. Mum laughs.

'Still as clever as ever,' she says, kissing my aunt on the side of the head.

'Yeah. Not that it ever did me any good,' says Edie. 'Hello, Ben. Make the most of your education, you hear me? I left school at twelve to look after my mother. Bang. Bye bye school.'

She's told me this a thousand times. But this time I listen a little better and try to imagine working as I am now for the past six years of my life.

'I can't imagine,' I tell her.

'Mum wasn't very well. She had us when we were old. She was disabled, as I've told you. Lost her arm as a child. Can you imagine? So she couldn't do much and when I was twelve she had a mini stroke. We didn't know what it was then but she lost some of the use of her left side, the side that had the arm. Cruel joke, life.'

'Happy birthday, Edie,' says Mum, trying to rescue the afternoon from doom and gloom, as some of Edie's visits can be drenched in it. She hands her a present. Edie smiles and says 'thank you, dear,' but puts it aside. I give her our card and she puts this on to of the present.

'One of those days?' Mum says. Edie nods.

'I hate birthdays. Can't possibly get any older, surely?'

'You'll outlive us all.'

'I bloody hope not,' says Edie. 'Oops. Sorry, Ben,' she says.

It's okay Aunt Edie, I want to say. I can't imagine being as old as you, at the end of everything, stuck here waiting to die. 'It's okay. I don't mind you swearing,' I say. 'I like a good swear myself.'

'Thanks Ben,' says Mum. 'Now, Edie. Shall we walk along together and get our tea?'

Edie, seeing herself outnumbered, surrenders her arm, and hauls herself off the bed.

For a woman who didn't want to eat, she packs it away. During coffee, after she's delicately polished off three courses, she sits back in her chair.

'That's better,' she says. 'I get grumpy when I don't eat.'

'Hangriness,' I tell her. 'It's got a name now.'

Edie smiles. 'Hangriness. I like it. Runs in our family. Your grandad – my brother – was vile if he didn't eat, if he missed a meal. I miss him.'

'Us too,' Mum says softly.

'That's really why I don't want to celebrate my birthday. Only half of me here.'

Mum nods. 'Of course,' she says. 'But we're here. Will we do?'

As if she's not spoken, Edie continues. 'We never spent a birthday apart until he died. It was our day. Mother used to say we should have been identical. She says we had our own language when we were small. After Father left – and you must understand, in those days it was an outright scandal – we'd to cope by ourselves quite a lot because Mother had to work. She took in washing. She had this amazing way of washing with one arm; had adapted mangles and things so that she could operate them. I still don't know how she brought up twins – and worked – with just one arm.'

'I wish I could have met her,' Mum says. 'I missed not knowing my gran.'

'Do you know what happened to his thumb?' I ask, as I have before, but she shakes her head. She seems to be lost in the past somewhere.

To cheer her up I start to talk about the job I've got. I tell her about some of the builders and some of the things they've said to me. I tell her how much I ache.

She looks up. 'It'll be nice to see that place built. Been nothing there for too long. Did you know my mother grew up there?'

'Where?' says my mum, confused. 'In the woods?'

Edie nods. 'In the orphanage. She didn't talk about it much. Wouldn't enter those woods for love nor money. Think on that, when you're busy working there. Say a prayer for her'

'I didn't know that,' Mum says. She sounds annoyed.

'I was told not to really mention it to anyone. I think she was ashamed or something,' Edie says. 'She wanted to be normal. With one arm, that was quite hard. With a husband who'd left her, it was harder. With those things plus the fact she grew up in an orphanage – well that was downright impossible. I think she just wanted to be invisible, and get on with life. I wish I remembered her better. She was always working, then she was ill, then she wasn't there anymore. You lot,' she says, encompassing, I think, my whole generation, 'don't know you're born. Don't know what work is.'

Edie falls silent and Mum and I look at each other. Mum signals it's time for us to be going.

We help Edie back to her room and she gets back into bed. She still doesn't open our card or present. Mum and I kiss her goodbye and leave the room. All the way home we're silent.

Mum parks the car. 'She's never told me that before. And Dad and I…just didn't talk much I suppose. Wonder what other secrets are hiding in that head of hers?'

'She seems so sad.'

'I know. Not an easy life. And my grandmother – your great-grandmother – she must have been so tough. To live with and through all that. I wonder where he went, your great-grandfather?'

'Why did he leave her? With baby twins? That just sucks,' I say.

Mum nods. 'Wonder how we could find out. Anyway I need to flop and put my feet up. Been a busy day. And you look shattered.'

By day five I'm stronger. I can feel it. I've chucked the gloves, decided my hands will be fine if I'm careful. And the chances of getting those grades? Nil. I know that now so I've stopped worrying. We don't hear from Suze and I realise how much I miss her. I imagine how it was to miss a twin, a super-sibling. I'm enjoying the work. The woods are noisy with human and animal life. The developer has put the preservation of the area up with the highest importance, so people are really being careful. There are strict rules about where machines can drive, and the place is tidy. The other builders stop giving us such a hard time as my mates and I prove ourselves. The pay is good and we all need it.

I've been shown the plans; the owner of the site wants us all to feel invested in these apartments. I like them; can imagine living in the trees. I decide to ask Mum if she'd move here one day, so I can visit her. Maybe I can buy shares or something.

While I'm working I try to imagine my great-grandmother growing up in these woods. She'd have grown up hearing sounds of bird and animals. No cars, no planes tearing up the sky overhead, life much simpler… life much harder. I think of the sheer amount of work that would have needed to be done every day. Everything by hand, every moment, work. Edie was right, our generation don't know we are born. I throw myself into the tasks more fiercely. Today I'm digging a channel around the edge of the outer ring of trees, to make where a small wall is going to be, that will mark the pedestrian zone. The owner, on page one of his brochure, tells the world that the inner circle of Chestnuts will be a "naturalist's paradise." One of the guys told me that if he could've got away with not allowing cars into the wood at all, he would, but he knew it would have put people off. Imagine not being able to drive up to your house… I quite like this idea and wish he'd been stronger and followed his instinct. Surely the car-dependent world has to be coming to an end? My great-grandmother's world had hardly any cars. They were just beginning to be known.

I wonder which of the trees here she would have looked at. Would she have climbed any? Maybe in those days it was forbidden for girls to climb trees. I imagined her having to leave here after it burnt down. How did she escape the fire?

'Scott!' It's my 'boss', Adam, the man slightly older than myself who's almost finished his bricklaying apprenticeship. He's teaching me about foundations today. I shake myself. He's probably seen me dreaming and not working. It's a complaint all of my teachers, ever, have had against me. I drift away, and end up missing what I'm meant to be learning.

'Yes?' I say, ready for a bollocking.

'Come and see this.' He's bending down over the trench I've been working on. I bet it's not level enough, or something. I brace myself and will myself to look bright and ready to learn, instead of pissed off. I tried really hard to get that bloody trench level.

I squat down next to him. He's pointing at something in the dirt.

Something shines up at us out of the bed of mud.

'You dug this up. Didn't you notice it?' he says.

I shake my head, unwilling to add that I'd been daydreaming about my great-grandmother and not paying attention. He reaches down and gently tugs at the shiny metal. 'It's gold. See how it's not tarnished?' he says. He dislodges it and pulls out a ring. 'You found this. Means it's yours. But we need to tell the boss. Any finds have to be reported in case there's a missing items list on this site. Sometimes, when we start a new build, there is a list of things that have gone missing over the years and we have to return anything we find that's on the list. On one occasion it was a bracelet, and I found it.'

I rub the ring against my jeans and it shines brighter. It's definitely gold; old yellow gold. Adam's away to find the foreman and I follow him, the ring warming in my hands.

The foreman takes the ring from me and photographs it. 'I need to hang onto it to get it checked. From what I remember there's no list on this site, but there might be a missing ring lodged with the central library. Sometimes that happens.'

The ring is almost hot in my hands and it's with reluctance I let it go.

Adam claps me on the back and tells me to keep my eyes open. 'You might be one of the lucky blokes who just finds stuff,' he says. 'Like my mate Jim – he's found heaps of jewellery over the years. Time for a cuppa and then back to it. Once we've finished this quarter it's over to the main build to work on the first foundations. We can't dig the rest of the trench until next week.'

I follow him to the worker's hut, feeling pleased with myself and anxious about the ring all at the same time. I want to see it again. There was something about it I liked. Something that felt right.

It's two weeks before the ring is cleared as not belonging to anyone. Reports going back years have to be checked in the library and at the police station. Half the records are on paper so apparently it takes ages. But I've almost forgotten about it as the worry about my results comes back to me whenever I have a moment of free headspace which, as it happens, I have a lot. Laying bricks gives me far too much time to think. My circular thoughts have made me realise how much I want my grades now. I wish I didn't change my mind so much – studying medicine is the one thing I've stuck to. My desire to be a doctor gets stronger with each passing day and by the time there is less than 48 hours to go I am aching with wanting the grades to be right. Adam has kept me as he says I work well; and am a "good bloke", which I take as a compliment, judging by what he says about some of his workmates. He says he wishes me well but also hopes I fail and decide to work under him. 'I'm a fussy bugger. OCD says my girlfriend, and you're just the same. Great skills for a brickie.'

The post doesn't arrive until 11am. So I go to work, not to school like a lot of my mates. I don't want my disappointment to be in public. Mum has the day off; she says by coincidence but I see her hope for me written on her forehead in frown lines.

At 11.15 I see the foreman hurrying towards me, with my mum running to keep up with him. In his hand is a small bag. In my mum's hand is an envelope.

They stand before me and I climb out of the foundation hole that we're working in. It's shallower than usual because we're working over the old cellars.

Adam follows me and stands next to me. 'What first?' he says.

I smile at the foreman. 'If that's what I think it is, I'll have that first please. It might give me good luck.'

'It's the ring,' he nods. 'Unclaimed. Means it's yours. It's about 90 years old; they told us in the jeweller's. They can tell by the mark.'

I open the bag and inside is a small box. Inside *that* is the ring, now gleaming. I slip it on my middle finger but it's too big. It fits my little finger on my right hand perfectly.

Mum hands me the envelope, with shaking hands.

There's a silence, as I open it. I skip all the words, trying to find the right letters.

C
B
A

My eyes find them.

'Well?' demands Mum. Silent, I hold out the letter and her eyes soften. She's telling me it's okay, before she even reads it.

'Scott!' she says, eyes having scanned it, through the hand which is clapped over her mouth. 'This is almost… This is fantastic!'

'It's not enough,' I say, but inside I'm ecstatic. I got an A! And if it's been a tough year, they might drop the entry level…

I kiss the ring on my finger. 'My good luck charm,' I say. I wonder whose it was. And whether it brought them luck, too.

Autumn

The dog has lived here for months. It escaped from a farm where it got beaten regularly by its owner. It fought its way through the town, got yelled at and ran away. It crept into the wood and hid, licking wounds, tail between legs. Nice smells here. Safety. It eats whatever it can scrape from the world of humans at night, venturing to the nearest bins. It scarpers back to the woods and hides back inside the old building. The leaves have fallen, and the dog makes a warm bed, turning itself around and around, until it is soft and warm enough to curl up on.

It hears voices, one day. It backs off, having heard too many cruel voices in its life. It cowers in an old fallen down heap of bricks, under an old post which has created a hole. It listens to the footsteps and voices coming closer. Four feet. To the dog, they are sounds that signal a warning – humans, feet, kicking.

'Here. This'd be the outer wall. Kind of like a city wall, keeping the riff raff out. Just inside this circle of trees. Inside, all the flats arranged as you're seen in the picture, each with their own bit of garden or terrace or balcony, each their own tree, if you like. There's a communal garden outside the 'city wall' (if the dog had noticed, he'd have seen the man raise his fingers in invisible speech marks) and you can imagine people strolling in and out of the trees, round and about…'

'I like it,' says the other man. 'Shops?'

'In town. You want people to venture out, not just stay in here or it'd be like a separate town. It's meant to be an exclusive housing area, not a prison. We want the town to do well, too.'

'Hmmm. Schools?'

'There are two, big rough one and smaller nicer one. One on each side of town. There's a catchment area. We'd make sure this development got into the good catchment area though. The other school – put it this way – if it was me on the wrong side of town, I'd move just to be near the better school.'

'That bad?'

'Just not that good. So. The name we've come up with is Chestnut Apartments. Sounds better than flats, not as big as houses, might attract more viewers. That's why we want to keep as many of the trees as possible, especially these ones here, planted in a ring. Around 80 years old, we think, but the orphanage burned down 110 years ago.'

'Interesting… wonder who planted them?'

'Maybe the old owner. It was a house way, way back, then a hospital, then became an orphanage when the owners died. They'd moved out before it became a hospital – guy was a philanthropist who wanted to do good for the town. Made his millions with mills, aptly enough. Guy built factories in Boughton and made a killing using cheap labour and imported thread, making cloth that went all over the world. Forget his name. Timothy somebody or other. Imagine being able to give a massive house like this away…'

'So it became an orphanage?'

'Yup. Then one of the kids burnt it down.'

'Really?!'

The man nods. 'Sad story, apparently. My gran used to tell me and my cousin about it when we were little. My cousin, who was a bit of a weirdo, got really taken by the story. He didn't do that well in life and ended up living here, as a homeless guy, until he went to the funny farm. He was a bit kooky in the head. The story is there was a boy with strange hands, extra fingers, I think, and everyone hated him. He went wild and tried to kill everyone by burning it down.'

'Nice,' said the man. 'Anyway. It's getting dark. Time we went back to the office. I need a coffee. Thanks for showing me the site. I'll take it to the investors and get back to you. You've got my vote and I can probably count on two others. This time we'll make sure it gets passed especially if you make that payment we discussed. Can I have a few more copies of the plans and the brochure? They're pretty interested anyway but anything else I can give them will help. My cut's what we discussed, yes?'

'Yeah, yeah.'

'Good. People will be behind this. Enough folk have brought ideas and then scrapped them – been going on years.'

Just then the dog whined. He'd been listening to the two men and the voices had sent him to sleep. In the dream he was chasing rabbits; one of the dreams that made his legs twitch and his jaw open slightly. In this dream he'd caught the rabbit, and was just about to dive into its juicy side with a drooling mouth when he whined in anticipation and woke himself up.

'What was that?' said one of the men.

'Dunno. C'mon, let's go.'

The dog, on alert and ready to run, relaxed again, and went back to his dream. When he woke up, it was getting dark, and the rabbits were out for a last minute feed on the patches of grass that grew here and there, in the rings of light. The dog pounced, and caught one, its dreams become reality.

It ate wolfishly but too fast and choked on a bone.

One last conker, dangling overhead, fell and landed, soft in the dog's fur.

Sapling

They can't find me in here. I'm in the middle of the woods, hiding behind a massive old conker tree. It's raining, I'm soaked and I'm bloody terrified. The Branford gang got me again on the way home from school. Gary Branford and his brother Pete, the toughest bastards at the comp and I had to run into them. I was at school late cos of detention, got caught smoking behind the maths block. Me mates ran and I got caught by Grimshaw, who dragged me off the head of year who put me in detention, cos it's the fifth time I've been caught this time. Up to six hits gets you increasingly longer detentions and number six gets you kicked out. Mum'd kill me if I got kicked out. I was only smoking to keep the friends that I've got safe as friends – without mates in this school, you're as good as dead. The comp is the bigger of two schools in town. The smaller one's better but I live on the wrong side of the woods to go there. They keep talking about building houses in the woods – then what'd they do about schools? If you were in the middle, would you get to choose? I know where I'd go, and it'd not be the comp.

'Blocker?' yells a rough voice. 'We know you're in there!'

I scrunch myself up closer to the tree. They'll not come in here. Too damn big to search. Once you go off the path, you could be anywhere. Surely they've got someone else to kick in?

'Blocker!' The voice gets closer.

'Fuck it, man. Get him next time.' Another voice, farther away.

There's some mumbling and a war-cry in my direction , possibly to scare me, which it does.

Silence.

Well, there's no silence in here. There's birds and trees blowing and branches waving and all the right sounds for a wood. It's where I come most. I'd never tell anyone at school, not even my so-called mates, that I like birds and nature. My gran used to spend hours with me in here when I was a boy, teaching me everything. She told me stories about the ruins which are mostly covered with trees. It used to be an orphanage and one of the kids burnt it down and tried to kill everyone. He had two thumbs on each hand apparently and was a bit crazy. He died in the fire, then came back to life and something else that I can't remember. Maybe he got married and lived happily ever after.

I wonder how it would feel to burn down a building? I've thought it about school often enough. That'd solve the problems. They'd have to send us to Fleetside, and put extra classrooms in. Everyone'd feel sorry for us and we'd be tough and cool. All the kids'd know and I'd be a hero.

Or I'd get banged up. I don't want to burn it down, anyway. There's birds that live in the gutters and some that build nests above the classroom doors. They build them out of spit and sticks. Now that's dedication. I couldn't kill a bird.

I close my eyes and try to imagine a huge great orphanage in the middle of the wood. What'd they build it there for anyway? It's weird, our town. The wood takes up all of the middle of it and the town's in a ring around the edge. In history at school they told us once, years ago, it was a massive old manor house and the people who worked there lived in small houses round the edge, and the house was so big there were a lot of people needed to work there, like a castle, and so the houses round the edge got more, and that's how the town was made. I think. I have to remember it all because reading's hard. That's another reason I don't have many mates.

There are heaps of conker trees here. Heaps. It's as if someone planted them cos they're all in a ring, more or less round the edge of the ruins. They definitely didn't grow like that by accident.

It'd be nice to live here. I wonder if they'd chop the trees down? I hope not. Maybe they could plant around the trees. The branches are thick above me when I look up, there's a ceiling of green and I see they couldn't possibly build without destroying them. That makes me feel sad. I've seen pictures of people tying themselves to trees so they can't be cut down. That's what I'll do if they ever come to build, and I'll be a hero then. The boy who saved trees. Mark Blocker, thirteen, saved the trees. I'll go down in history.

I think about the boy with four thumbs who burnt the place down. I wonder if he came out here. Did he stand right here and watch it burn? I shudder, and feel that the shadows are a bit longer than they were when I came in. It's darker. How long have I been here? Gran will be angry if I'm home late. I'm at hers tonight cos Mum's working. Dad's still away. Mum says he's not near the war but if he's trying to negotiate peace how can he not be near it? Because he's in the government, Mark, I hear her say, again and again. And the Americans have borrowed him to be there, not here. I don't get how if he's a big shot government person the Americans can steal him and how come we ended up in a dump like this, not in a big house nearer London? Because he's not important enough yet. But he will be. How can he not be important if he's negotiating peace? I ask her but she tells me to shut up and rubs her eyes. I wait for the rubbish comment, 'you'll understand when you're older, Marky'.

To distract myself from thinking about them, I decide to collect conkers. Maybe I can plant my own forest of them at the back of our house, on the wasteland bit where the tramps hang about at night. The bit Mum tells me I must Never Go. She wants to move, but she doesn't want to do it without Dad. I'm sick of thinking about it all.

I wonder what it'd be like to have a brother? We could talk about all this stuff. If he was younger I could tell him how to do stuff. If he was older he could show me how to do stuff. How not to get chased by the Branfords.

I fill my pockets with conkers. Shadows are bigger. Time to go. Just as I turn, something catches in the corner of my eye. I turn back; nothing there. That's enough for me: I leg it out of the woods, and straight onto Limekilns Ave, which will take me home quickest. Behind me, I imagine the boy with four thumbs, hands outstretched, chasing me.

I turn to look one last time, and see how the woods are closing around me, shutting me out. When I turn back, I run smack into something solid as bloody stone. I go down with an oof, and for a while I actually see stars, just like they do in Tom and Jerry. It felt like this last time the Branfords got me and punched me in the side of the head. I sit up, and look for what I'd run into – it *is* stone; an old pillar. Huge square thing, covered in ivy. I've never seen it before, not in any of the times I've been here. I stand up and run my hands over it to see what it is. It's flat on each side. Like a castle gateway or something. Then it hits me – the old house. Would have had one of those big drives. I pull the ivy aside. It's sandstone – see, I did learn something at school. Woodwork teacher takes us out looking at buildings all the time. I like Woodwork. Very faint, I see some letters. I pull more of the ivy off.

Goodbye Janey
Sorry

Very very faint, but I think that's what it says. Weird. Usually it'd be a swear word or 'so and so loves so and so'. I shrug, arrange the ivy back across the pillar and go on my way, off to Gran's.

Germination

Strange man. Looks at me as if he knows me. Ugly, but kind. Gives me things to wash that aren't dirty. Makes me wonder if he's after something else. If it was anyone else but me I'd think that was right but it's me, worked almost to death, one arm taken by a machine. The pain will never go. The memory of the pain as it happened will never leave me. I almost died; it was only Dottie's knowledge, passed down from Matron, to tie something round the stump that saved me.

My life has been work. Days at Chestnut Manor are like a dream. Why am I thinking of it now? It was a dream. Life there was good. Not all work work work. Afterwards, after the factory, I had small job after small job. Learned to use my left hand. Saved enough to buy this hut, which is my business and my house. I don't need much.

I don't own a mirror. I used to be pretty. I used to be admired, by the boys. It tickled me. Matron used to tell me I'd find a rich man to marry, with my face. Ha. If she could see me now. But she can't, because she died, two years after the fire. Died working in a hospital, caring for people with consumption. Kind Matron. Like a mother to all of us.

The strange man brings me a bunch of flowers one day. He almost runs, after delivering them to my hand. They're withered, wild flowers that he's found by the side of the road. I put them in a jar in my hut. I ask him his name and he says, James, like it's not really. The name doesn't fall from his mouth like it would if it was really his.

I don't know so many people here anymore. The town has grown, slowly eating up the countryside around it. Where Chestnut Manor used to stand is just a big wood, now, where I never go. There's talk of building a new something-or-other, but it's just talk. And the town grows outwards and the wood grows bigger so we're all expanding.

I ask James where he's from and he says some town I've never heard of. Near Newcastle, he says. But when I check with William at the Crown he says the man told him Yorkshire. So I confront James and he admits he didn't speak the truth. He tells me he lost his family in a fire and at this I understand. Grief. I know grief. I tell him about Chestnut Manor and the young boy who died who I barely remember and the suspicion that it was the cook that started it, because later it was told that he'd had a dispute with Matron and the Missus and wanted to get his own back. James shakes his head like this isn't true and then his face changes and he said he'd overheard some men in the Crown talking and I say Who? And he can't say.

He is a strange man. But he talks to me and he brings me flowers and the way he looks at me is new. And old at the same time. Old like it's the way the boys used to look at me but new because here I'm not seen. I'm just One Arm Jane who washes dirt away. I would have liked children. A home and a husband. But here men want a woman who is strong. Who can farm and birth babies and pull lambs out and calfs and cook and clean her babies' noses. What woman with one arm can do all that? And yet, look at what I *can* do… I don't care. I'm old already. Forty-five. Those days are no longer in my reach.

James comes one day with a shirt that I can tell hasn't been worn and I tell him so and he looks like a sheep and says he comes because wants to see me. Then he looks at the ground. I look at his scarred face and his strong arms and know he's not a bad man. Not an honest one, but a good one. And I whisper that he can come and see me anyway.

And that's how it started.

All the things Matron warned me about, all those years ago. She told us girls about men and our bodies and how the two can work together to make life. We giggled but she shushed us and told us to be careful. I never understood it but here in my body now something strange is going on. It's calling out to this ugly, dishonest man, who looks at me like he knows me. He's working at the Inn, taking care of the horses and the rooms and fixing things. The Crown starts to look smarter. James stops hiding his face and I see how the scars intercross each other. I ask him how he got them but he won't tell me. One of those shadows that covers his face comes across him and soon afterwards, he leaves.

I don't see him for two days and this time when he comes, he brings more flowers – in a vase.

We go walking.

'I like this town,' he tells me. 'I want to stay.'

I nod. He'll stay and find a wife and I'll be a memory. He just talks to me because he pities me.

'I want to go,' I tell him. And I do. But where would I go? I'll be here til the day I die. 'I want to start again and live in a big house and have a maid and a cook. And someone to do my washing!' We laugh. We laugh a lot together. Our walks become weekly events. People start to watch us.

One day he takes my single hand.

I pull it away, shocked. Yet inside, something strange is happening. Like hunger. Like the feeling I used to get when the boys wrote me notes. Like a birthday day. Fluttering.

One day he says, 'How many people from Chestnut Manor still live here?'

So I tell him. 'All of them, except the ones who've passed on. Like Matron.' When I tell him this, he trips over, as if his feet have suddenly stopped working.

I'm almost an old woman. Yet when I bend down, to help him up, my face is close to his and for a second, time stops. I'm aware of his breath and of mine. His face, scarred and lumpy, looks somehow lost. As if he's as confused as I. Yet he must have been with women before? I'm an old woman but I feel younger.

'Janey,' he says, and I start.

'Nobody calls me that anymore. How did you know?' And I pull back.

He shakes his head. 'In the Crown. Said you used to be called that. One of the men who was in there…' His voice tails off and I stare at him.

'Jane and James,' I say, and smile. And this time when our faces go close, I don't draw back.

I stop him quickly. If someone should see us! We are too old to be chaperoned but still, if we were seen – I would lose my trade. People would think I had other ways of making my money.

'You're beautiful,' he tells me after that kiss.

I shake my head and look down. Beautiful. Not me. 'I've got to go,' I say and I walk, fast, away from him.

That first kiss stays with me. I don't wash my face that night. He doesn't come for five whole days and I have to almost tie myself to my bed to stop myself from going to the Crown. All this, at my age.

110

When he does come, it's with a ring.

Words I thought I'd never hear fall from his lips, like a plea. I hardly know him. He does not have a house. He has money, but I care little for it whilst I can make my own. It's his kindness that wins me over in the end. His face, so much hidden. The scars that tell stories. I've got enough stories of my own.

When the words come; words I thought I'd never hear, it's as if I knew they were coming. The silence between us grows heavy and in the seconds before he speaks I know exactly what he's going to day. How do I know this? I don't know. We're in the woods and it seems like even the birds go silent whilst the words hang between us, where the heavy silence just was. In the seconds before he speaks, when I know what is coming, I also know my answer. Something in me is afraid but I put it down to nerves, simple nerves and tell myself that the air of mystery around him doesn't matter. We can get to know each other during the hours sitting by our fire, with children around our feet…

When I say yes he is dumbstruck for a good few seconds. Then he smiles and embraces me as if I am made of glass.

Then we laugh.

James has bought a house. A small house, on the outskirts of town, as far away from the woods as he can. I am grateful for this; it is as if he understands my ancient grief and wants to protect me from it. He asks me if I'd like to leave but Dottie, June, Elizabeth; all my friends are still here.

We laugh a lot whilst we're planning it. I never knew life could be like this. It is light and colour and joy and laughter. More laughter than I've known since Chestnut Manor days. He stops me washing and he goes to work but we still have more money than I understand. He must keep it hidden and I don't know where.

The wedding planning has to be brought forwards. It's my fault; I didn't want to wait. I've waited long enough, I tell him, and this fellow obviously feels the same, I say, stroking my belly. My friends are horrified, all except Dottie who had exactly the same thing happen. Twenty years ago… My age, says the doctor, will be a problem.

The night before the wedding, I pack my remaining goods and move to Dottie's for the night. James wants to keep my hut, says he has an idea for it. I take one last look around its dusty corners and say goodbye to my small life.

Dottie, my oldest friend, says she's happy for me. She says it, but I see it doesn't quite see it in her eyes. She doesn't know James that well yet. When I tell her this she mutters, 'neither do you' but it's all right. I know he is a good man. I can feel it. He is generous and kind and the stories written on him are no worse than the ones written on me.

I feel younger, even as my baby grows, sapping my strength. The very fact that my body can make a baby makes me feel powerful, even when I am weary of the day. Dottie tells me the weariness will go, soon.

'Do you?' says Mr Simpson, the vicar, and we say,
'Yes.'
And he kisses me and I have a husband.

Life changes. I move to James' new house. My possessions are few and he insists
on taking me to Boughton, to the shops. I point out the factory. He strokes my stump
and takes me to the dressmaker. He asks her to make a dress with no sleeve. I look
at him in horror and he tells me, 'There isn't anyone like you. Let me buy you a dress,
just for you.' And I see his point and I smile and say, yes. He orders me special dresses
for pregnancy. That day, I feel like a queen.

James works hard. He makes our tiny house better. He builds a cot. He brings me
flowers. He starts to look different himself. As I bloom outwards, it's as if he blooms
inside. His smile gets wider.

One day I ask him, 'Why did you come here? You came out of nowhere.' It's
a question that has been bothering me for a while. He has no family. He's got no
friends here, no connections at all, that I can see. Dottie asked me the same thing
once, with suspicion in her voice.

At first he doesn't answer. I press him again. 'I knew you were here,' he says. And
he kisses me and I am satisfied with that answer. He has his secrets. I'd like to say 'I
have mine,' but I don't. I am an open book. He is slightly more closed. His thumb, for
example. There is a strange scar on it. He tells me it was an accident with a knife so I
ask him what happened and he stumbles over his words. Something about skinning
a rabbit.

One day he comes home with a bag full of horse chestnuts. He doesn't know I'm
home. I catch him trying to hide the bag behind the wooden bench that sits along
the wall in the kitchen. The only place horse chestnuts grow is the woods around the
old manor.

'What are they for? Where did you get them?' I ask him.

He is silent for a moment then says, 'I want to plant trees for our boy.' He is so
sure it's a boy. 'So he can climb them when he's older.'

'And what if it's a girl?'

'Then,' he says, 'I'll teach her to climb too.'

'Where?' I ask him again.

'From the woods,' he says. What was he doing in the woods? He's been at work
on a farm today. 'I thought I'd bring a little bit back with me. Because you must miss
them. Because they were a part of your childhood.'

'I don't want any...' But then I stop. I stare at the bag and remember collecting
conkers with the other children. Putting holes in them – more jobs for Matron – and
playing. I nod.

'Thank you,' I tell him, my thoughtful husband. He is right. I loved those trees. The
only place horse chestnuts grew was in that wood. The colours of them; the signalling
of winter that they did. Always the first trees to go, yellowing and browning and

bringing in the winter and the long nights.

'Take me with you, next time you go,' I say.

'After the baby,' he replies.

The months go by, faster. I'm not ready when I feel the first pains. James rushes out to call the doctor. Dr Simpson is the vicar's brother and the son of the doctor who used to come and see us and treat us at Chestnut Manor. He looks worried, tells me again I am too old for this.

And it does feel as if I am. The pain. Rips me in half. Ruins all of our good sheets. Makes me scream. Makes James' scars knit together as he frowns. He wants to be there but the doctor bans him. Mrs Murphy arrives and shoos him out of the house. In between pains she tells me I'm too old. She tells me I'm strong. She tells me I'm lucky. She tells me other women have been watching my rise through life, from nobody to lady of the house. I can't reply; let her prattle on whilst my body and I converse in pain and I take whirling trips deep down inside myself, to where there's a chain connecting me with my invisible mother and all her invisible ancestors, a chain that connects right to this being who wants to tear me in two.

Mrs Murphy gives me a piece of smooth wood to hold in my one hand, wipes and examines and probes my most secret places. She shouts things at me, indecipherable things that make me angry. I scream at her to pull it out, that I cannot bear it, that I am going to die. Time tilts and I've been in that room on that bed for years; can see myself from above, years of my life bleeding away there. And then I drift away when the pain mercifully fades and allows me to catch my breath and stare at my huge belly and scream, No, when the pain comes back.

Then she's yelling at me to push and I push – as if there is any choice, my body is pushing for me and I'm really tearing in two this time and I'm going to die. I am going to die.

Then, a rusty scream.

'It's a girl,' says Mrs Murphy, wrapping something bluey-red in a blanket and handing it to me. Out of the folds peers a tiny face, purplish and squashed. I break with love. Mrs Murphy grabs her back and lifts my nightgown and puts the tiny face to my breast.

The pain rips through me again and I scream and almost drop her, my one hand not enough.

'Mrs Ingram, I do believe there's another one in there,' says Mrs Murphy, matter of fact, catching the baby as my body lurches and pushes, the pain coming back so intense I know I cannot bear it.

When I wake, it's dark. I am in agony down below. This pain is worse than the one after my arm went. This is beyond anything I've ever experienced. But next to me is my husband, his lumpy face lit with love in the candlelight as he gazes down at not on, but two tiny sleeping faces on his lap.

He sees me awake.

'Thank you, my darling, clever wife,' he says, and he leans over and kisses my forehead. 'We have twins,' he says.

'Two girls?' I say and he shakes his head. 'A girl and boy,' he says. 'One for each of us.'

He leans sideways and helps me hold my babies, both tiny beings cradled in my one good arm. I stare, wonder how on earth I'll manage with one arm and two babies. But my heart is bursting with love. The children I never thought I'd have, here with me, snuggling into me. My body will feed them. My husband will look after us both. I gaze and gaze, their tiny faces scrunched up and peaceful. Then one of them – I don't even know if it's the boy, or the girl yet – opens its eyes and its tiny mouth and starts crying. I look at James helplessly and he smiles, takes the other one to his knee and helps me arrange the baby for its first – or second – meal. I expected to feel embarrassed, feeding my child in front of him. I'd talked of it to Dottie who tells me she's never let her husband watch her feed her children. James doesn't even ask if he can stay. He simply makes himself indispensable and tells me he will help me, for as long as I need it. He looks at the window, cuddling the baby, whilst the other one suckles. It hurts, but after the pain is an incredible feeling, of connection and love so strong I know I will kill for this life.

I lean backwards so I can cradle her better and as I do so the blanket falls open, revealing the fact that I'm feeding my son. I look at his tiny body, drink in every inch of him. His hands are so small that…

His hands. His thumb.

My scream brings James' head whipping round so fast he hits the bedpost with his forehead. He curses.

'What is it? What's wrong?'

'His thumb,' I whisper. My head is full. There's something wrong, here. It's not just his thumb, there's something else. Some understanding that my fogged up mind will not make.

Until I see my husband's face. He goes white, like Dottie used to when her curse came. White, with shock. And ever so slowly, as he brings his eyes to mine, understanding begins to dawn on me.

Thumbelina.

The fire.

'Get out,' I tell him. I can't think beyond this. 'Leave me!'

'No, Janey, no. I'll explain…'

'Out!' I am screaming now, sitting up in bed, my son's head flopping backwards as my breast is ripped away from him. 'Go! Leave us!'

James' face loses something, then. His eyes fall from mine. He looks down at his still sleeping daughter, at his son, who is screaming, then back at me.

'I'm sorry,' he says. He places my daughter in the crib and he leaves the room, dipping his head through the too-low doorway.

There are feet clunking up the rough staircase. There're exclamations and mutterings from James. Dottie appears in the doorway, looking questions at me. Then, and only then do the tears come.

He's a coward. He's gone.

I can't think beyond the first few days of screaming and feeding and no sleep. My babies are beautiful. I try not to look at the boy's thumb. It's not the thumb itself that bothers me. It's the fact that it reminds me of his father and his lies and the whole wrongness of it all. I don't sleep much. Dottie sends me her eldest daughter who looks after me as if I am a child, making me rest and feed and heal. She has brought up siblings and is good with babies. Dottie lends me her crib and my two babies lie side by side in the room that lightens and darkens with passing hours. I lie there in between the slices of day, crying, sometimes, but mostly shaking with anger.

It's Peter from the Crown who tells me he's gone. The story comes out, bit by bit. The truth of everything that happened thirty years ago. There are many who remember him; those who still live here. Those who are still living. Fliance, which isn't even a proper name; it's something that somebody heard and spelled wrong. Banquo's son. Fliance. Fly. Flee. He has flown. There is no sight of him anywhere in the town and it's this that hurts most. No explanations, no apologies – not that I would have accepted them – nothing. James – Fly – has gone and left me alone, plus two.

After a few days I'm strong enough to walk into the woods. I never go in. I walk to the centre of the woods, to where the house used to stand. And there, I take off my wedding ring with my mouth, fight the urge to spit it out and stamp on it, hold it up to the light so that it surrounds the sun, and then throw it, as hard as I can, towards the ruins.

Then I turn and walk back into my life.

Conker

The flames leap upwards and outwards quicker than Fly expected. This isn't the small fire he'd imagined; this is a monster, leaping from his fingers onto material that it guzzles, greedy and relentless, rushing away from him, running towards the house, crackling and roaring as it grabs dry bushes and trees and shrubs, jumping from one to the other until it reaches the house.

He stumbles backwards, his skinny, strong legs propelling him into the safety of the trees as he hears the first shouts, the whistles and the screams. His fire is now eating the building itself, grabbing hold of wooden beams and climbing towards open windows and curtains. He wants to scream but his voice has been taken from him by the hungry fire, taken with the wind that is building and fanning it upwards further. His voice is there, yelling inside the fire as it burns and burns. The flames are beautiful and he's caught between wonder and horror as he sees figures come rushing out of the house, sees people grabbing buckets and flinging them pointlessly at the wall of fire.

He backs further into the safety of the trees. He hears people shouting names; trying to do the register as they do every morning out on the same patch of grass. He hears more screams and for the first time he realises what he's done.

'Stop,' he whispers. 'Just stop. I'm sorry, just STOP!' His voice builds to a shout that falls to a sob and he jams his fist in his mouth. He's killed them all. The fire is spreading too rapidly now, it's going to eat them all. Burn them alive in their beds. All the other children, and maybe the masters too. Maybe the women, the kindly women. Maybe Matron, with her fierce strong hands and sausage fingers that can swipe and can wipe up blood.

What have I done?

He'd only meant to scare people. Show them what could happen, if people were nasty to him. He'd meant it to threaten. *Be nice to me, or I'll burn you all...*

He can't see who has got out of the house. He can't see faces, just orange blurs with wide mouths screaming noise and fear.

He has to run.

Fly, real name Fliance, after some long dead foreign ancestor (it was on a piece of paper, an explanation like an apology, in the basket that contained him when he was placed carefully on the steps), turns from the monster he's created and runs into the trees, letting the darkness swallow him. Coward, he tells himself over and over. Coward...

It will be years before he sleeps properly again. He will dream of this fire night after night, remembering every detail. In some of the dreams he tries to stop it; grabs a bucket and joins the futile efforts of the staff to put the fire out. In some of the dreams he lights the fire inside, and stays to listen to the screams of children burning in their beds.

It's only the news that the fire claimed nobody except Fliance Smith, known as Fly, that everybody got out except this poor child, that means he can sleep again. He hears this completely by chance, in one of those strange coincidences in a tavern two hundred miles away, by two travelling men talking about plans that are in place for the ruins of Chestnut Manor, formerly a manor house, hospital and lately a children's home. The plans won't take shape but the men are excited, as they are stakeholders, in the tavern on the way north to visit other possible investors. Fly listens as they talk about the memorial that will stand there as a tribute to the sole boy killed in a tragic fire that took the whole house and all of the outbuildings.

That night Fly sleeps for the whole night, no dreams that he remembers, waking with the sour taste of ale and feeling more tired than he's ever done in his life. But for weeks afterwards, the words, *nobody died,* roll around his head, a gift, a tiny piece of joy that brings a rare smile to his face.

Fly is no longer the skinny yet strong and fast boy who earned his nickname by being the fastest boy in the school. He had to be, or he'd have received more beatings than anyone else. He's strong, now, years of manual labour having bulked him out; scars on his face, each the story of a fight, hiding his own face. He looks different. He's unrecognisable. Gone is the fear that haunted his childhood and gone also is the thing that earned him some of his beatings.

'Devil-spawn!'

'Mutation!'

'Eleven!'

'Thumbelina!'

He heard the taunts for years. In the end he took a knife and a good deal of ale, and he cut the offending extra thumb off his right hand. It was the only thing that could have rendered him seeable. Without it, he can go back. The bleeding was bad, but he was ready. He remembered all of Matron's lessons about cleanliness and infection and he took care of himself well. All that is left of his eleventh digit is a small scar, like a burn. Fittingly, like a burn.

Fly packs up his small sack of possessions. He pays a week's rent ahead of time as an apology for leaving Mrs Black's so suddenly, and he starts to walk. The walk will take him weeks, but it is the only way that feels right. If he walks, it is some kind of penance.

As he walks, he makes himself think of each and every child who lived at Chestnut Manor. He makes himself picture all of their faces. There were fifty-nine of them and he can remember every face, except one. Janey. The same one he's been drawing for years, the one he can't get exactly right. He'd made sure she was safe because beforehand he'd sent her a note, telling her to meet the boy everybody knew she was in love with, outside, by the barn. Just in case his small fire got bigger. He couldn't risk her. She'd never even looked at him, small Fly, fast running Fly, so fast he was just a blur. All the boys loved her. He'd hear them at night, making crude jokes about her, jokes that made his face burn with shame for her and her pure soul.

He tells himself it isn't Janey he is going back for but every time he tries to picture her she slips away and his usually brilliant memory fails him. And he knows with each step he walks, that one glimpse is the reason he is going. To see if she is still as lovely. To see if she is still there. For he has no idea what happened to all the children after the fire. He has had no idea until recently how many survived. He's got to see her face. Just one more time, then he'll go away.

The journey takes him thirty-three days. He takes a rest, every now and then, sometimes spends a night in an inn drinking ale. Some nights he finds a place so quiet that he stays and lets his memories wash out, reminds himself again and again that he didn't kill anyone. As he heads south the air warms by tiny amounts and the land around him smells different. His sleeps last longer and he finally stops feeling tired. One morning, waking up under a hedge, he feels so full of life that it scares him. He runs across the field, his large muscles slowing him down, but the speed still in his heart.

When he sees the first milestone for Boughton, the nearest large town to his destination, he feels sick. When he sees the last one, the one that says *1 mile*, he stops for the night. He skirts around Boughton, stopping only once to buy a good hat and a neckerchief with which to hide his face, and a pair of gloves, so that the scar is hidden.

He walks through the farms to the south of Boughton and finally, frighteningly, there is his destination. Hillridge, under the hill that gave it its name; a collection of houses that is deceptively small until you realise that half the town is hidden on the other side of a large wood, in the middle of which used to stand Chestnut Manor. Fly decides to walk around the outside of the village and climb the hill, spend the night in one of the caves up on the ridge. If the caves are still there. If he can remember where they are. From there he can wait, and watch. And decide if he dare enter his old town, the town he arrived in aged three months, in a small basket, with a note attached telling the world his name and how he acquired it. An apologetic note, one that asked for forgiveness and love for the child, despite his disfigurement. And from there Fly grew, not much, but enough to live and earn nicknames and be the sport for the other boys. Fly became smaller inside, and afraid, and nervous. But he never told on anybody; never told Matron the names of those who had kicked and punched him and made him bleed. Because if he did, they'd told him he would die.

Fly sits under the ridge and looks down at the town. He sees houses he remembers. He sees trees he doesn't remember. Where Chestnut Manor used to peek out of the treetops, there are just trees. The wood has grown strong, just like him. He imagines the ghost of the house sensing his arrival. Imagines it telling the trees that they have to trap Fly inside the wood. Imagines the house alive again, with windows that are black eyes and doors that are entrances to hell and all that he remembers. Why has he come back? He asks himself this again and again and for that first night, he can find no answer at all.

The following morning Fly walks down off the hill and into the town. He sees how much it's grown, sprawled outwards from the green centre. He cuts quickly across streets, doesn't meet questioning eyes (he guesses they don't get many strangers here) and tips his hat over his face, only removing it when he meets the sigh of green in the centre of town. He lets the trees close around him, much as they did after the fire. He waits for them to grab him, hold him; give him what he deserves. The wood is thicker. Paths cut here and there. And there is evidence of people. Small fire circles, clearings, some glass bottles in a pile. He pushes forwards, and after a few minutes clears the ring of growth that was the grounds of Chestnut Manor and finds the site of the house. There isn't much left. The ruins are low and covered in creepers and bushes. Where has all the stone gone? He imagines people picking at it, taking materials bit by bit, until there are just a few piles left. Evidence of walls. Broken tiles. He stares at it, swallowing down the intense emotions which rush up from his middle. His inner voice reminds him, *you did this.*

Fly walks to where the front door used to be. It was grand, with curled steps than fanned inwards and drew you inside. He remembers the flowers that they all planted every spring, which grew and coloured the front of the house. He looks up, out of old habit, to where his dormitory window is, and sees branches and sky. Trees grow right in the centre of the house. Small trees, that are slowly taking over. *You did this.*

He looks to where the lawn used to be, where register was held on fine days – and occasionally wet days, if Sir was feeling aggrieved. He thinks of all the other children, the only home they'd ever known taken away from them. By him. Where did they all go? Why didn't anyone rebuild Chestnut Manor? Then he remembers the conversation that has led him here; the investors who spoke of plans that aren't quite taking shape. He thinks of the chance of hearing that conversation and wonder if somebody has led him here. But for what? And who? It's thirty years since he was here. He's a man now; a man with no future. Maybe he can do something good here. Work on the project that the men had spoken of.

For the whole day, Fly sits and gazes at the building. He listens to the animals who live here, observes a fox, some feral cats, numerous birds. It is tranquil, but too tranquil. When Fly imagines the voices of children as they used to be, the silence is terrible. *You did this. But nobody died... just you.*

It's hunger that makes Fly rise and walk down what used to be the grand driveway, tree lined by the chestnuts that had given the manor its name. The gravel is gone, creepers have crossed over from side to side, bringing the wood closer. The paddocks that used to lie near the entrance have gone, turned into overgrown fields.

The gateposts still stand. They are smaller than he remembers, until he realises it's him that has grown. He stands with his back against one, feeling its solidity. These gateposts will still be here long after he's gone. Strong stone. You can't burn stone and who could move such large things? Nobody. He feels glad *something* of the house remains as it was.

The Crown Inn used to stand not far away. As a boy, he used to watch the men stagger out of it, afraid of their red eyes and their manners. Matron, or whoever was taking them out would click her tongue in disapproval and hurry them past. Frowning. He remembers Matron's frown. Where did she go? All of those people whose jobs he destroyed...

The Crown is still there, exactly where it used to be and in this road, not much has changed. For a moment he forgets where in time he is and is afraid to go through the doors, until he brings himself back to the present. He still has money, having had not much need for it in Yorkshire. He worked and ate and drank and saved. For what, he doesn't know. His money is hidden in the bottom of his sack and on his person he carries enough for two days at most. He's big, but still no match for more than two people.

The inn is quiet. Two men sit in dark corners. Behind the bar is a face he's sure he knows, but then he's expecting that with anyone he meets and here is the first one.

'I need a room and a meal. How much?'

The man looks him up and down. 'Where are you from?' he asks.

'I've come from up North. I'm looking for work,' Fly says, because what else would he be doing?

'Won't find much here. Lots of men looking. Room's a guinea. One meal included.'

Fly nods and hands over the money. He orders ale and retreats to the only free corner where he slips into the dark. He realises how much his heart is thudding but he's safe. Nobody has recognised him. Thirty years have passed; half a lifetime. The ale slips down too fast and he orders another.

'Where can I get clothes washed?' he says and the landlord nods to the door.

'Out there, left to the river, small house with washing bloody everywhere. Ask for Jane.'

At the mention of the name, his heart stops. He grabs the ale and heads back to his table. *Common name*, he thinks. *Impossible.*

After eating he heads up a creaking staircase to his room. It's bare and cold, but it's got a bed. As he flops down on it he can't stop himself thinking, *I'm home...*

He removes his stiff, dirty clothes and adds them to the other dirty items. He makes a pile by the door, climbs into bed and thinks that tomorrow, he'll get them cleaned. Tomorrow, he can start again.

He wakes late; the bed comfortable and his body tired after the journey. He picks up the bundle and walks straight down the stairs and out of the door before he changes his mind. The washing flags the house, announcing that she might be there. Fly slows his pace and stands for a while, looking at it. Janey had been the most beautiful girl in the house. She was headed for big things, they all knew that. She'd get adopted by a rich family. She'd work for a rich family and marry the son. She'd do well. How could she not? She was Janey.

Fly resists the urge to run when a woman appears, a bundle of washing swinging by her side, ready to hang out to dry. He sighs, mostly in relief. It's not Janey. He doesn't notice her arm right away, because her sleeve hangs down over it but when she begins to pick up the clothing, piece by piece, he sees the empty sleeve swinging by her side. He shrinks backwards; any kind of physical affliction making him feel ill. Ever since Thumbelina, he can't bear it. He decides to look elsewhere to get his washing clean but she calls out.

'That for me?'

And in her voice, he hears it. A ghost, a long-vanished voice. It's her.

He can't find his voice. He nods.

She reaches out her arm. It's brown and strong and rough, a working arm. A hard-worked arm. An over-large hand. He is repulsed and she shakes her head.

'I won't bite,' she says. 'What's wrong with you?' She strides towards him and grabs the bundle. 'Two days,' she says. 'Penny a piece.'

He nods and turns and walks as fast as he can back up the road to the Crown. The ale helps. When he's worked up enough courage, he goes to the bar and stands against it. The inn is busier today so he feels safe enough to ask the landlord, 'That washerwoman…'

'One Arm Jane?'

Fly nods. 'What happened to her?'

'Factory work. When she was a child. Got her arm stuck in a weaving machine over in Boughton.'

Fly stares. 'How old was she?'

'Twelve. Used to be in the children's home. Til it burnt down. Those that were old enough to work went to Boughton.'

The inn keeper walks away to deal with an argument brewing in a corner of the bar. Fly drinks the rest of his ale in a long gulp. *You did this.*

And suddenly, he knows what has called him back. He was stupid, to be repelled by her arm. As stupid as the children who used to tease him. He knows, as surely as if it's been etched on his heart, that he's come back here to put things right. Janey is Janey. And he will help her. He will put it right.

Eye of the Storm

There's a storm forecast for tomorrow. Today the sea is restless, choppy in all directions at once, as if something is brewing deep down under the surface. Grey blue water flashes and swells, haphazard. The gulls seem out of sorts, as if they sense it too, dipping down and hitting the water, flying high, cawling at each other and heading back to the waves. Or perhaps they're just looking for food, working on instinct, getting on with living. I shudder, imagine being flung about in that nightmarish water, with no control. I haul the coal inside and shut the door again. I've lit the fire, and Cat and I are making the most of it. We'll probably lose power, so if I get the house hot now it'll hold some of the heat when the storm hits us and I've no electrical back-up. I check my torches have batteries and that there are enough candles in the cupboard.

The air is ominously still, despite the churning sea. I put on my coat, and walk to the harbour along the coastal path. The horizon makes me catch my breath; it's blue black, as if something is coming to swallow us up. The storm is coming faster than it was supposed to, and as if to prove it, a chilled breeze lifts my hair and plays it around my face. I shiver and pull on the hat that lives in my overcoat pocket. At the harbour fish shop I buy pieces of salmon; long tail piece for me and offcuts for Cat. I buy eggs and potatoes, the only other two things Peter sells.

As I'm leaving he tells me, 'It's going to be a bad one, Laurie.' I love the way he pronounces my name. I nod and tell him I'll be fine.

'If you need anything, I'm just up the brae,' he says. I wave and smile my thanks and feel his eyes watching me as I pick my way through the scaly puddles of the fish house floor. I like Peter and I know he likes me. But I don't need or want pity, or anything else.

The wind has ice in it as I walk home. It's not often I'm glad of my involuntary non-working status, but today I am. I can hole up and keep warm and not feel guilty I'm letting anyone down. The storm's forecast to last almost an entire day. Twenty hours, they reckon. I feel a thrill in my abdomen; I love the drama of wild weather, especially here, where I live on the edge of the land. Then guilt does go through me, for the people who will undoubtedly get hurt in the predicted hundred and twenty mile an hour winds.

Every year someone gets swept off rocks, too – a fisherman up from the city, naïve; someone trying to take dramatic pictures of waves; kids, playing dare. I hope it's wild enough to be a spectacle, but safe.

Inside, I check all the windows and doors, shove towels under the back door, gather as much wood as I can fit in the log basket through the front door to add to my coal supplies, bolt the door and seal my cocoon. I drag a duvet down to the sofa and curl up with Cat and a book. We listen to the wind, first playing with the tree branches, then beginning to whistle around the house. I feel the energy picking up around me. The phone lines will probably go so I get up and check my e mail, immediately wishing I hadn't when I see the third mail from Stu in a week, this one with the subject OUR SETTLEMENT. My eyes are pulled to the brown envelope on the windowsill. I get up and close the curtains. I click 'Delete' without opening it, reply to a few family mails explaining I might be cut off for a few days and not to worry, and check the Met Office website. The weather warning has been upgraded to red, a huge scarlet blob with my house, I imagine, right in the middle. The storm is coming.

I shut down the computer and unplug it. I think, what the hell, and unplug the phone as well. If there's lightning they'd only get fried. I decide it wouldn't hurt to switch my mobile off, too. I stroke Cat and curl up beside her once again, with nothing to do now but wait.

When I wake it's to the wind howling. It's dark and my fire's burned low, now nothing more than glowing embers. I've always been able to sleep deeply and I wonder how long since the storm started. Cat's nowhere to be seen and I bet she's hiding under my bed, in a shoebox I leave there just for her. I try the lamp next to me and it works, but flickers. I build up the fire and go through to the kitchen, get my candles and torch on the table and cook myself some beans on toast. I haven't the energy to do the salmon now. Hail starts pelting the window and the tin roof of the lean-to that is my utility room. I wonder how many tiles from the main roof will be torn off. The wind howls louder. I can hear the sea crashing even over the wind and I send out a wish for all the fishermen to be safely home.

The towel under the back door is already sodden. I check my anemometer and see the wind's gusting at sixty. Long way to go yet and the windows are rattling. For the first time a flicker of worry stirs within me. I close all the curtains and go back through to the lounge. I hold the duvet around me, bank up the fire and try to sleep, no longer excited by it. I just want morning to come.

Sleep is not possible; it's too noisy. I lose power at one-thirty and I try to doze with the torch in my lap, afraid to leave candles burning. I want Cat to come and be with me but she's stubborn and ignores even her treat packet being rattled. I float in and out of consciousness, fear alternating with weariness, and at one point, to my shame, tears of self-pity dripping down my face for me having to spend this night on my own. I think of Peter, only a few hundred metres away but I've never been one to take advantage. I will him to come and knock at my door nevertheless. Nobody comes. Although I try not to, my eyes stray to the curtains, behind which I know sits a brown envelope addressed to me, within it Stuart's freedom.

I want it out of my house.

The wind's died down slightly by the time I see the first grey light in the room. Rain still hits the window, but the darkness has lifted, after this very long night. I am in a hurry, now, and throw on jumpers and coats and boots, grab my strongest torch and pick up the brown envelope by the corner. I don't even want to touch it but I have to, to shove it into a plastic bag. I kick the sopping wet towel out of the way and shove the door open against the wind. Going down on the rocks would be madness but I need to make sure the pages in here don't get blown back to the land. I want them out there in that churning, boiling rage that is the sea. As I'm about to leave I remember something, and turn to grab a photo that's been face down in a drawer for the last six months. In it Stuart and I are sitting on the very rocks I'm about to walk to, heads together, the sun making us squint but nothing diminishing the smiles on our faces. My mother took it, the day we moved in. I shove it into the bag as well and make my way against the wind and the rain, out toward the small headland that keeps the house protected from the worst of the waves.

Out here the world is deafening. The sea is roaring, the wind makes my ears ache and the trees have a screeching music all their own, branches trying their best to hold on. I notice in the half-light that my chair and table have blown off the deck and are goodness knows where; all of the pot plants are rolling side to side across the patio and tiles are flapping in the wind. Several already lie broken on the ground. I'm annoyed, now. This'll cost me, to fix. As if funds were not already too low. I grit my teeth and make my way out of the gate and onto the rocks. It's hard to stand upright. Sea water lashes my face and I think of the people I read about who get blown off rocks and how stupid I think they are and yet what am I doing? I imagine the headlines and know what people would think. Heartbreak and betrayal and depression. He'll not get that satisfaction, I promise myself. No way I'm letting myself get flung into there. I wedge myself between two rocks and squat down. I open the bag and withdraw the envelope. It's wet already; the bag must have had a hole in it. No matter. I rip open the top and am glad it's too dark still to read the writing. I've been told what it says and I don't need to remember the wedding again or any of it. I just want the pages gone. I let the first one, which I'm sure is a solicitor's letter, fly out of my fingers. I watch it get ripped away and dragged into the sea where it's taken immediately by the white foam. I take the next leaf, page two of the letter, perhaps, and let it go as well. I give this one a wave.

Something isn't right inside me. The pages are gone from my sight instantly. But what I feel is wrong. I wait, for elation or relief to hit me. Nothing happens. I'm wet outside and empty inside. I wait to feel something. Even anger. But there is nothing. I cram the rest of the pages and the envelope back inside the bag, and crush it to my chest.

Inside me is our whole story. What am I meant to do with it now? For him, there's been a Book Two. For me, the end of the book has been torn away. Like when you find a book in a hotel on holiday and start reading it, only to find the last couple of pages missing, slipped away by a pool or on a beach, unnoticed.

I sit and watch the weather the same way I've watched too much television these past months, not quite taking it in. The storm breaks and it begins to die down. When full light arrives I'm still sitting there, soaked and cold, clutching the bag to me, waiting for tears that aren't going to fall now because I've none left. Still I sit. Hunger growls inside me and I watch the tide go out. I crouch lower in my rocky hollow, in case anyone from the village sees me and thinks I need rescuing. As the tide recedes it leaves gifts: plastic fish boxes, tree trunks, rubber gloves, shoes – random bits of random lives – thrown together. In front of me is an old Fairy Liquid bottle, round and white like they used to be years ago. Where has it been all this time? I imagine it doing circuits of the world, washed up on beach after beach. The writing is faded, but still readable. The trees too, once strong and rooted are at the mercy of ocean currents. How did they end up in the sea in the first place? I'll never know where they came from and I want to know their history. Were they cut down and then did the land flood until they were washed away? Sometimes they're still connected to an intricate root system, showing they fell by accident on some far away shore. I wonder what kind of trees they were, who climbed up them, how many lovers lay underneath staring at the leaves above and at each other. I wonder how they felt when they fell, when they crashed down. Did they see it coming? Now all their power and strength is gone, given up to the endless ocean. They have been defeated by life, like everything is, in the end. None of us has any control.

I give a yell which startles me because I don't feel it coming. It comes from deep down inside, builds up and bursts out like the winds in the storm. I yell, almost against my will, a couple more times and then I do feel tears on my face, hot against cold, before they're blown away and part of me is given up to the sky. Inside me is my own churning sea, my own winds, my own rain, fighting their way out, pulling me in different directions. Feelings I'd forgotten I had surface and make me gasp aloud, clench my fists, tilt my head upwards. Let it rain on me, then. Rain some more. I can take anything! But the sky is stilling, the waters are drying and the storm is dying.

I want to be back by my fire. I get up, stiff and sore and rock-cold. My feet are asleep. I stand and let the feeling come back. I look in the bag. The papers are wet, but salvageable. I get out the photo and with cold, shaking hands, undo the clips at the back. I take out the picture, careful not to damage it. I look at it one last time, look at the happiness in my face and in his. I will never know where it went. I hold it by the corner, until it flaps in the wind. The rain has almost stopped but a few drops fall onto the glossy colour. The photo dulls. I let it go slightly more, until I'm holding onto the very tiniest minute triangle, then I just open my fingers. I watch it as the wind picks it up and carries it away, a kite without a string. I watch it until it falls to the sea and is taken by the hungry waves.

I shove the plastic bag inside my coat and walk along to the harbour. I want to make sure the boats are okay, see if anyone's around, wade through the foot-deep sea foam which will have covered the road. The wind's dying fast, now, though the waves still pound the shore. Here, the rocks don't erode quickly. Granite and conglomerate rock resist the sea and erosion takes thousands of years. The people in this village are a little like that, too. I admire them; this ability they have to withstand pretty much anything the world throws at them. I lift my chin a little higher. I'm part of this village too, now. There was a time when I wanted to run and move, as this was supposed to be *our* new home, but I've stayed the worst, and just as the village will renew itself after the storm, so will I. There are a few folk out, tutting at broken tiles; the sagging telephone cables; our rubbish thrown back at us by the sea and the haphazard way the boats have been pushed in the harbour. Already, with the storm in its dying stages, people are working to get back to normal so they can get on with life. People greet me and wave across gardens and I wave back, hesitant at first and then confident, calling their names if I know them.

Back at home I light the fire and lay the papers out on the carpet in front of it. I put the enamel kettle on the stove. I go back to look at the kitchen and see it properly for the first time in a while. It's like the beach; bits and pieces of everything washed up from my life and discarded. Piles of papers and unopened post cover the table, all except for the corner where I eat. Every surface is covered with clutter of some kind. The tide of my life has brought things in and dumped them. I take a bag, and, whilst I wait for the kettle to boil, begin tidying up. I find a black biro amongst the chaos.

The pages don't take long to dry. I sip my tea and take note of the places I need to sign. Stu's signature is already there. Although the pages have gone crinkly as they've dried, they're still legible. I sign four times. I hesitate, but only for a second, on the last page. This last one, with our names sitting side by side is just like or wedding certificate. The signatures then were strong and hopeful, a promise of a new chapter starting. On this last line, I make sure mine is strong and hopeful again. If it's got to be the end of the beginning of my own story, I want it to be purposeful. I find a clean envelope, address it to my solicitor and put my boots back on. Cat reappears and curls around my legs, welcoming me back.

I open the door and breathe in salty fresh air. By the look of the sky – brighter, lighter – the clouds will soon be gone. Things look cleaner, as if a layer of the world has been removed. Into this newness I go, my steps feeling solid against the ground.

At the post box, though, I falter. My hands start to shake and I feel the bitterness back in my throat, trying to make its way out in an ugly yell. I've been through all this, I think, and come out the other side. Just this morning, I sat and fought as the wind fought the rocks and I won. I won. I raise my hands up, willing them to stick the envelope through the slot. It just won't go and I know I'm weak, after all.

The post van draws up beside me.

'Braw day, now,' says the postie. It's a woman I don't recognise.

'Where's Graham?' I ask her.

'Stuck at home. Tree through his roof,' she says. 'I'm covering, just for today. Funny how things can just happen like that.'

I nod.

'Want me to take that?' she says.

I shake my head, but hold it out to her. 'It's my divorce,' I say.

'Ah,' she says. 'His idea, or yours?'

'His.'

'Want my advice?' she asks as she gathers the letters of people braver than me.

I nod, again.

'There's no dignity in not facing it,' she says. 'Tell you what. I'll go down and do the other box. I'll be about ten minutes. Make your peace, and give it to me then. If you want,' she adds, and she drives away.

I try to summon the person I was just minutes ago, last night, this morning. Like the storm, I'm changeable. I can't keep up with myself. I sit on the memorial bench near the post box. I want a sign. How do I know, at the end of the day, that what I'm doing is right? If I can feel so strongly one way, then another, almost in the same breath, how can I trust what I'm doing?

The wind lifts my hair and strokes my face. I've missed that, I think. Being touched.

As if he's been summoned by the wind, Peter appears at my side.

'You're okay,' he says, and I can hear relief in his voice. 'I went down looking for you. Found this on your doorstep.'

I look at what he's holding. The envelope, addressed to Stu.

'But…?' I say, and look down at what's in my hands. It's a plain, empty envelope. I must have picked it up by accident, and dropped the right one.

As he hands it to me, Peter can't quite meet my eyes.

'If this is what I think it is, you're doing the right thing to send it,' he says.' I'm biased, I know,' he looks down at the ground, 'but you deserve better.' He gives my arm a squeeze and leans over and kisses my cheek.

The kiss is a jolt of lightning; I'm thrown out of myself for a second. He can't look at me as he turns away, and walks back down the hill.

I touch the place where he kissed me. I notice my breath, faster, and there's a feeling inside me I can't place. Yearning? Loneliness?

If I'm the storm, and he's the lightning…

The postie comes back.

'You're all pink,' she says.

I can't speak as I shove the envelope towards her, smile and run down the hill, after Peter. Electricity can come out of seemingly nowhere, strikes randomly, lights up the sky. This might not be the ending I imagined, but it's one that's nevertheless appeared, as lightning does against a dark, heavy sky.

His face, when I call him, shines as he turns. His smile, I see, could light up a dim room. I return it, a spark jumping from another spark and making a fire inside me.

Around us, the air swirls invisible but I imagine us in a cloud, a negative and a positive particle, coming together, flashing to the ground, charged with a new energy, all of our own. I feel my smile stretching and love the way it pinches my cheeks. Just like this, out of nowhere, I think, and I know that in this instant, I am doing the right thing.

And that's all there is, thousands of instants, pushed together. Some of them create explosions. I take a breath, and reach for his hand.

Snowfall

Grief has cut me in two. There's my head, which knows he's gone, and my heart, which hasn't got a bloody clue. Every single day my heart gets a fresh battering as I see his hat, or find a note he's written, or simply think he's about to come through the door.

Slowly it feels like my heart starts to freeze because it just can't take all the shocks and that's perfect because we're due for the worst winter in hundreds of years. Or something. I hear this on the radio and file it in the back of my mind and pay it no attention, despite the fact I'm living halfway up a hill in the middle of nowhere with a two-wheel drive car and no friends close by. It doesn't penetrate the veil I'm living behind, the one that separates me from the rest of the world.

Sally, who's my dad's neighbour, has tried several times to peel back the veil but I don't let her in. The last time she stood at the door like a daylight ghost calling me.

'Bella… Bella, I know you're in there… I've got something for you…' She may mean well but there's no way I'm letting her in, to stare at all my dad's stuff, just sitting there not going anywhere when I should be moving on and sorting it out. I'm not letting her anywhere near me so I wait until I see her car go out before I leave the house. My dad had relied heavily on Sally before I moved in and it's as if she feels more of a claim to grief than me, crying more loudly at the funeral, making desperate tiny gestures at the edge of the grave.

The first snowfall has me unprepared. Sally comes to my letterbox and tells me through it, in a narrow voice, that I don't know what Scotland is like in the winter (I do) and that she can help me if I want (I don't) because she has a four wheel drive. I've heard that sometimes people hear the voices of their loved ones after they've passed on but it's never happened to me. But I can *imagine* what Dad would say, so in the end I tell her okay, yes, I could do with some supplies.

On the way out I pass my sad little Fiesta, it seeming to say sorry for only being small and having two wheels and making me have to sit in Sally's Range Rover Obnoxious, and listen to her talk about my dad as if she'd been close to him.

'Such a wonderful, wonderful man,' she says.

'How your mother could have left him…' she laments.

'How lucky you were to have a father like him. My own father, he wasn't like that…' she says, eyes brimming.

I look at the whitening world around me and it's as if I'm in Narnia. Almost unrecognisable. I let myself fall into the brightness and drift away. My dad used to read CS Lewis to me. He read to me every single night until he was kicked out. He was an excellent father, not a good one. Fifteen years ago kids stayed with their mums most of the time so it was never really considered I'd do anything else. I missed him every minute and the visits every other weekend weren't enough. As soon as I was old enough I moved to Dad's. And then, it felt, my life really began again.

My father's name was Richard Goodman, and he lived up to his name. He was good in every way: good to the homeless on the street; good to everyone he served in his shop; good to strangers who needed help; good to animals; good to me. He was fun, trustworthy and, he told me often, my biggest fan. And I was his. He urged me to go away to college and broaden my horizons, despite knowing I'd probably never come back. And I didn't. I worked during the holidays and stayed in my digs; and after that moved in with Tan, my boyfriend. When Tan and I broke up I went travelling and my visits home got shorter and shorter. I feel awful about it now, of course, every one of those missed moments haunting me dreadfully, but Dad encouraged me. Until he got sick.

We've arrived at the supermarket. My tears have misted up the window where my head's resting and Sally puts her hand on my arm.

'Are you okay?' she says, pointlessly.

In answer I open the door and march across the car park, seeing, rather than hearing my dad's disapproval. Sally looked after him, cooked for him, shopped for him and listened to him for weeks before I arrived. My fury at finding out he'd hidden his cancer from me was nothing compared to the fury I'd felt that she'd been there looking after him, when it should have been me. Of course he was trying to protect me.

When I'm in the tinned section, I see the undertaker. Mr Gregg. I duck and pretend to be looking at baked beans along the bottom shelf but he's seen me.

'Bella,' he says. 'I've been trying to get hold of you. Your dad's phone doesn't seem to be working.'

I stand up and raise my eyebrows in a 'oh, really?' sort of way. I've unplugged the phone.

'We found your father's ring,' he tells me.

I'd nearly killed him when he told me they lost it and now I want to hug him.

'It had gone down one of the drains, where we…' he remembers in time and shuts up. 'We found it three days ago, when we were clearing an, er, blockage.'

'I'll come and get it,' I say.

'No need,' he tells me. 'It's in my car outside.'

The fancy car struggles on the way home up streets that have become treacherous since we were inside the shop. I've apologised to Sally and she's patted my arm again. We're good. The ring is on my thumb, the only digit it will fit on. Even then it's a bit loose. She doesn't talk on the way back but I see her looking at me looking at the ring, engraved with RG.

Life's okay again.

I've bought enough food to ensure I don't have to go out again. It takes ages to shift the bags from the drive to the house because the world's turned into a huge ice rink and the snow is falling faster and thicker ever minute. By the time I've finished I'm freezing, exhausted and faint. I shut the door after Sally's offers of more help and sit at the kitchen table and then I notice it: the ring's gone.

Later on I'm sitting in the lounge crying as if he's just died all over again. I've been outside, searched every inch of the ground between drive and house with no result. Sally helped. The snow is inches thick already and there are footprints and there are tyre tracks and there are tears. We can't find it and I'm so cold and it's so dark that in the end I have to give up, and shake my head at Sally and go in. It had been as if I'd found part of him again. That ring was on his finger for his whole adult life. It was given to him by his father when he took over the shop and it was never off his finger. I fall asleep eventually wearing one of his old shirts and wrapped in a blanket, on the sofa where he spent his final hours.

The snow falls for days. My father's house is remote because at the end of a day serving people he liked perfect silence. In the snow it's beyond silence, it's like being underground. The snow fills up my doorway so I can't open the door, it covers the tiny cottage windows, it sits on the roof and slides off when it gets too heavy in whumps that wake me in the dozing afternoons. I sit it out. I feel close to my dad here but though I wish and wish for him to come, he doesn't.

Sally does though, banging on my kitchen window every day. I wave an 'I'm okay' and she leaves me alone again. I should be grateful.

The freeze goes on and on. I get up later and later, and sleep more in the afternoons. I don't even try to go out. I'm aware that I'm not right, but I do not care. I keep the phone unplugged and wave at Sally and the days pass. I look at my thumb often, at where the ring was, for so brief a time. Whilst the rest of the country rages at the sky, I lie down with the snow, and do not care.

It's a different sound that wakes me. Drip, drip... I don't want the thaw to come. I roll over and stuff my head into the pillow and will it to snow again. But the dripping continues and after two days of sun, there's Sally, banging on my door.

'I'm okay,' I whisper through the wood. I don't want her to see me; there's enough of me left to know that the lack of washing will be a problem. I know I'll get back to life again, in my own time. Just...not yet.

But Sally has other ideas. The knocking continues and when I don't answer she opens the door. I forgot she has a key.

'Bella,' she says and in her tone is disapproval and care, in equal measures. She holds her hand out. 'Come.'

I don't want to go out but she takes my hand and tugs it, ever so slowly.

'Look,' she says, and pulls me to the doorway.

The light hurts my eyes. I stand in the doorway and let them become accustomed to the brightness. The world is so noisy: dripping, trickling, water, birds…Sally is waiting for me to do something so I try hard. Is it that she's waiting for me to notice how full of life, life is? Does she want me to feel something thawing within me? Say something?

She pulls me forwards and points at a rose bush. My dad loved his rose bushes and to see them all dead and brown and withered hurts me. Reminds me of him, dying. Sally looks at me. What the hell does she want? I want to go back inside but as I turn to go, something catches my eye. In a world of white and silver and ice there is something yellow caught on a lower twig of a rose bush. A perfect circle of gold.

'Sally?' My voice, so unused, so buried, is croaky.

'All these weeks, it was here waiting for you,' she says. 'It wasn't on the ground, it must have landed here.'

I bend down and pull it off the twig. I look for the sign he's sending me – a new bud? Spring, coming? But there's nothing, just brown broken dead twigs of a rose bush that may or may not survive this dreadful winter. That's no message. Is it?

'I don't understand,' I say.

'You're not meant to understand,' says Sally. 'None of us are.'

I close my fist over the ring. It's freezing and I think of all the nights it's been here waiting for me. I smile and it feels weird on my face.

Sally puts up her hand and brushes my cheek. 'That's better,' she says. 'Now put it on. Before you lose it again.'

I push the ring over my thumb then change my mind and take off the necklace I'm wearing. I fumble, with stiff fingers.

'Let me,' says Sally. And she takes the ring, weaves my necklace through its perfect centre, and fastens it around my neck once more.

'Thank you,' I say. 'For everything.' And I don't know if it's joy that makes my voice strong, or the fact that my father's ring is around my neck, right where my heart is.

The Shapes of Us

As I'm staring at the images on the camera the security guy, Rod Small, according to his badge, is trying to make excuses.

'So, you see, he is an expert. Whatever system we had running, he'd have been able to find a way in. We've contacted his department and he's in for questioning as I speak, but I would like you to know, Mrs. Singleton, that we take our business very seriously and we can assure you that-'

'Tell me again what he took,' I say.

Rod Small nods and swallows. He reads from a list: 'All of your son's drawings, his reports and medical notes, his teddy and a jacket he left at Bright Days on Friday. Oh, and a dummy which was at the back of his tray.'

I look again at the furtive figure moving in time-lapse jerks across the screen. His hair is dark and he's stocky, which all looks familiar, but not uncommon. Coincidence, perhaps. It's his face though. There is only the quickest glimpse of his face as he turns from Sonny's tray and heads for the door, but in those high cheekbones, that fine nose, his strong chin, I see a face I know better than my own.

I think of running my hand down Sonny's profile as he slept in his cot, back when I was first getting to know him, when I wondered about those features.

Rod Small opens his mouth to give me more reasons why this couldn't possibly be CareSafe's fault and I speak to stop him.

'What happens now, Mr Small?'

'Well,' he says. 'Now you have a choice. The police department would like to make their own investigation to find out why an officer has done this, but they have made it very clear that if you would like to press charges, you will have their full cooperation.'

I don't speak.

'Mrs Singleton?'

'I need a little time,' I say. 'I need to think.'

Outside, a wind is blowing. The pavement is scattered with leaves which dance around my ankles. In Autumn Sonny was born and I added the temperature to the list of other worries I had, constantly. The main one was always, *What if something happens to you, Kath? What then?* I'd answer myself: *This was what you wanted. You should have thought about that then. About the fact it was just you.* The problem was I hadn't anticipated the huge mountain of responsibility that rolled down on top of me in an avalanche of sleepless nights and anti-depressants. The fact that I, and only I, was all that stood between Sonny and the world. I was all he had. And I was terrified I wasn't up to the job.

Three years on and the fears are still there, but I am more confident in myself as a mother. The terror about something happening to me has never left though. At the clinic, way back when it all began, they asked me about this and I'd blithely answered that being on my own would never be a problem. Look at all I had accomplished with my life! A political career, several books, a big house. I could give this baby everything he or she needed. Money would never be a problem, I could cope, I would be fine, I wanted a baby.

There had been an element of genetic choice. Not much, for we're not clever enough yet to design our own babies, but I could pick certain traits. A high IQ. I wanted height and a strong physique. I wanted a baby with dark hair, preferably, to match my own. My skin colour. A quick procedure and nine months of eating exactly the right foods at exactly the right times, according to the development books, and there was Sonny. All mine and yet not all me.

I pick up Sonny from my mother's. He comes flying down the steps towards me, a little hurricane, and my heart constricts with love.

'Hey Sonny-boy. How 'bout an ice cream?'

He squeals all the way to the café.

I watch him covering himself with chocolate goo and see the grainy time lapsed face again, superimposed on Sonny's. It makes me shiver. The man didn't look dangerous. But what if I didn't press charges and he did something worse? How would I feel? Other things are bothering me: the man would have known he was being filmed – he was a cop. He didn't wait until night; he was at Bright Days in full light on a Saturday. My head is whirling with it all.

Sonny falls asleep on the way home, dark hair tumbling over his beautiful face. I wonder how it would feel not to know him.

I drive to the police station.

I park facing the door, engine running. I sit and stare alternately at the door and at Sonny. After about fifteen minutes, a man comes out and sits on a bench. He lights a cigarette and as he bends forwards, dark hair falls over his eyes. But as he looks up, I see it's a different face.

The man looks out at the car park, then he sees me and his eyes lock onto mine. As he walks over I hit a button on the door and a *clunk* locks us in. He comes right up to the car and stands by my window. I put the car into gear and am going to pull away when he smiles. In the smile is Sonny. I stop the engine and lower the window an inch.

'Can I help you?' I manage to keep the shake out of my voice.

'I'm Thomas, the brother of Chris Goodchild,' He has a soft voice. Not threatening.

I shake my head. 'Who?'

Thomas looks at me. 'Chris. Yesterday he was arrested for breaking and entering. At Bright Days.'

'Oh.' I don't know what else to say.

'The thing is, Chris is a good man. He's just been a little mixed up, and a little lonely. His wife just left him, you see, and he'd always wanted kids, and she didn't want any, and he feels it's too late and,'

I put up a hand, stopping him. 'Whoa – slow down.'

'Sorry.' Thomas looks down. 'I'm just worried for him. If he loses his job, as well… The thing is, I know who you are. Chris is a good officer but he's abused his position to track you down. I need to tell you something.'

'I know who he is,' I say softly.

Thomas doesn't look surprised. 'Chris said you would, as soon as they called you.'

'But, why? If he wanted to meet me, then why do it like this?'

'He's been having a rough time. Not thinking straight. I want to ask you a favour, Mrs Singleton.'

'It's Ms,' I say. 'You're going to ask me not to press charges.'

'I am indeed. It would wreck his life. He's not a bad person. Please,' he adds.

In the back, Sonny stirs. I think about the time last week when he asked me why he didn't have a daddy.

'Why did Chris, erm, donate?' I manage to blurt out.

'He needed money. He did whatever he could to get through school. They were offering a financial incentive to those who fitted the bill so…' Thomas shrugged. 'He was young. Recently life got him wondering if any of what he sold got used, so to speak. He found your son.'

'Just him?'

Thomas nods, before grinding out his cigarette and going back into the station, one last plea in his eyes.

It takes a couple of phone calls to straighten things out. Everyone seems relieved; far less paperwork and publicity this way, I guess. I want to leave but Sonny clicks himself out of his seat just as I'm about to pull away.

'Sonny, no,' I say firmly.

'Wee-wee,' says Sonny.

We're in the middle of potty training and I can't just ignore this. Breathing out heavily and reminding myself that none of this is his fault, I unfasten my belt and stop the engine. I take Sonny behind the car. When he's finished I pull up his pants and whoosh, he's off, out of my grasp and across the car park.

'Sonny!' I shout after him, but he doesn't even turn his head.

He's shouting '*Nee-naw!*' and making straight for a police car parked by the entrance.

I catch up with him as the main doors swing open and Thomas exits, with his arm around his brother's shoulders. They both stop and stare at Sonny.

'Nee-naw!' shouts Sonny, up at them. 'Pleecemens!'

'They're not police,' I start to say but am stopped by the expression on Chris Goodchild's face. It is soft, like Sonny's, when he's asleep.

I wait for Sonny to turn and run to me as he often does with men he doesn't know.

He stares back at them, at Chris in particular. And smiles.

Heartstone

All I can think is: he would've hated this. The minister has a captive audience and is going on and *on* about God and Jesus, about how Robbie is with them now, about how we all must pray for him. Robbie was an atheist.

I glance about at the rest of us; we're all thinking the same thing, I can tell. Unfortunately we're all on display in the front row, so we can't whisper to each other. I know because Sophie, next to me, tried and all she got was more brimstone and fire-speak injected into the speech from the minister, who directed it right at us, as if hell was a cert.

That was one of Robbie's expressions – going to hell in a handcart. He got it from his mum. It was one of the few things he had of hers, he used to tell me, apart from her eyes.

Robbie was gold. His mum might've turned gold, too, if she'd not topped herself. But if she'd not topped herself, we'd not have had Robbie, and Robbie made our home a home. Selfish of me to think that, probably, but Robbie told me himself he'd found it hard to live with her; she loved drugs more than she loved him.

If he'd not bought that stupid bike, he'd be with us still. I knew it was a bad idea. Robbie was a speed freak on a *bicycle*.

'And so we pray for Robbie's friends; all those at Richmond Nook, and his carers. We pray that they may find the strength to continue God's work without him. We ask that you, oh Lord, protect them and be with them, as they...'

I tune the minister out and think of Robbie as he was that last night, sitting on the beach by the fire at Chris's farewell, listening to Davo's guitar, passing a joint around. We'd been talking about our plans after we left. Chris was heading to college the next day, moving to a hostel. Flying the nest, Don had said, tears in his eyes.

Don was like a dad to all of us. He was the only carer who'd come and join in the beach parties and even though he didn't smoke, he never objected when we did. Don was our favourite, but they were all good. I look over my right shoulder to where they sit, ashen-faced. Don's cheeks are wet; Paul and Mez are holding hands, sobbing. Rebecca is holding hers in. She comes across as tough, but she's a big softie underneath. She sees me looking and gives me a sad, half-smile and a tiny nod, before looking back at the minister who's now going on about how Robbie is with Jesus.

Honestly.

If Robbie could hear this crap he'd be really pissed off.

But, it makes me think. Where *is* he?

The last time we were all together was on the beach. Around midnight, Don had shambled off, singing an Oasis tune, turning back once to tell us not to be too late.

The beach was part of our grounds so it wasn't like we could get into any trouble, but still it was good of him to let us enjoy our farewell parties. We'd followed half an hour or so later, one big hug with twice the legs as us, lightly stoned, a small, tight family of our own making.

By mine and Sarah's room, Robbie stopped. Sarah hugged him goodnight and slipped away, leaving us together. Alone.

'Want to come into town with me tomorrow?' he said. 'I'm going on an early morning bike ride, but when I come back?'

I thought he'd never ask.

I couldn't speak but I nodded. He smiled and came close to me, giving me a kiss, right on the lips. Then he put up his hand, stroked my cheek, turned…

…and was gone.

I didn't tell anyone about the kiss. Or about why I'd cried the hardest.

When it was time to put him in the ground the minister really went off on one. She raised her arms and her voice went with them. She did the whole ashes to ashes thing. We became that hug with twice as many legs again, but with one pair missing.

The carers lowered him into the hole and the silence was awful. Except for the minister. *Her* silence was good.

I thought about coming here to visit him and sitting by his headstone in years to come, but I wanted something I could *keep*. My own stone. A heart-stone.

There was a thing back at the Nook afterwards. Social workers, friends, carers, us. There was nothing nice about it; we just had to get it over with.

I went to bed early, finally able to give in to tears. Only Sarah, perhaps, guessed, because she left me alone to grieve.

We are back on the beach. But this time, I'm sitting between Robbie's knees, leaning back against his chest, his arms around my front. His chin is on my head and he's humming along to Davo's music. I turn up and to the side and he kisses me, for longer than the first time.

'Where did you go?' I ask him.

'I'm right here,' he says, and he holds out a stone. It's heart-shaped, smooth and cool. He places it in my palm. 'But I'll be away, soon. It would've been gold, Mish,' he says.

'Michelle!' I opened my eyes to see Sarah's face inches away. 'I dreamed of Robbie. He came to say goodbye. When I woke up, my bed…' She pointed over to her side of the room. Sand trailed over the floor, onto her sheets. She was sobbing, as she lay down next to me. I felt the grittiness come in with her.

I put my arms around her. My right fist was closed as my hands met.

Wrapped in my hand, the stone was warm. I could feel it.

1 + 1 = 2

1 9-20-15-16. I can just make it out. The screen is so wet I can hardly see it, though Nate's shoving it in my face.

'We *can't* stop,' I tell him. 'More snow's coming.'

20-9-18-5-4.

'I'm tired too. But if we can make it to those trees we'll be safer if this turns into a blizzard. If it stops, we'll carry on to the bothy and call it part of the adventure.'

Nate stops. He holds out the calculator. 14-15.

No.

I bite my lip to prevent myself screaming at him, shaking him. But what sort of a mother would I be then? I'm already doing a terrible job, dragging my son out on this badly planned journey. I've failed him. I've failed us both.

All right, the snowfall wasn't forecast. In Scotland, though, things can change several times a day and I should have known it was possible. I remember my words, coaxing him into the car this morning: It'll be fun! We'll stomp through the snow, stay in a bothy and cross the hills. It'll be a challenge – no phone signal, no other people. We'll make a fire. In the morning, we'll look for the treasure.

I gently pull him along and thank God, he yields. We make it to the trees as the sky unleashes a thick whiteout on us. It's supposed to be May. I can almost hear Danny's voice: *Scotland doesn't have seasons. Every day, everything is possible. It can snow in Summer and be t-shirt weather in Winter.* At first, the unpredictability was fun, until Danny turned as changeable as the weather and suddenly it was me, and Nate, and nothing could be trusted to stay the same.

I read about this journey in the dark weeks after Danny left us and decided that one day, I'd take Nate. It's a path that winds through the Highlands, taking in an area where the Campbells were supposed to have buried stolen MacDonald gold after the battle of Glencoe. I imagined Nate holding a metal detector with a smile. Instead, here he is, shivering, frowning and clutching his calculator as if his life depends on it.

We sink down against the back of a tree.

I close my eyes and wish us home. I wish the last eighteen months hadn't happened. I wish my son would speak to me, instead of using code numbers. I think I know why he does it; Danny was a mathematician and this was his first calculator and somehow Nate's connected the two. I've had to learn his language.

He taps me. I open my eyes.

9-7-12-15-15.

'Igloo?'

His big dark eyes fix on mine.

'I don't know how to build an igloo,' I sigh.

He looks upwards, at the sky falling on us. I follow his gaze. If we don't get shelter, we're going to die. I see that the snow's blowing up against two trees right in front of us, creating a drift as high as my waist.

'Will you help me?' Please say yes, I will him. If you're there, Danny, help me.

Start, and he'll join in. I taught him to build a snow survival cave once. He called it an igloo.

It's almost as if he's spoken but it can't be. Half-remembered words float around my head all day most days. I never hear *I'm sorry.*

I shrug off my pack and crawl to the drift. I begin to pack snow together around the edges and shore up the sides, concentrating on making a windbreak. At first, Nate just watches, then he holds out his calculator.

13-15-18-5

'More. Okay, I'll get more. Can you help me?'

He starts grabbing clumps of snow and dumping them by me. Despite everything, I smile – he's *with* me. The snow sticks easily and soon the walls are quite high. Nate moves away and my heart sinks before I see him around the back wall, adding thickness and strength with huge glovefulls of snow. We work quickly against the freezing wind and soon we have something that looks exactly like an igloo. Except for one thing: the roof.

Nate's ahead of me, though. He disappears for a couple of seconds into the white and I start to panic, but he returns right away with some branches which he lays over the walls. I do the same, and soon there's enough support to fill in the gaps with snow.

I drag our packs to the door, beckon him in and make a barrier across the door with our stuff. Outside, the wind picks up. I open our packs and use my waterproof rug and sleeping bags to make a bed. We've lots of snacks and I lay these out. Nate grabs a cereal bar. We eat, listening to the wind. I know there's nothing else we can do except wait for morning.

'It's quite cosy,' I say. The light inside is blue-white; it feels safe. I try to pretend we're playing at this, in our garden, but in my head is a running commentary of all the ways I've screwed up.

Out loud, all I can manage is 'I'm sorry,' before tears take over. Nate sits, solid and cold beside me. Then slowly, he moves a little closer. And closer. He lays his head on my shoulder. I daren't move. My tears stop and I think of all the things I've never told Nate, and all the things he's never told me. A mountain of things, unsaid.

'After your dad…' I begin. I still can't say *suicide.* 'I really want to talk to you, Nate. I've got a lot to explain. After Dad…' Inside our igloo it's silent again. 'I wish I knew what you thought. I wish…'

Dammit. I need to do better, *be* better.

'Nate, if I talk, will you listen? Will you try and talk to me?' My voice is firm.

He picks up the calculator, hesitates, then keys in 25-5-19.

'Thank you,' I breathe. I lay my head on top of his and begin.

Small Talk

'She said the cat's been chatting to her again,' says Jenny from the hall, where they're doing the changeover. There's a titter from the next carer and when she speaks I realise it's the one I hate; the big boned matronly nurse who's rough and doesn't do small talk.

Where's Marlo, when I need him? On cue, in he strolls with a twitching mouse in his jaws, which he drops on the threshold of the kitchen.

'Nice one, Marlo,' I say. We both know what Big Bones thinks of mice.

In walks Big Bones. 'Mrs Johnson,' she says. 'How are we today?' Without waiting for an answer, she's away towards the kitchen.

I smile.

She screams, and runs back into the lounge and through to the hall. I hear the front door slam.

Marlo jumps up onto my knee. 'Think that's the last we'll see of her,' he purrs.

Snails

The day after he left me I evicted all the snails from our garden. He'd kept them there to ensure a balance in his own little ecosystem. I took a bucket and hunted for two hours, under every stone and hosta leaf, behind the bench, in the dark little space between the garage and the wall. I put pink nail polish on each shell, just out of interest.

I carried the bucket to the old railway line, quite a walk from my house, and there liberated them, one by one. They didn't seem to notice it was different, just peered out and rolled off in random directions. I watched them leave and walked home, alone.

I made myself tea and sat in the garden. I smiled at the hostas. I thought about how I didn't have to cook dinner. How I could do what I damn well pleased. When the tears came I walked inside and switched on the TV and hid under a blanket on the sofa.

The hostas recovered but my garden was too quiet.

'I'm sorry,' I told the birds sitting on the fence, looking, I imagined, for shells. 'But they had to go.'

By the time the hostas were strong again I was watching less TV. And when they were back sleeping in the earth, I'd taken up belly dancing and Spanish.

The day after he tried to come back, I saw the first pink shell. Then another, and another. Like him, they slimed their way back in. Unlike him, I let the snails stay.

The Thinking Place

I looked at my watch as I hurried along, worried that I would be late. I couldn't miss this appointment. I wondered if I'd even remember the way; it had been years.

I felt butterflies of excitement as I thought about what lay ahead. Would she recognise me?

Arthur Jewel had told me the place was magic the first time he caught me trespassing. I'd been eleven years old, brave, bolshy and ready to start breaking rules. Arthur found me when I was halfway down the wall, after I'd discovered the clearing for the first time.

'I don't mind you going there, but be careful. The place holds a special kind of magic. And sometimes, it can be a good place to find answers...' he'd said in his quiet, gentle voice.

To an eleven year old, these words were temptation itself. I made the clearing my own special 'thinking place' and in all my years of going there, I never met anyone else.

Arthur was an extremely kind man. Curator of the Ambleton museum for thirty years, he was known to everyone in the town. He once told me he'd like to take all of the stuffed animals and cruelly pinned insects from their display cases, bring them back to life and set them free.

Arthur saved my life that day. If he'd prevented me from going to my thinking place, I don't know where I would have gone when I needed refuge; there I was safe.

And Arthur was right. The place certainly was magic.

I checked my watch again; I still had half an hour to spare. After a quick glance down the lane to make sure I was unobserved, I slipped through the gate which led to the walled-in yard at the back of the museum.

Nothing had changed. Arthur had died when I was at university, and it seemed the museum still lacked sufficient funds to make any improvements. Just as I remembered, the yard was full of ancient farming machinery, old rusting engine parts and disintegrating sheds.

I squeezed behind the biggest shed and looked for my tree. Climbing it was harder than I'd imagined but I managed to pull myself up and through its branches, until I could drop down on the far side of the wall.

Already I was in another world.

Dense woodland gave the light a greenish tinge and thick leaf litter made my steps soft. I touched trees as familiar as friends, brushing aside twigs and branches, until I found the way to the stream. In one leap I was across.

A small animal path ran alongside the stream. I followed it, breathing deeply the clean, summer scented air.

The path twisted away from the stream and took me across the top of a small ridge. I looked for the old pine tree which marked the way, skidded down a small ravine and then came to a standstill. I had arrived.

The clearing was surrounded by trees. On one side was a stone pagoda, built next to a large, kidney shaped pond. Back in the 1820s when the museum was a house, this had been part of the grounds.

I made my way to the back of the pagoda and reached down, brushing aside shrubs to reveal the well-weathered carving in the bottom left hand corner. There it was: ***M and M - 26/6/07***

I sat on a rock, looked at the words and smiled. Now all I had to do was wait.

* * *

The girl came crashing though the trees into the clearing. I heard her make her way to the pagoda and sit down. She burst into tears and sobbed loudly, taking great gasps of air in between cries.

I had to time this carefully.

I waited until she'd stopped crying, begun muttering angrily to herself, and decided to make my move.

Quietly I crept around the edge of the pagoda and walked around to the front, as if I had just arrived.

The girl jumped up with a small scream.

I drew in my breath. She was so young; so very young. Her skin was smooth and her eyes clear. Her hair was thick and glossy and she wasn't wearing glasses. She was shorter than I'd imagined and wore clothes I'd forgotten existed; lots of pink, accessories everywhere, tight jeans and boots. I remembered how it was to be her age, wearing the desperate fashions of a fourteen year old trying to find her own style.

I drank in her youth.

Her mouth dropped open as she stared back at me, her face registered recognition and confusion. I knew exactly what she was thinking.

We gazed at each other. Finally, we shared identical smiles; mine surrounded by a few more lines.

We sat down, neither knowing quite how to begin. Eventually, it was she who spoke.

'Tell me what to do,'

I took a deep breath. I'd been rehearsing this speech for years.

'Firstly, wipe your face.' I handed her a wet-wipe.

'Secondly, forget about running away. Thirdly, stop feeling sorry for yourself. Yes, I know that's what Gran would say, but it's true. She didn't get through her life by pitying herself. To fully understand what I'm going to tell you, you need to be strong.'

She sniffed, and nodded.

'The women in our family have always been strong. Speaking of Gran, you should spend as much time as you can with her over the next year or so. Tell her how much you love her.'

Her eyes filled with tears again.

'Stop,' I said. 'Just accept it and enjoy her. There's nothing you can do about it.

'Now, I know what happened today. I remember.' I touched her cheekbone, where I knew a bruise was forming.

'This is very important. At the moment, you have three choices about the kind of person you can turn into. You can be a victim; you can use this as an excuse to be a difficult teenager and go off the rails. Or, you can become a bridge between other members of the family and help everyone get through. The choice is yours. I know how bad you feel, how confused, how angry. So, I'll just stick to the facts.'

She was listening carefully. I breathed a sigh of relief.

'Right. Whatever your dad says over the next week, month or year; this is *not* your fault. Your parents' marriage is ending because of a whole load of reasons, none of which are to do with you.'

'But –' she said.

'I know. But it's not true and if you believe it *is* true, trust me - you'll be dragging that guilt around with you for years. Don't listen to either of them too much, because they are very bitter. Make up your own mind.

'Try as best you can to remain friends with your dad, however hard it gets. You'll want to get angry, but it will only worsen things. He will never hit you again, today was the last time. In his way, he is already very, very sorry but he has *no* idea how to show it. If you learn to forgive him and to master your own temper, who knows, he might learn too. You can still have a relationship with him, if you try. In a few years you could still be father and daughter, not strangers.'

I took a deep breath.

'I know about Kevin. It was a huge mistake, but you don't need to keep on making them. Your body is *your* body, you can say no to whoever you want.'

She opened her mouth to say something.

'No, no questions. Because some I won't want to answer, and you'll read the truth in my eyes.

'Don't drink too much at university – don't look so surprised, you *are* going to go. You won't blossom fully, until you leave Ambleton. By all means, experiment, but keep a handle on things. Too much alcohol will stop you being all you can be.

'Friends are incredibly important, but don't waste time by hanging out with people you can't be yourself with. They'll only hold you back. You *know* who I mean… In a few years, a good friend will ask you out for a farewell meal before you leave town. You'll want to put him off as you are busy getting ready to go, but *don't*. Go out with him.' I felt tears in my eyes at the memory of Rob. I hurried on.

'Do *something* about your anger. Find a way to keep a lid on it. If you don't, it'll only get worse.' I stopped.

There was one last, big thing I had to tell her but I was afraid of hurting certain people's feelings if I said it aloud. I whispered in her ear.

Her eyes widened, then she swallowed and said, 'Okay, I'll be careful.'

I could have told her how to get rich. I could have warned her about which 'plane not to get on, which beach to avoid in December 2004. But I'd survived, and lots of money wouldn't help.

She put up a hand and touched my face. She ran her fingers over the deep frown line between my eyebrows and the faint scar on my forehead.

'Worry,' I said, indicating the frown line and, 'Anger,' pointing to the scar.

'Glasses,' she said, slightly disappointed.

'Inevitable,' I nodded. 'Forget contacts, they'll never work for you.'

'Can I ask just one thing?' she asked

'Go on,' I said, remembering.

In a small voice she asked, 'Will I be loved?'

I smiled and touched her shoulder. 'You are loved *now*. It just doesn't feel like it. But you are very definitely loved. You just need to learn to love *yourself* and then you'll notice how much more of it there is in the world.'

'What about big love... a boyfriend...'

'There is someone very important in your life, but not for years. Have fun in between. Don't worry, you'll know him when you meet him.' I gave a great big grin, and touched the ring on my finger.

'There's one more thing we've got to do before you go home.' I took her hand and led her to the back of the pagoda. The wall was lichen stained and blank. I took out my knife and in the bottom left hand corner I scratched into the stone: *M and M - 26/6/07*

She gasped. 'So long!'

'It'll go really, really fast.' I turned her to face me. 'Live it well, *live every minute.*'

We looked at each other and both thought about the years in between.

'Now,' I said. 'It's time for you to go. They are worried, especially your mum. She is only doing what she thinks is right at this time, for everyone. She doesn't need the added worry of you being lost. And she loves you, don't ever forget it.

'Go and give your brother a hug. One day you'll be living half a world away from him and you won't believe how much you'll miss him.'

She turned to go. 'Is this the only time?'

'I think so. Arthur told you this place was magic... don't forget to thank him sometime. Remember what he said, about finding answers? This is a crossroads for you.'

We hugged. 'Be strong. Oh yes, and try to pass your Spanish exam.'

She raised her eyebrows. She smiled, saying, 'Travel?!'

'Lots of travel,' I replied.

'Thank you,' she said, and then she was gone.

From the pagoda, I watched the reflection of the sun shining through the leaves onto the surface of the pond. I felt relieved, lighter in being.

Suddenly, I heard the rustle of leaves. An elderly lady appeared in the doorway. She was wearing a pink tracksuit and trainers. She had on the most outlandish glasses; sparkly pink frames, with purple tinted lenses. In between her eyebrows was a deep wrinkle. She winked at me.

'Thought I might find you here. Pig of a place to get to nowadays, what with the new highway.' she said. 'Anyway, few things you ought to know…

Home Grown

The tomatoes were the reddest I'd ever seen. I took the box from the woman who grew them for us and thanked her; it was out biggest order from her yet. As usual, she hastened away, as if afraid to stand there. The label on the box read 'Thea Allbright, Organic Produce'. It had been me who found her when I took over as manager of Greenacres Home for the Elderly. I wanted to do something different. Instead of keeping them alive, I wanted my residents to Live. Good food was the start of this and already I'd seen tiny improvements; more smiles, less illness, more friendships. Although Thea Allbright had only delivered small quantities until now, it was a start and I intended to work with her to help her produce more.

Supply and demand and cost and funding – Economics wasn't my strong point but I could learn. I'd already persuaded the very tight owners of the home to increase my food budget, explaining that it would decrease their medications budget, if people were eating good, healthy food. Thea's food was the best I'd ever eaten and already I'd seen a difference, after buying from her for only two months. My residents looked brighter, were more talkative and active, and seemed to have gained a glow. All of it unquantifiable, but I knew it was there.

The tomatoes were for a summer salad I was making myself. I tried to work in a different part of the home every week. This week I was on kitchen duty. I think the staff found me a bit barmy, but I didn't care. My job was to improve lives, and to do that I needed to know how every inch of the home worked.

Whilst I was chopping the tomatoes I couldn't resist eating a few. The scent took me back into my childhood and my dad's greenhouse. The colour was deep summer sunsets, late in the evening, staying up far longer than I should have because the adults murmured, made soporific by wine; I'd be forgotten. By the time they remembered I'd be dozing in the hammock under a crocheted blanket, secure and happy. My childhood never stayed like that, of course, but then childhood never does. As I bit into the flesh of the tomato I could hear my father's voice, calling to me...

'Jenna?' said Mark, our chef.

I came to. 'Sorry. I was miles away. The taste of these...'

'Matches the expense,' grumbled Mark. 'The supermarket ones were perfectly fine.'

I sighed. 'Just taste one, and you'll know what I mean,' I said.

Mark took a small tomato and popped it, whole, into his mouth. He closed his eyes as he chewed. His frown disappeared and his face became smoother, suddenly attractive. Mark spent so much time looking cross that I'd never seen him like this. He looked, suddenly, younger. He opened his eyes, and smiled.

'You're right,' he said. 'I could taste my working holiday in Spain. Best time of my life.'

He went back to peeling carrots and started whistling. I'd never heard him whistle before.

I usually ate with the residents, moving tables each day. This way I got to know everyone more. I urged the other carers to do the same but so far, only one of the nurses had joined me. Today, I noticed, Caroline was already sitting with Mrs Littlewood, looking awkward but sitting there nonetheless. I smiled to myself. Things were changing, slowly but surely. Caroline was one of my less cheery carers. A woman who seemed to begrudge everybody everything.

The salad was perfect. Mark had made a real effort with presentation, for a change. I saw him hovering by the kitchen door, watching. I nodded at him and mouthed, 'thank you'. He nodded back.

Today I was sitting with two sisters, Emily and Edith, and a newcomer to Greenacres, Mr Smythe, who so far hadn't settled in very well and was unseasonably grumpy, cloudy in summer. I longed to get him to smile but so far, had failed, instead getting a catalogue of things that were wrong with his room, with this place, every single day.

Mr Smythe wasn't going to have any salad until I held the bowl out to him, and out of some upper class politeness, he took it. As with Mark, when he ate the tomatoes, he closed his eyes and his face changed. I held my breath and watched as his face seemed to grow smoother, just like Mark's. His frown disappeared and he smiled.

'Delicious,' he said. 'Just like my grandmother's home grown, back in the thirties... she used to supply the school, you know. I got to taste her tomatoes every day during the summer term. What memories...'

The two sisters were chatting, their faces lit.

'Do you remember we used to steal from Tom Sergeant's greenhouse?' giggled Edith.

'Oh I do... I recall him chasing us out of the garden that time, just after the war when he was short of seeds. Oh! Do you remember his face?' Emily covered her mouth.

'Like a thundercloud!' Edith squeaked and they both dissolved into peals of laughter.

All around me, I could hear memories being relived. There was laughter, exclamation and joy in the room. Like children, I thought. As if they had fallen backwards into their lives. Even Caroline, her face usually grim, was laughing.

'This was such a good idea,' she called over to me. 'I am enjoying myself!'

I noticed that Mark was still there, by the door. He saw me and smiled, shaking his head slightly, as if in disbelief. I got up and stood next to him.

'The tomatoes,' he said. 'Like magic. Look at them all!'

We watched the room. Soon the salads were gone, and slowly, the laughter faded and everyone quietened down. 'That was amazing,' I said. I went through to the kitchen, picked up the phone and called the number I had for Thea Allbright. She answered as if she'd been sitting right next to the phone.

I explained what had happened and asked if I could order double the amount of tomatoes for the next delivery, in three days.

'I can do that. But... this effect you talked of. It probably won't happen again,' she said. 'I find sometimes thing like this can happen, with a special crop. But it tends not to happen twice. It's as if you get immune...' Her voice had gone dreamy.

'What do you mean, immune? What effect? Do you know what I'm talking about?' Until then, I'd not even been sure that what I'd witnessed wasn't just an effect of the summer sun, the changing season. Not food... But she knew what I was talking about.

'Immune? What?' she said, her voice sharper. 'Sorry, I'm not sure what you mean.'

'About what you just said. the effect of the food?'

'All I said was I might not have enough for a second crop so soon. Remember I only grow in small amounts,' she said.

'Right. Well, I'd like to talk to you about that,' I said. 'I'd like to maybe buy more.'

'That won't be possible,' she said. 'I'll deliver cucumbers tomorrow as your chef ordered, and peas, and also some early potatoes.'

We said our goodbyes and I put the phone down, confused. I watched Mark, chopping with a fury for the evening meal, and decided I'd imagined the whole thing. He was frowning; life was normal once more. I looked into the dining room and everyone was quiet. Caroline was clearing plates ready for the second course, chicken breasts and cream sauce. I helped the rest of the staff clear and serve the food. Nothing unusual happened and as I watched the quiet room, I could hardly remember how everyone had laughed, a few short minutes ago. I shook my head, to clear it.

The following day it was hot again and salad was the menu I chose. Pasta salad with raw peas and cucumber, mixed in with a gentle sauce of creamy herbs.

Thea had dropped off the order, again almost running away after she'd delivered it.

I took a cucumber, and regarded it. I cut the end off, and bit into it. I wasn't a fan of cucumber, but this was different. It was crisp and tasted... bright. I couldn't describe it any other way. I closed my eyes...

... and saw my dad, before he got sick, sitting in his green house door, trousers rolled up, cucumbers on green stems twirling around the shelf, dangling off it. My dad smiled at me down the years and I remembered how he smelt when he came in from the garden: earthy, fresh and sun-kissed...

'Are you all right?' Mark's voice held concern, not something I'd heard before.

I realised tears were running down my face. I nodded.

Suddenly, I dreaded lunch.

I handed out tissues one by one. The two sisters hugged each other. My Smythe sat and wouldn't talk to anyone. I walked from table to table, comforting.

The phone rang. I took the kitchen extension. I recognised the voice, that was speaking very fast.

'The cucumbers, not the right ones. I got the orders muddled. Please don't eat them; they were meant for a wake. They were... never mind. Just please, can I have them back?'

I held the phone out towards the dining room. 'Too late,' I said into the mouthpiece.

It took me ages to find the farm. And when I got there, it was less a farm than a smallholding – a very small, smallholding. I knocked on the door but nobody answered. I walked around the building. Out back there were raised beds, greenhouses, plots with green growing in neat lines. Wheelbarrows stood between plots, loaded with various produce. One held potatoes, one held courgettes. I walked over to the one filled with potatoes. There was a piece of cardboard on top, saying: 'First Earlies. Your Grandmother's Hugs. Happy, Childhood.' I put the sign back and went to the next wheelbarrow, full of courgettes. The piece of paper in here said: 'School. Memory Enhancers. To be hidden in soup (give kid-friendly recipe).'

I walked to the first greenhouse. The piece of paper on the door said 'Cuc's. Generally, fathers. Generally, sorrow. Good for grieving.'

The tomatoes were next. I'd already guessed what the sign would say: 'Happiness, childhood, great for the elderly – Greenacres?'

'Hey!' a voice startled me. Thea was running towards me, yet it wasn't Thea. The Thea I'd met had been young and pretty. This woman was older, wrinkles ingrained with dirt surrounded big, sad eyes. 'You can't come in here,' she said. And she grabbed my arm.

'Who are you?' I said, resisting.

She was bending down and pulling me along. As we passed a wheelbarrow she plucked something from it. It was small and purple – a plum. I had time to read the piece of card on top: 'Plums – to forget. Good for dealing with anger, transgression.'

'What you have to understand,' she said,' is that for years my family have been persecuted. I've been happy, settled here for years. I do not intend to have that spoiled. I won't be punished, or investigated. I help people. That's my calling. It runs in the family and I will not be stopped.' She held out the plum to me. The voice changed. 'Eat this, and be a dear,' she said. 'It's the easiest way. Alternatives are... messy.'

⚜

I walked up to the door, Chef Mark's order in my hands. 'Can you deliver this tomorrow?' I asked.

The woman who took it was attractive. 'Potatoes? For Greenacres? I've got the perfect ones,' she smiled, bright teeth flashing.

Snowslip

On Sunday evening he doesn't come home. The climbers' forecast that morning had warned her: strong winds, blizzard conditions on higher ground. She sends a whispered prayer north to the mountains. She paces the lounge. Impatience rushes her to burn dinner – which she can hardly eat – scald her tongue on coffee, take a yowling step on the cat.

Through the window she looks into darkness and tries his phone again, imagining him digging his way out of an avalanche to get to her. At ten o'clock she calls mountain rescue and describes his clothing and tent to the tiniest detail. Even the colour of his socks. She shudders as she says, *red gloves*, seeing cold blue hands inside. She imagines that strength, dead.

She takes a pill and tries to sleep, the phone next to her pillow. It's a fitful sleep full of cold white dreams in which she's sledging, terrifyingly fast and free, the wind howling wildness in her head.

There's no news on Monday despite helicopters circling clear skies; rescuers scouring the tracks. Neighbours come, sympathy in their eyes as they take in her sloppy clothes and her tense, stripped face.

On Tuesday afternoon she takes a cardboard box from the attic and packs some of his things, just to see what it feels like. She's writing Red Cross on it in pink pen when the phone rings.

Once she's replaced all his possessions she stumbles up the stairs and paints her face with shaking hands. She dresses properly. Whilst making dinner she practises her smile.

Wetherby Pie

N ote: The quantities needed to make this pie vary according to how many you are feeding and how big their appetites are. Generally I allow 2oz of meat per person, or three pieces, or more if you are feeding men. If you use 2oz, double the quantities of the other ingredients, and so on, saving an extra filling for tomorrow's stew. If meat is not available this can be made without, just as well.

Steak
Onion
Garlic
Swede
Carrot
Parsnip
Salt
Butter (if available); Lard, if not.
Ale – dark
Fresh herbs: parsley, marjoram, thyme, dill, oregano and fennel: 1small tsp (if no fresh use seasonal – see notes at back on complementing flavours)
Dried: chives, rosemary, pepper: ½ tbsp. and 1 bay leaf
Note: follow recipe EXACTLY re quantities of herbs

(Double quantity of my grandmother's pastry – see front of book)
(Stock – use meat stock my mother made – see previous recipe)
Flora, 1947

Susie has eaten Wetherby Pie many times, but never made it. It's part of their family lore; a recipe passed down through generations, invented long ago and captured by her grandmother Flora on paper. Wetherby Pie – named after the town where her family had lived, years ago – is meaty, strong, and fragrant all at once, crowned by delicate, layered pastry. It makes her think of the past; the good bits of her history: family meals and laughter and in-jokes. It makes her think of the worse bits too; the in-fighting, which, like the in-jokes, are half-told stories that everyone knows. They usually came at the end of the meal, after too much wine. But she doesn't have to dwell on those. She can't remember the last time she had the pie. Certainly not in adulthood, for when a family breaks up the family stories get lost along the way.

She looks at the mountains of food on the work top and swallows, hard. Couldn't she have done bangers and mash? There's a chance he won't even remember, with his selective memory and internal gaze. She thinks it would destroy her, if he doesn't remember. She flings open a cupboard and crashes out a pan. She's not ready for this. She looks at it all, clenching and unclenching her hands. She picks up the recipe book and bites a nail as she reads it.

She puts the book down, walks with purpose to the oven and switches it on, ignoring the uncomfortable whirling in her stomach. For unless she tries, she'll have even more regrets.

She cubes the meat and browns it, rolling it to get every side equally caught. The smell of the fat crisping makes her want to eat it right now. Like the way they always eschewed low fat spread when it became fashionable and continued with butter, her family has always eaten the fatty bits, fought over the skin of the chicken, enjoyed the rich flavours. She lays the meat aside and goes to work on onions and carrots, frying them slightly before adding dark ale, sending the vegetables dancing in the bottom of the pan. She consults the book and lets it cook on for three minutes more, before adding the herbs. This bit is the secret bit that Gran used to make jokes about; the secret ingredients that only women could pass to other women, when they were old enough. Susie got forgotten in the break up, only finding these secrets a few weeks ago when she got the book. She's surprised; some of the flavours aren't ones she'd have thought to combine. She's got all the jars lined up, the fresh green herbs ready chopped in neat green piles. She sprinkles and spoons according to the recipe and closes her eyes as the herbs' scents climb the steam to her nose.

She adds more ale and watches it simmer. Then in goes the colour: yellow-orange squash, lilac garlic, gentle sunset swede and a little creamy parsnip – chopped small. Finally, it's time to return the meat. The stock is a secret, too, and took her a while to concoct the previous night, when she'd hunched like a witch over the pan. She pours it in, turns the heat down and steps back from the stove. She wipes perspiration from her forehead and decides it's wine time, to help her relax. Otherwise it won't matter what the meal is like; she'll mess it up by being tense and edgy; the girl she's always been around him.

Susie pours herself a glass of Merlot. She's tempted to add some to the pan, but it's not in the recipe and for once she's going to follow the rules. She scans the book. She reads, mixes, and tries to add some magic as she turns the spoon. *Please, let this work. Let him enjoy it. Let him notice,* she thinks, over and over. Mike tells her she shouldn't bother, after everything, but he's her dad, after all, and he's ill. Shouldn't she try one more time?

The pastry is where it could all go wrong. She's never been any good making pastry and usually cheats with ready-rolled stuff. But the recipe had a few surprises and the result was soft and connected, behaving like pastry should, not crumbling. It's been in the fridge, the 'cold place' mentioned in the recipe, written before fridges hummed heartbeats in every house. She unwraps and kneads it, until the pastry is soft and workable once more. She drinks more wine while she waits for the filling to cook.

It's hard to get the pastry to look how she remembers it should look; thumbed up around the edges, neat and professional-looking before it goes in for its first bake, but she does the best she can, which was always one of Gran's homilies. Unfortunately, her best has never been enough before but she won't give up, which, she's been told, was one of her grandfather's, whose mind didn't give up until his body gave in to the cancer that was now consuming her father. She sighs, wishing she'd known him, wishing she could have asked him what to do to make it all right, to make her father like her the way he should; the way she's always wanted. Before it's too late.

When the pie is in the oven and the vegetables are all stacked up for steaming, she gently closes the recipe book and strokes its cover. It's a soft, stained, blue leather, which, she imagines, has absorbed the emotions and aromas of thousands of meals across the generations. She wonders at the conversations it has been witness to; the sorrows, the joys, the fears. She thinks of all the events that unfolded in the world as this book sat in kitchen after kitchen. She wishes she could listen to it. Touching it is like holding hands across the years, time travelling and finding a different version of herself using copper pans, a hand whisk and an enamel bowl. She can remember Gran using it, watching her as she squinted at the tiny writing of her own mother or her mother's mother, smiling at her own memories. Last night, as she'd allowed the aromas drifting up from the stock pot to her to spirit her away, to the past and the time to come, she thought saw her own future children, sitting, watching her cook while they drew at the kitchen table. She thinks about her father as a boy sitting watching his mother, too, a young woman Susie's never seen except in photographs. Gran's familiar, worn face was the only one she knew; the one that had lived so much already, the one whose laughter and whose sadness had already written themselves on her face, had tired her, had sapped her energy her too quickly. She places her palm on the cover of the book, knowing her grandmother had once done the same, knowing it's the closest she can come, now. Her grandmother's funeral was one of the few times she can remember her father holding her; awkward and stiff, he'd attempted a hug.

She wonders what her father was like as a child. He's still childish, a petulant five-year-old in an old man's body. Or is that too cruel? That's the angry part of her speaking, the one he's hurt. He's an enigma, one she's spent her life trying to crack. She must think with love, mustn't dwell on her anger whilst she's in the kitchen, or it could seep into the meal and embitter the delicate flavours, the ones she wants to soften him with. He's living proof that nature overrules nurture, that however much love you feed someone, they can still grow up as if they'd been deprived of its light. Or perhaps she's not tried hard enough to find him, inside his thorny shell.

Susie's added to the book, as its most recent custodian, and she's happy there are still lots of blank pages left; yellowing, slightly crispy pages, which are a crinkly joy to write on. She's added her name to the list inside the front cover and made sure there's plenty of space underneath. It was Hilly who hid it from him, handing it to her with a secret smile on one of her visits. She'd tried to push down the rage and the horror she'd felt that he could throw this away, like so many other things she'd been too late to save. Anger simmers again and she pushes it away with a mouthful of wine, swallowing red feeling away with the burgundy wine, a stronger red, one that can overcome it.

She lays the table, looks at the time, checks the recipe book, turns down the oven and turns on the potatoes, broccoli and cabbage ready in their steamer to go on top. She looks down at herself and wonders if she should change. Her clothes are splattered with food and she's hot, but no, he won't notice anyway and she feels comfortable enough as she is. She sits, and clock-watches. Twelve minutes to go; two until they arrive. Her father is never late.

They arrive as Mike does, harried, from the office. He kisses her and gives her an 'it'll be okay' squeeze, as she collects herself and tries to look confident. It's a few weeks since she's seen her dad and she notices right away he's lost more weight. He looks grey and he's somehow shrunk. She's surprised by the tears that blur him suddenly, and she blinks them away – for he never could deal with emotion. Her father gives her a barely-there air kiss on the cheek, followed by Hilly, who's always more tactile and gives her a hug as well.

'Smells gorgeous,' she smiles.

Susie takes the coats as Mike rushes up to change.

She never knows what to say so sticks to safe ground. 'Good journey? You found us okay? I know it's harder to get to than our old house but-'

'Where's the toilet?' her father asks.

'Fine thanks, dear. Yes, no problem.' Hilly says.

'This way, Dad.' Susie leads him down the hall, noticing him not noticing anything. Back in the kitchen Hilly's unloading wine from a bag and explaining they're going to stay at the B and B down the road. Susie expected this, especially when he said they didn't want to stay with her because they needed to be getting back. He's good at making up some excuse and then acting as if he's never said it, as if it doesn't matter that he's lied. She has learnt to let this go, let it waft away on her breath as she exhales the slight away. Never mind that this house has a spare bedroom, never mind that there would be plenty of room. She'd hoped, briefly.

'Out of his comfort zone,' Hilly manages, guessing her thoughts. 'You know...'

'It's all right, Hilly, I know. It doesn't bother me anymore.' Susie pauses. 'How's he been?'

'Stubborn, awkward, thinks he knows better than the doctors. Tried to tell the nurses how to take blood the other day.' They both smile at this.

Something hisses from the stove top and Susie swears under her breath and rushes over, turning knobs on her cooker as if she's conducting an orchestra of steam.

'Need a hand?' Hilly asks.

'No, it's all under control. Mike's in the lounge, I think. He'll get you a drink.'

Hilly touches her on the shoulder and strides out of the kitchen. Susie's no idea how Hilly lives with her dad, with his singular, self-involved self, his way of doing things, his temper. He even seems to do what Hilly says, sometimes. She doesn't understand how, but they seem to be a good fit.

She suddenly remembers the plates, cold in the cupboard. It's right there in Gran's writing – *serve on hot plates* – a little afterword in faded ink at the end of the recipe. And she's glad, because the distraction takes away her annoyance, rising up, always there, always ready to spoil everything, boil the atmosphere as she tries to stick up for herself, reverts to her childhood self, the one who was always, *always* wrong…

'If you're here tonight, I need your help,' she says, looking back at the recipe book. 'I just want…' But what did she want? A lifetime of love, condensed into these few last weeks? An apology? A thousand apologies? Money for all the therapists she's seen? A plaster for the bruises, both real and spiritual? Perhaps a compliment and an evening of peace would be enough. Perhaps, just a moment of connection with him.

'Actually, Gran, just make this meal as good as yours. It's my gift to him.'

She shoves some plates and serving dishes in the top oven and grabs the strainer, then stands and waits for the timer to beep, counting down her feelings with it.

By some miracle, Susie feels, it's all ready on time. She arranges the serving dishes around the pie, and stands back. It looks okay, she thinks, but the vegetables might be overdone and is she sure the pie is ready? Maybe she should put it back in for a few moments to make the top slightly browner? She turns around and knocks the recipe book from the side. Susie bends down to pick it up. The page that's fallen open is overleaf from the pie recipe and has a few words on it, written in her grandmother's copperplate: Wetherby Pie – Perfect for family reunions and other events. This recipe always works to bring people together. Susie smiles, touches the words softly with her finger. She looks back at the table. She nods.

She puts the book back on the shelf and stands by the door. 'It's ready,' she calls, pleased at how strong and steady her voice sounds.

There's a brief pause in the air, a gap in which anything could happen. Susie stands on the kitchen threshold, eyeing the front door. Her legs twitch, as if to take her running away. She hugs herself, and waits.

Her father's voice comes ahead of him. 'I hope she's remembered I can't have bread, or anything too fibrous, or… Oh!' He stops in the doorway as Susie steps back, and looks at the table. 'Wetherby Pie?'

'I made it for you,' Susie says.

Her father looks at her and looks back at the table. 'I…'

'Susie dear, this looks wonderful!' Hilly sounds genuinely impressed.

Mike winks behind their backs, and gives her a thumbs up.

'Please, sit anywhere,' she says.

Her father sits, making a show of trying to get comfy on their lumpy chair cushions, habitual frown settling in to the grooves on his forehead.

She picks up a serving spoon and takes a breath, breaks the crust of the pie. She spoons some onto a plate, making sure her father is served first.

'You've forgotten the salt and pepper,' he says.

For a second, Susie wants to react, just tip over the table and walk away, leave them all there. But violence is his thing, not hers. She picks up the salt and pepper from the worktop and smiles as she puts them down.

'Please start,' she says, when all the plates are full.

Her father's frown has gone again, and he's looking at his plate. Susie watches him as he slowly cuts into the Wetherby Pie. Meat and vegetables fall onto his plate, released, steaming from the pastry. He scoops it onto his fork and watches it every millimetre of the way as he brings it to his mouth. As he chews, he shuts his eyes, and gives a small groan. He swallows, then opens his eyes and looks directly at Susie.

He can see me, she thinks. *He's going to say something nice!*

'It's very good,' he says. 'But not as good as Mother's.'

Hilly looks up, her mouth working to chew the food quickly and speak, but Susie shakes her head. She can feel his words in her stomach, as if they've hit her. She should say something. Make it all right. Show everyone she's not hurt by the remark.

Susie opens her mouth but shuts it again as she realises she has nothing to say. It's just his way, she reminds herself, over and over, her thoughts red and sore, he'll be gone, one day soon. She starts eating but the food tastes wrong. He's right, why did she think she could cook as well as Gran? She should have done her own thing, not a poor imitation of someone else's. It tasted good, but not as good as she remembers. The meat's too hard; the parsnips are...

Mike's kicking her under the table. She looks up and he inclines his head across at her father. Her dad is chewing, slowly, nodding. His face is red and his eyes are watery. She notices, as she hasn't for a long, long time, that his eyes are exactly the colour of hers. He's taken another mouthful and the food is caught there, in his mouth. A tear escapes and rolls down his cheek. Susie stares, unable to look away. She's never seen him cry.

He chews the food, swallows and looks at his plate. 'Mother used to say-' is all he says, before he covers his mouth with a hand. He shoves his chair away from the table and leaves the kitchen.

Mike coughs. 'It's the most delicious meal,' he says.

Susie's staring at the door. 'I know,' she says, and she stands up. She follows her father down the hall, the rich smells of the pie following her in waves, like hands carrying her, guiding her along. As she walks she feels the blood in her calling out to the blood in him, knowing that this time, she's reached him and she's going to take his hand and explain why she created this meal and what she wants him to tell her. She feels the absence of fear like a drug.

'Dad,' she calls. 'I'm here.'

Cellular

There's dust all over our house. It's been there since well before you went out of the door one day and couldn't come back.

It's got deeper, more real as the years have passed. My own dead cells are sinking in with yours, mixing and settling, together. I wouldn't let anyone clean it, even if there was anyone that came.

They cleaned after you at the hospital, swept you up at the crematorium and I scattered you into the air. Now don't be hanging on to me, you'd said, not even a little bit. And don't leave me on the mantelpiece like an ornament.

You knew me very well.

So I didn't. But I stopped cleaning.

Every time I come home I say, hello, to the dust. And sometimes the dust motes rise, float through the air like stars and I imagine it's you saying, hello, back to me.

Get Your Motor Running

I was starting to think the whole insane plan might work, when my brothers Bill and Jim dropped the coffin. *Took off* without the coffin would be more accurate, as the bike and sidecar shot out from underneath it like a rocket, leaving it to crash onto the road. Behind us, twenty bike engines fell silent.

Bill halted the Harley and looked back.

'Woops,' I heard Jim say, as he began to climb off the bike. He'd got one leg onto the ground and was beginning to swing the other over, when he let out a yell and froze, one leg up and one down. 'My hip's gone,' he gasped.

'Hang on, I'll help you,' Bill said and I was about to object on the grounds that Bill could barely walk himself, but he was off the bike and giving Jim a well-practised hip-relocation shove before I could speak. I got off my own machine and hobbled – I'd just had four hernias fixed – over to the coffin.

'We'll just have to lift him back on,' said Jim.

'I did my back in, putting him on there in the first place,' complained a voice from behind us. I guessed it was our friend, Gerry. It was hard to tell because everyone was in full 'Skullcrushers' garb: denim waistcoats, leather jackets and identical helmets, black, and covered with skulls. We'd had the same outfits since 1969 and *Easy Rider*, when, though a fog of marijuana smoke, my brothers Frank, Bill, Jim and I had formed the Skullcrushers with some friends. The only drugs we took now were Viagara and blood pressure pills, or perhaps an Aspirin. We'd not ridden for years, but when Frank decided he wanted to arrive at his own funeral in a Skullcrushers cavalcade, we couldn't argue.

'Come on,' I said.

'I've knackered my shoulder,' said another voice.

'Told you we should have tied him on,' said Bill.

'Look. This was Frank's last wish. For God's sake get over here and put him back on. We have to be there in ten minutes.' I'd promised my sister-in-law Eva that we'd be there, on time, with Frank. Intact, obviously.

With a few groans and popping knee joints some Skullcrushers hefted the coffin back onto Bill's sidecar. It didn't seem to balance as well as before, leaning drunkenly to the left and away from the bike. We started our machines.

The route would take us around town, onto a few miles of straight road and then down a lane to the church. I fell into line behind Bill and Jim, and off we went. Bill pulled away more slowly this time, and Frank wobbled, but stayed put.

With the roar of twenty engines behind me, I felt young again. The way that everyone was revving their engines made me think we all felt the same: sad, yes, but proud. Perhaps even happy. It had been a good excuse to take dust sheets off bikes that had survived years of nagging wives to live on in the garage, dreaming tarmac dreams ('You're never going to ride that thing again. You can't get a leg over it, for starters.' Turned out we all could.) All at once I realised that was probably Frank's plan all along; to get us all together again for a long-overdue ride out. I was just out on the road with my big brother Frank.

I hit a huge pothole and for a second, fought for control, hearing several shouts over the noise of engines behind me. I glanced in my mirror, braced for a pile up and saw that everyone was still upright. I exhaled. Not far to go.

We turned onto the straight and I said a small prayer. This was the bit I'd been dreading.

Just before the end, when Frank told me about the funeral parade, he'd said he wanted 'one more little favour'.

'Eva,' he whispered, 'hasn't let me drive the car faster than forty for years. I want to get up to eighty, one last time.'

Right on cue, Bill opened the throttle and the Harley and sidecar pulled away. Behind me, twenty engines growled. We started to speed up. I alternated between watching my speedo, my mirror and the coffin, waiting for something to go wrong. The needle quivered as it climbed to fifty, sixty, seventy... Eighty! Yes! Frank's wish had been granted and the Skullcrushers were back, for one last glorious ride.

For a few moments, I thought we'd done it.

That was when I saw the woman and the dog. It was a puppy, bouncing and straining at the leash. As we came close I saw it jump up at the woman's legs, and then everything went into slow motion.

The woman fell over. She let go of the leash and the puppy raced straight towards the sidecar. Bill swerved to the right.

The coffin kept going straight ahead. For a few seconds Frank flew through the air and then for the second time that day, he hit the tarmac.

This time the coffin didn't stay intact.

The lid flew off, and Frank bounced out. There was a lot of squealing rubber and crunching metal as arthritic fingers fought with brakes, Skullcrushers slid into each other and time stopped.

The woman screamed.

Somehow, I stayed upright. With shaking hands I turned off the engine and dismounted stiffly (scuse the pun, I thought manically, mind racing. Or trotting. I kept seeing images of myself explaining all this to Bea, wishing I'd listened to her. Bloody woman was right again. I swore that if we all survived this, I'd sell the bike and buy a new pair of slippers.)

I walked over to Frank. He lay, face to the sky, waxy, but undamaged. Jim and Bill arrived, breathless at my side.

'Thank God he's not hurt,' I said.

The three of us looked at each other. Bill's face creased first and we laughed like we hadn't done in years. So hard that we had to hold each other up. Even Frank looked like he was smiling.

'Still glad we didn't bother with rope?' spluttered Bill and that set us off again.

I looked behind me. By some miracle, everyone seemed to be all right. One of the Skullcrushers had the puppy in one hand and an arm around the woman. A queue of traffic had built up behind us and drivers were honking.

'Eva's gonna kill me,' I said. 'Do you think we can repack him?'

'He's not a bloody suitcase,' said Bill.

'Sorry, Frank,' I said to my brother. We tried to be gentle, but just as we got him over the open top of the coffin, Jim's hip went again and we dropped him. Luckily, he landed with all his limbs in the right place.

Putting the lid back on felt awful.

We arrived at the church two minutes late but with engines roaring, just as Frank would have wanted.

Eva stood at the door, dabbing her eyes with a tissue. We parked up the bikes and stared at the coffin.

'Here he is, then,' I said.

'Thank you, Barry,' Eva said. 'I didn't think… Well, you managed it. I was worrying about nothing. Thank you. It's what the crazy old sod wanted, you lot to ride together, one last time. Though how you did it, I'm not sure, what with the state of you all. But thank goodness, no mishaps.'

Bill snorted laughter and turned it into a cough as I fought to keep a straight face.

'No, no mishaps,' I said. 'Absolutely none.'

'Let's get him up the aisle, then,' said Eva. 'Remind me who's carrying him?'

'Um,' I said, thinking of my hernias. I'd forgotten about this bit.

My son, Philip, appeared at my side with his cousins. 'We've got it from here, Dad. Wouldn't want any of you to hurt yourselves, or,' he added in a whisper, 'drop Uncle Frank.'

'How…?'

'We were a few cars back. I was just about to get out and help when you had it all sorted. Think Uncle Frank would've found it hilarious. Don't worry. You secret's safe with me. Though maybe it's time to hang up the helmets?'

'Not a chance, Phil,' said Jim, coming up behind us. 'Heaven forbid this is the beginning of us all popping our clogs, but if it is, Frank here has started a new tradition. I think he would've enjoyed this.' He gently tapped the coffin.

There was a small thunk, followed by a scream. I looked down. Apparently the coffin had sustained slightly more injury than we'd first thought. Frank's hand had flopped out of the side of the coffin which had opened like a magician's box at the 'reveal!' moment.

But the way his hand had landed looked exactly as if he was giving us a thumbs up.

'Yup,' I said. 'He did.'

A Man of Means

I'm a king.

My throne is by the graveyard gates on Union Street in Aberdeen, where I sit in my flowing robes, watching over my citizens. Some of them lay tributes at my feet; most ignore me – I am in camouflage, after all. I see the same people every day. I know all their names and their roles in my kingdom. They don't know I'm a king.

I protect them all. I watch them all.

Sad Lady has a hungry face, worn shoes and a stapled-together handbag. She reminds me of someone: a woman I failed, in the hot empty desert, in the dark days before I became a king. She works at McDonald's, right opposite my throne.

Every morning she brings me a cup of coffee and a smile. One day I tried to refuse the coffee for her sake but she smiled and said softly, 'We're all one family'. I thought about that statement a lot. It made me feel light as air, that she'd said it. So for a day I pretended I wasn't a king, that we were indeed all one family, but then someone kicked me and someone else spat near my cup and I thought, *No, Sad Lady, you're wrong about that. Just you. You can be in my Royal Family.*

The richest ones are usually the rudest. Jealousy, maybe. There's one man, Tweedy, who's never acknowledged me even when I smile at him. He stalks past in shades of grey-green every day and disappears into a swanky upstairs office just down from McDonald's.

One day I've been given more tributes than usual so I stand up, thinking about buying a burger from Sad Lady. As I move forwards, I see a running blur to my right, coming right at me. I have no time to move and someone crashes into me, almost making me fall. I get my balance back and see that it's Tweedy, breathing hard, down on the pavement. He makes a gasping noise so I go to help him, as a king should. I'm duty-bound to help my subjects. As I reach out to him he sees me and flinches away, barking, 'Don't touch me!'

I stand back and watch him pick himself up and walk away. On the ground are some pieces of paper that must have fallen out of his pocket. I'm picking them up and am about to shout to him when I notice a scratchcard with loads of matching 000000s. Very quickly, it goes beneath my robes. I leave the rest, go back and sit on my throne. In a few minutes he's back, eyes wild, searching the ground. I decide it's time for that burger, before he remembers I exist.

Sad Lady's upstairs at McDonald's, clearing tables. She doesn't see me as I pass her, no more than a whisper in the air, and slip the scratchcard into her pocket.

Signs

The empty road stretched ahead of Laura as she sped along, sodium lamps lighting her way, nudging the speed limit but not going over it. Her job depended on her having a clean licence. She'd run away, again, and though she felt ashamed, she didn't know what else to do. Driving helped her clear her mind. She'd been on the road now for an hour, and she was tired, but was afraid to stop because then she'd have to think.

Laura had loved driving since the moment she got behind a wheel aged seventeen, for her first driving lesson. As soon as she touched the accelerator, she knew this was what she was meant to do with her life: drive. She took her advanced driving test aged twenty-five, and soon started her own driving instructor business, aimed specifically at nervous women who'd had problems with driving in the past. Laura could turn them from terrified drivers who'd failed their driving tests, to confident, smooth drivers who passed every time.

Now, she concentrated on the road, on taking the perfect corner, braking before it and accelerating out of it, smooth and steady. If only life were as easy as driving. If only life had rules to follow – do this and do that and get from A to B easily. Life was difficult and complicated and she was stuck.

Everything had been fine. She was in a steady relationship with Kenny, a man she adored, she had a successful business and a dog and a nice house and friends and a social life. She was happy. And then Kenny had ruined it.

Last night, at eleven o'clock, he'd proposed.

She should have seen it coming, and made different arrangements for the evening. It was their one year anniversary, and eleven o'clock was the time they'd met in a cinema foyer, as they each tried to compose themselves after a sad film which they'd both gone to see alone. They'd been wiping their eyes and they'd seen each other and giggled, embarrassed but drawn to each other. They'd started chatting and the next film they'd seen, they'd seen together.

She'd told him about her past. So why had he gone and ruined it?

Poor Kenny – she'd left him standing there with the ring, whilst she grabbed her handbag and jumped into her car. She'd switched off her phone at the first set of traffic lights, and concentrated on driving. She drove onto the motorway heading north and sat back in her seat, switched on her cruise control and watched the miles tick past.

Her concentration was disturbed by one of those huge overhead signs flashing orange ahead of her. She leaned forwards and squinted at it, hoping it wasn't an accident warning. She taught her drivers safety and cringed every time there was an accident, thinking that most were preventable, if drivers were careful.

The sign loomed closer and she stared at it.

TERRIBLE LONELINESS AHEAD

said the sign, in big, orange letters.

'What?' yelled Laura, swerving as she watched the letters disappear overhead. At the last moment, she realised the sign said

TRAFFIC RESTRICTIONS AHEAD

She shook her head and rubbed her eyes. She must be more tired than she'd thought. She sat up straighter and popped a sweet in her mouth. She always kept some handy in the central cup holder in case she felt tired and wasn't able to stop. She didn't advocate it to her students, but it worked for her.

She drove on. Soon, another orange sign glowed up ahead. Laura slowed down. The sign came into focus.

YOU'RE GETTING OLDER: ARE YOU FEELING TIRED?

the sign asked her. This time she slowed still further and stared at the sign. She read it again:

WEATHER GETTING COLDER: CHECKED YOUR TYRES?

'I'm seeing things,' Laura muttered. Ahead, she saw a Welcome Break sign so she indicated left and pulled in.

The coffee focussed her. She'd driven almost 70 miles. She was exhausted, and it was two in the morning. She looked at her phone. She reached out and turned it on. Immediately it bleeped, telling her she had messages.

L, call me.

I love you, Laura. I'm sorry.

Come home and we can talk X

L please let me know you're ok XXX

Poor Kenny. He'd be worrying about her. Kenny liked to be her hero. She'd told him many times she didn't need a hero. Told him she was absolutely fine as she was. Why hadn't he just left things as they were? Weren't they happy? She could look after herself and she didn't need a shoulder to lean on.

She sent him a quick text: I'm fine. She hesitated, added an X. Took it away again. Pressed 'send'.

She clicked on her seatbelt, popped a sweet into her mouth and drove back onto the motorway. She thought about the past few years.

Soon after she met Kenny she'd told him about her two engagements. The first had been James, her boyfriend of five years, since she'd been sixteen. He proposed to her on her twenty-first and as she said a breathy 'yes', she knew she'd found her true love. She ignored anyone who said she was too young, argued with her mother who told her to wait and began looking at wedding dresses straight away. When James broke it off, two weeks before the wedding, nobody said 'I told you so'.

Laura picked herself up, dusted herself down and worked hard, telling herself she'd be more careful with her heart next time.

A year later, she met Rod, who was teaching the course on car mechanics that she attended on a Wednesday evening. Rod was nothing like James. He was older, wiser and, he told her, had fallen head over heels. At first, she resisted, but bunches of flowers and romantic cards won her over and they began dating. When Rod proposed, she took a breath and said yes, thinking, things can't go wrong twice. That was when Rod's other fiancée came round, banging on her door.

After that, Laura said, no more dating. She lasted almost three years this time, busy with work, happy walking her dog, but then she met Kenny. He was lovely. And when he kissed her, she knew that he was different.

Laura thought of his kiss now. She'd miss him. The past year she'd been happier than ever. She'd not wanted anything to spoil it; she'd wanted things to carry on just as they were. What now? She'd be fine on her own but there were so many things about Kenny she'd miss. She shook her head, as tears came into her eyes.

The next sign said,

PAIN FORECAST

and she felt the tears pool in her eyes and then run down her cheeks. As she passed under the sign its letters came more sharply into focus and she realised it said,

RAIN FORECAST

Laura shook her head. All of a sudden, she wanted to be home. She didn't want to be driving about in the rain, in the middle of the night, alone. She thought of Kenny, on the sofa in her house, worrying about her and her stomach gave a little lurch.

She looked for the next road sign to tell her exactly where she was. To her horror she saw she was now 120 miles away from home. She took the next turn off, went over the bridge and headed back onto the motorway, back south. Back home. Kenny would have gone back to his flat by now. In the morning she'd call him and explain she couldn't see him anymore. She wasn't sure he'd even want to see her, anyway, after what she'd done this evening.

None of this was Kenny's fault. She'd told him she'd been engaged before but perhaps she'd not explained well enough what had happened. Otherwise, why would he have asked her to marry him? Wasn't it obvious what would happen?

FASTEN YOUR SEATBELT

flashed past in big orange letters. *At least the signs are making sense now,* thought

Laura. She found herself remembering a time last summer when she and Kenny had gone on a roller coaster and her seatbelt hadn't worked properly. Kenny had fixed it for her, then kissed her and said, 'I'll always make sure your seatbelt works,' and she'd smiled and known that he'd meant it, he'd meant that he'd always make sure she was okay. She'd have jumped off the roller coaster and run away, if he'd not been there to make sure she was safe.

Just like she'd run away this evening.

The world blurred as her eyes filled with tears. She brushed them away and concentrated on the road, on the radio, on anything but her thoughts. There were hardly any other cars on the road now. Laura usually loved driving on quiet roads. She sometimes took her more nervous students out on motorways late at night, so that they could get used to driving on empty roads. It was a technique that had raised a few eyebrows, but one she knew worked. Tonight, though, the roads felt *too* empty. She began to wish there were other cars on the road. She began to wish there was someone else in the car with her.

I need another sign, she thought, *to tell me what to do*

She could explain it to Kenny at least; she owed him that. Perhaps she could ask him to pretend he'd never said anything. Maybe she could go and speak to someone and get over this fear of engagement. Perhaps she could ask him to use different words. Or, her inner voice suggested, you could just try saying yes, and see what happens.

She indicated to overtake a lorry and, through force of habit, checked her eyesight by reading its number plate.

YE5 KNL

She blinked as she overtook.

Well Laura, she thought, *you did ask for a sign. Nothing could be plainer*

She calculated: it'd take her two hours to get home. She'd be tired; she could grab a couple of hours' sleep before work tomorrow and afterwards she could go and see Kenny. She'd apologise for running away. Her heart leapt at the thought.

'I want to see him,' she said aloud, to try the thought out. She pushed her foot down on the accelerator, ever so slightly. 'I'll never know, unless I try. Isn't that what I tell my students?'

As she drove, moments from the past year flashed through her mind. The way he made her laugh. The way she felt complete, when with him. The happiness she felt in his company, even if they were just watching a movie at home. The miles passed and her tiredness lifted, giving way to butterflies in her stomach.

She thought about how it felt to be wrapped up in Kenny's arms, in the safe haven between his strong shoulders.

She stopped the car and dashed off a quick text:

Coming home, wait for me. X

She was two miles from her junction when she saw one last sign approaching.

HARD SHOULDER FOR EMERGENCY USE ONLY

it said.

'Actually, you're wrong,' said Laura, giggling, to the sign, 'hard shoulders are *not* just for emergencies.'

She was still laughing when she arrived home and saw him, standing on the step, watching for her. Her laughter turned to tears as she ran towards him. He wrapped her up in a hug and she rested her head on his shoulder.

'Ask me again?' she said.

Strings

Weak for musicians, I go throaty and flirty, dancing, finding their eyes with mine.

Mick played the fiddle with his soul and I'd never moved like that before. His beautiful fingers stroked life from the strings and I saw notes hang in the air between us before they found my feet.

The next morning I was on the ferry to work like every other day before, the scent of him on my skin, the memory of my hands in his hair. A shiver in the morning cool as the sea called and the ferry blew its leaving fanfare and I thought of my fiddler warm in his hotel bed. A feather landed on the deck at my feet. I reached for it, ran it across my lip.

Our farewell had been full of what ifs. If I stayed; if he stayed.

I thought of the grey meetings coming. The ferry revved beneath my feet as she readied to leave. I switched off my phone and ran back, all the way, to find him loading the van, ready for the next island pub.

His fiddle sat on his lap where my hand rested too, the feather a promise in my fingers.

The Worry People

For the first time in eighteen years, I was moving to the spare room. I saw it in Paul's eyes then: defeat. He gave up arguing and watched me pick up my pyjamas. We broke eye contact at the door, both aware that if I stepped into the hall, a line would be crossed.

I stepped into the hall.

Whilst part of my mind yelled at me to go back, I kept walking. I held the tears in until I'd closed the spare room door and was sitting on the bed, then I let them go.

The ending was beginning.

Once I started, I couldn't stop crying. If Paul heard me, he didn't come in. And why would he? I was the one who'd left our bed; made my own bed. But somebody heard me, the one person I had to hide this from – Amy.

'Mummy? Why are you in here?'

I drew a breath and looked up at the door. Silhouetted in the light from the hall stood Amy; a small angel who carried a hug and brought it straight to me, just the way I'd comfort her. I had time to be proud of her, and of myself for teaching her to be like this, before I dissolved into grief once again.

'What's wrong Mummy?'

I couldn't say anything. With all my will I gathered myself together, wiped my eyes and looked at her.

'Did somebody die?' she asked.

'No, no, sweetie. I'm sad, because Mummy and Daddy had a fall out.' We'd always said we'd be emotionally honest with her.

'I heard that,' Amy said, disapproval in her tone. 'You were shouty.'

'I'm sorry,' I said. *Lame, Laura, so lame,* I said to myself. 'I'm sorry you heard it.'

'I hear you a lot,' she said. 'You argue when I'm in bed.'

'Amy, honey, do you mind if we talk in the morning? I've got a bad headache and you've got school tomorrow. I love you,' I added, wishing that love could magically make it all right.

'Are you getting divorced?' she stared at me until her eyes were all I could see. Paul's eyes.

I shook my head, but I wasn't sure if it was a denial or not. 'No. No, of course not. I just grown-ups...' But my words failed me. How could I explain it to her? How could I explain that Paul and I had forgotten how to make it work? 'Don't worry,' I said. 'I'm not worried,' I added, 'everything will be fine.'

Amy looked at me, cocked her head to one side and pursed her lips. 'You look worried,' she said.

I forced a smile. 'I'm tired, sweetie. I need to sleep.'

'Wait there,' Amy said. She dashed from the room and returned seconds later. 'I got these on our school trip to the market yesterday.' She held something brightly coloured out to me.

The school trip. I'd not even asked her how it went, preferring to text Paul furious messages most of the afternoon.

'I'm sorry, I' I had nothing to tell her. I held out my hand for the object.

Amy thrust it towards me and said, 'These are called Worry People. You put them under your pillow and tell them all your worries. And in the morning, whoosh! All gone. They'll help you, Mummy.'

'Is that right?' I smiled at her. 'Thank you. Now go on to bed, okay?' I gave her one last hug and a kiss and she left the room, glancing back at me from the door. I couldn't read her expression. I tried to remember how many of her friends' parents were divorced, where she'd learned to say the word so clearly.

I didn't think I was going to be able to sleep. I looked at the Worry People. They were stuck along a small piece of wood. They fitted into the palm of my hand, tiny cloth figures that were stitched together in a row of colour. Their faces wore miniscule smiles, half-hidden under little bowler hats. I sighed and put them under my pillow so I could at least tell Amy one truth in the morning. I heard her talking to Paul and though I didn't feel tired, an exhaustion overcame me and I fell back onto the bed, unable to think about anything anymore. I just wanted oblivion. I'd not slept well for days, waking up in the night to think about Paul and me, and what we should do. I wasn't sure I even loved him any more, and I didn't understand where it had gone.

As I fell asleep I half-heard a voice say, *help me*, and I thought it might've been my own, but I was drifting away, feeling myself sink down into the mattress.

'¿S?' said a voice.

I opened my eyes.

And screamed. I was sitting on the apex of the roof of our house. I grabbed the tiles for support as the world wobbled around me.

'¿S?' said the voice again.

I looked around and saw a small woman, perched just behind me, knitting at a furious speed. I twisted around to face her. I tried to speak, but my words wouldn't come out.

'What do you *want?*' Her voice was impatient and she made a tutting noise as she dropped a stitch.

I looked down from our roof and saw my jungled garden from above with the washing I'd forgotten to take in against the backdrop of sodium lights and stars.

'I'm dreaming.'

'S, y no,' said the woman. 'Yes and no. You called me, I came. What's your problem?

Because I'm pretty busy tonight.'

'You're – the Worry People?'

She looked around. 'Person. You see more?'

I shook my head. I gave myself a surreptitious pinch. I remained on the roof.

She sighed. 'Okay, okay. I know already. You don't know if you love your husband anymore. I help. Easy to fix.' She laid her knitting on her lap and took one of my hands in her shiny brown ones. She stroked it. 'Shut your eyes,' she said. 'Now tell me about Paul. Anything.'

I did as I was told. I didn't know I was going to speak until the words started coming, as if pulled from my soul. They fell over themselves, tangled up their letters and tumbled down off the roof, telling our story as they went. I told her

all about our wedding which was the happiest day of my life and how when we danced, I cried and held Paul and knew I was safe

about meeting him for the very first time when I was single and cynical and didn't believe in love at first sight and then I saw Paul and suddenly I did

and about when he first kissed me under a tree in a park, the bark rough against my shoulder as I turned to feel the tenderest kiss I'd even known

all about giving birth to Amy, how Paul and I looked at each other and communicated thousands of things without any words and how even though I was on gas and air I knew I meant every look that said we're together, our souls, this is real and this is love and I love you, I love you

and how we held Amy, afterwards, this baby we'd waited for, for five long years, this tiny perfect human who completed our circle and bound us together, forever, and I told her the promises we made to our daughter as we named her and stroked her miniature hands and felt her warmth and life

and later, years later, when we found out Amy would never have a sibling, how we held each other and sobbed because we wanted to multiply our love all over again because that's how it felt, having a child

I told the woman how love had begun to change and that we didn't know how and that we didn't know why and that we seemed powerless to stop the arguments.

Then I told her about how I noticed Carl one day at work, and he made me see how old I'd become by making jokes I didn't understand and flirting with me. At first I was confused and didn't know when to laugh but gradually, I relaxed. I couldn't remember the last time I'd felt attractive, but when he smiled at me, I felt beautiful. When I looked in the mirror I didn't recognise myself anymore. My wrinkles stood out. My smiles looked forced. Carl made me laugh – when was the last time Paul and I had laughed? I began to wear more make-up to work and think about my clothes in a way that made me feel young again. I'd enjoyed it and I'd make excuses to have to visit Carl's desk. He asked for my number and, pleased and blushing, I'd given it to him.

One day Carl texted me, a silly, flirtatious text, and I'd replied, and Paul had seen it and that had created a whole new level of arguments.

'Stop,' the woman said.

I opened my eyes.

'No, keep them closed.' She put her hands on my head and twisted them slightly. It hurt.

'Ow!'

'That's better,' she said. 'Now, continue.'

So I tried to tell her about Carl again, and our arguments but somehow the words wouldn't come. I couldn't see Carl's face. I didn't *want* to see Carl's face. All I felt inside was how much I loved Paul and how stupid we'd been to let all that good feeling go. The arguments really were trivial; instead I recalled how soft and warm Amy had been when she was first born, this child that was half of each of us, our love brought to life. I tried again, to say that we couldn't communicate any longer and shouting was a part of our day but all I could see were his eyes during our wedding dance, as we slowly twirled and the lights flashed by and the cheering of the wedding guests spun us faster until all we could see was each other.

I wanted to tell her how I believed it would be easier alone, no fighting, no misunderstanding, no bewildered silences in which we once laughed, but all I could see was Paul and me at a charity comedy night, laughing so hard and having to clutch each other in order not to fall off the plastic chairs.

I opened my eyes. 'I love him,' I said, and the words surprised me.

'Of course you do,' the woman said. 'You just forgot for a while, and let life get in the way. The more love you start with, the easier it is to find again if you lose it. You had lots. Lots of love. That's how it should be. Now, I go.' She let go of my hands.

From somewhere in her bulky skirts she pulled a stripy bag into which she tucked her knitting. She stood up.

'But,' I began.

'Easy. Now I have somebody else to see. Shut your eyes, think of your bed. Sweet dreams!'

There was a pop in the air and a hole where she'd been, before the air moved with a shimmer and filled the space. I stared, shook my head. I was left, alone, in the dark.

I closed my eyes as she'd instructed. Instead of the spare bed, I saw mine and Paul's bed. It looked far too big for just one person.

In a second I felt my familiar soft pillow and duvet tucking me close to Paul's warmth. He snored gently, a sound that had lately been driving me nuts but was like music, just now.

He stirred in his sleep and murmured, 'Worry Person? Mm? What?'

I slid my hand under his pillow and felt the cloth figures, just like mine.

Amy. We'd have to have words with her in the morning. Tell her how much we loved her

Dust

The first layers are not extraordinary: village celebrations, coffee mornings, memorials, birthdays. I'm used to these emotions now, and I breathe them away softly, gently. They're familiar. I'm not as good at Graham at judging time so at first I go slowly, afraid to miss anything. Sometimes I stop and breathe deeply, knowing I'll be coughing for a week, knowing I've no choice. I let myself get drawn in and I focus and drink it in and draw it to a date. Stella couldn't remember the exact date but I can guess: Anna was in early pregnancy, with me. 1998, summer.

It's hard to judge and I stop frequently, my eyes sore, my throat harsh.

It's three o'clock in the afternoon before I find them.

I was seventeen when it happened. I didn't know what it was, at first, but the look on the face of the workman holding the machine told me what I'd wanted to know for years: that I was special. Not just different, but special. Mum and Dad had tried, but I knew they were biased.

Our village hall was built in 1864. We once did a project on it at school and I'd always loved it; loved its uneven planks, the smells as you first walked in that were part primary school, part coffee morning. I loved the windows and the old tables and the feeling that there was more air inside than out.

I didn't tell anyone all of this; I tried to be like my friends, slightly disdainful of the village events that we had to go to. My shared history with them was ripped away when I found out what *adopted* actually meant. Mum and Dad had never hidden it from me, but I'd always assumed I was as much a part of the village as anyone else, that my parents' shared genes that were part of the pathways around where I grew up were my genes too.

That I was, actually, an outsider, an incomer, was harder to take than the final understanding of the reasons behind our differences. My dark hair against their blond; my height that kept me growing past them. My siblings were part of the village. I was not.

Lucy's sixteenth ('Of course not. It's just that when we found you, and then she came along, it was like more magic. Of course we don't regret it.') birthday was in the hall. We'd been lucky to get a booking because the village had finally raised enough money for some renovation work and having the floor cleaned and polished was the priority. It was dull, from years of use, its wood buried under dirt. The hall would be closed for weeks, and Lucy's birthday was the day before the work began.

I'd had some of the smuggled-in punch, gone home feeling sick and had left my bag and jacket in the toilets. I'd rushed back as soon as my room stopped spinning, thinking that I'd be too late and my stuff would be stuck in there until the work finished.

The doors were open. I stepped inside, into clouds of dust. My favourite smell was gone, replaced by

my tears, as I stood all alone, not wanting to be held or comforted like my siblings. Mum was raw, Dad solid, holding her, lips pursed. It felt as if my heart had been torn out, that if I carried on crying I'd break. When comfort did come it was from Lucy, unexpected, her hand on my back, her head on my shoulder, this sister-not-sister who I fought with all the time. You were her favourite, she said, and that's OK. Don't shut us out. We loved her too. And I turned and hugged her and felt our connection, aged thirteen, these things unexplainable at the time but now as I remembered it I felt it all over again and knew we were family, really

'You OK, love?' I was pulled back to the present.

I stared. The man was covered in dust. He pulled off his mask, looking at me as if he wanted to see right inside me. It wasn't creepy, not like Mr Roberts' low probing gaze in the sweet shop.

'I left my bag here last night.'

'Right. You looked a bit peaky there for a moment. Mind if I carry on?'

All I could do was shake my head because

I was twelve, it was our primary school leavers' disco and it was the last time I'd see Jason because he was going off to a different school in a different county and all I wanted was one dance to take back home with me. But Laura, my best friend, grabbed him right at the end and there they were, gliding past, heads close. I couldn't blame her because she didn't know about Jason. He was my secret, one I kept all to myself when they were all giggling over boys. And I remembered leaving the hall, the cool blast of air on my face and the hot angry tears that ran down my cheeks all the way home

'I need to sit down.' I'd never fainted but the room was blacking at the edges with billowing shadows and my head felt like it was rolling.

The man took a chair off a stack and then I was sitting.

'Put your head down, between your knees,' said the man and I did, but the dust down here was different, and

now I was with people I didn't know. Old people. There was the clatter of cups and a shrill voice, telling everyone the talk about Norway's fjords was about to begin

'You feel it,' said the man. 'Don't you? Well I'll be damned. I've never'

'Don't know what I feel,' I managed.

'I thought it was just me,' he said, staring at me like he wanted to pick me up and hug me. He laughed.

'This morning I've had birthdays, coffee mornings and wakes. Oh, and toddler groups, jumble sales, parties, film showings and discos. My masks help.' He reached around to his back pocket and pulled out another mask. It was grubby, and I didn't want to put it on but he didn't give me a choice as he placed it over my mouth. The air cleared, and so did everything else.

'Tell me,' he said. 'Tell me what you felt.'

The idea came later. I'd gone home, overwhelmed, tired and still hungover, not sure that what I'd just experienced had been real. I'd lain on my bed and stared at the ceiling, waiting, as the idea glimmered and grew.

'Mum' I approached her in the kitchen where she was sitting with a cup of tea, dinner on, the most relaxed she got in the afternoons. She'd been waiting weeks for me to tell her what I was going to do next. Halfway through my A-levels I was struggling. I wasn't academic like the rest of them and trying to keep up wasn't doing me any good. It was Mum who'd suggested taking some time out to work, and see if I found my calling. Her name for it. Seeing as I didn't even know who I was, my calling was going to be extra hard to find. What had my birth parents been? I burned with questions but didn't want to hurt Mum and Dad.

'I think I know what I want to do,' I said, sitting down and pouring myself a cup from Gran's teapot. And I told her.

The next day, I went back to ask him. He was sitting on the low wall outside, smoking. He didn't look surprised to see me and before I'd got the words out he was nodding.

'I didn't think there was anyone else,' he said, smiling at me like a long-lost relative.

If my parents were bemused by my off-the-wall idea, they hid it well, relieved, I think, that I'd made some kind of decision. College was put on hold and Graham, who'd told me his name with a handshake that made my fingers tiny, picked me up every morning. His 'patch' was huge, most of the north of England and the borders of Scotland.

He began by testing me, smiling when tears ran down my cheeks, saying, 'Yes. That's it,' and crying with me, if it was a particularly bad one. We laughed together over comedy nights and we stood, solemn, as eulogies were read out. Sometimes they were just glimpses, others, the whole evening came back in colours so bright they burned our eyes along with our emotions. He taught me to use the various sanding machines until I felt comfortable with not only them, but what we helped them reveal. He taught me to deflect the emotion, not be too affected by it.

At the same time, I put the other part of my now fully formed plan into action.

At first, the questions were gentle and casual. 'So, how old was she again?' and, 'And what was his job?' or, 'Do you know where they lived, when they met?' I had to be careful because Mum was suspicious. I'd never wanted to know much before, but now I needed to know everything. However, it turned out she didn't know much at all.

I didn't tell Graham, either, worried he'd think I was using him. I wasn't; I loved learning from him. And there was much to learn.

'Smell this,' he said. 'Wait for the memories to go then sniff again. Can you smell it? That's pitch pine. Hundreds of years old. Well-seasoned before it was laid. Beautiful, it is. I'm gonna take off my mask and breathe it in. You don't get floors like this anymore. You try. Tell me what you smell'

Graham said things like 'I still can't believe it,' and 'it's fate, it is,' often, as we worked, side by side.

When it was time for me to work on my own, Graham let me loose on my first solo job. I wasn't only nervous; I was terrified. Sometimes the memories came at you so fast they nearly knocked you off your feet, and the kaleidoscope of human feeling was intricate and complicated. Emotions I had no name for floated up to us, and the amount of them sometimes, layer upon layer and woven into the wood itself (sometimes we even felt the tree: ancient, solid, noble) was almost too much. But I got stronger, and I was ready.

It was a newer floor than most we did, and the polishing only took a day. It was a long day, and I'd kept my mask on the entire time, just in case something came up that I couldn't deal with.

When I went to drop off his van, Graham looked like a proud parent.

I knew it was time.

There was only one thing I knew for sure: they were both dead. I didn't know about the wider family, their friends, their jobs or lives. I also knew – from Mum – I'd been adopted by a private agency that was now closed and may not have been entirely legal. My mother's name was Anna and my father's was David. There had been something about drugs in their pasts. And that was it. My birth mother's last address was listed as Ansterwood, two hundred miles to the south. This was where I headed for the first of many journeys, physical and through cyberspace.

As I park up outside Ansterwood Hall, I think about the long path to get here. I found out how my parents died, taking the same batch of heroin that was too pure. Mum had inferred drugs were involved, but she'd not known much. Finding it out

182

was a shock, but it was a relief, too. I'd imagined, in the sleepless nights, suicide or murder, but it had been an awful accident. I was in the squat at the time, asleep in a cot. When the police arrived, hours later, I'd still been sleeping. My parents weren't the only ones who'd taken drugs, although at least they'd had a choice.

Newspapers were helpful, but I really got lucky four months into the search when I found one of Anna's friends, Stella – now a social worker who'd turned her life around after Anna and David died. She gave me some family names which I'm keeping tucked away for later. First, my parents. She filled in the most important blanks for me and she gave me the information that's brought me here, today. They'd got engaged, and they'd had a party. It was better than anything (their attendance at a town event?) I'd hoped for.

The hall is of a similar age to the one in our village. This usually makes me happy as it means an interesting job, but today it fills me with dismay. How will I find them? There will be too many layers and theirs might be thin, or too diluted.

The machine I've brought is our smaller one. It's not as heavy and it's the one I use for jobs when it's just me. The village council were hard to persuade, but I've a portfolio of before and after pictures and the lie about the rare pitch pine and a new type of polish that we needed to trial worked well. Graham knows I'm up to something, but not what exactly. I might tell him. For now it is my secret.

What comes first is the familiarity. Like the glance of a shining head of hair disappearing, swinging around a corner, I catch her. My mother. The feeling is one I know, yet have never had before. It's like recognising myself in a mirror, in the semi-dark.

She's happy. I get that immediately, a strand of her joy reaches me as the machine glides soft over the wood, swishing up the dust and the memories to me. I catch them, and breathe it in

Anna looks at Dave and I see him for the first time. He's got long unkempt hair and an air of melancholy. I can't see myself in him except for in his determined chin. Anna has a tiny bump in her belly, her skinny frame not looking strong enough to hold me. But her happiness glows like a light, yellow-orange light, and seems to come from all over her. She touches me often, tucked away safe inside her and I can feel the promise of the future in her touch. Dave kisses her and hugs her and smiles, and in them I sense determination and a need to get it right, this time.

I'm pulled further in. I run the machine just a little, not enough to take the whole layer away but enough to take me further back.

Anna sits on his knee. Some of their friends are drunk. Some are worse than drunk; eyes pinned and hands floppy and smiles zoned out. I can feel Anna's need, but her deeper desire to do it properly, for her child. For me. Dave holds her hand and when a mate comes and offers him something in foil he shakes his head and looks down but I can see the fear in his face, the fear that says, I dunno if I can do this.

Anna takes his chin and turns his head and takes his hand and places it on her belly. She kisses him and whispers something that I can't catch, but I can feel the emotions inside it. Think of this, she's telling him, guiding his hand to where I'm kicking and making her laugh and I see him smile back and nod. People are leaving, staggering out. I wonder at their bravery, having this party, at the statement they're making. I look for people who look like me but it's all friends. Where are their families? Alienated? Dave pulls Anna to her feet and holds her and I'm tucked safe in between them both.

My people. My beginning.

Anna's thoughts reach me: she wants to be a teacher. She wants to train when I'm older. Dave's I can't read. What does he want to do? There are engines in his mind. Metal and heaviness. And craving. I can feel his craving as he fights with it deep inside, hands shaking as he leads Anna around the floor to Extreme's *More than Words* and I know it's their song from years before when they first met, straight out of school, before the drugs.

I am with them, as they move, as he sings and she sings. I feel their yearning. I feel their need for me, this baby who has come along and who is going to save them. I sit down and lay my hands each side of me. I want every last memory of them, before I turn it into dust.

And it's here, flowing into me, their love, their love for me and the beautiful knowledge they wanted me. *Anna* wanted me. Anna wanted me and wished for me and I came, to be there with them, a sum of them both, and their love. I'm their gift, Anna is thinking, something else they can choose. She's going to get it right and make it up with her family and marry Dave and have a wedding. She's going to wear a dress, one that doesn't cover the track marks because they're her battle scars against an evil she's beaten with love. She touches me and I feel it stronger than ever as I concentrate on our connection. *My mother wanted me* and I know then that it doesn't matter what happened next; I don't care what led them back down the dark path. Right now I know I was wanted, needed, and I came willingly. And just for a second, there is a space into which Anna looks, and for a second our eyes meet and I gasp because they are *my* eyes. She smiles.

First Published

'Your Lifejacket is Under Your Seat' was first published in *A Tail of a Mouse, An Anthology from Michael Terence Publishing, 2017*

'Wordsmith' was first published in *'Wordsmith' – The 2016 Just Write Creative Writing Competition, in association with Writing Magazine and John Murray Press, 2016*

'Leucothea' first appeared in *Journeys Beyond, Earlyworks Press, 2016*

'The Perfect Stroke' was first published in *Sixteen and All That, Plymouth Writers' Group, 2016*

'Small Talk' was first published in *The A3 Review, March 2016*

'The Thinking Place' first appeared as 'Gateway to my Past' in *Take A Break's Fiction Feast, February 2008*

'Wetherby Pie' first appeared in *The People's Friend in March 2019*

'A Man of Means' first appeared in *Grindstone's 2018 Anthology, as well as on their website*

'Signs' first appeared as 'Follow the Signs' in *The People's Friend, February 2019*

'Strings' was first published by *Reflex Fiction, on line, 2018*

'The Worry People' first appeared as 'Sleep Tight' in *The People's Friend Special, 2018*

Earlier versions of some of the stories first appeared online on the *Hour of Writes* website under the pseudonym 'Seaside Scribbler'

I apologise for any errors or omissions in this list